The
Immaculate
Conception

ALSO BY GAÉTAN SOUCY

Atonement
The Little Girl Who Was Too Fond of Matches
Vaudeville!

Gaétan Soucy

The
Immaculate
Conception

Translated by Lazer Lederhendler

ANANSI

First published as *L'Immaculée Conception* in 1999 by Les Éditions du Boréal
First published in English in 2005 by House of Anansi Press Inc.

This edition published in 2007 by House of Anansi Press Inc.
110 Spadina Avenue, Suite 801, Toronto, ON, M5V 2K4
Tel. 416-363-4343 Fax 416-363-1017 www.anansi.ca

Distributed in Canada by
HarperCollins Canada Ltd.
1995 Markham Road
Scarborough, ON, M1B 5M8
Toll free tel. 1-800-387-0117

Distributed in the United States by
Publishers Group West
1700 Fourth Street
Berkeley, CA 94710
Toll free tel. 1-800-788-3123

The poem on pages 47–48 is taken from *The Fables of La Fontaine, Translated From the French by Elizur Wright, A New Edition, With Notes by J. W. M. Gibbs* (1882).

House of Anansi Press is committed to protecting our natural environment. As part of our efforts, this book is printed on paper that contains 100% post-consumer recycled fibres, is acid-free, and is processed chlorine-free.

11 10 09 08 07   1 2 3 4 5

LIBRARY AND ARCHIVES CANADA CATALOGUING IN PUBLICATION DATA

Soucy, Gaétan, 1958–
[Immaculée Conception. English]
The Immaculate Conception / Gaétan Soucy ; translated by
Lazer Lederhendler.
Translation of: L'Immaculée Conception.
ISBN-13: 978-0-88784-783-7
ISBN-10: 0-88784-783-8
I. Lederhendler, Lazer, 1950– II. Title. III. Title: Immaculée
Conception. English.
PS8587.O91314413 2007   C843'.54   C2007-902664-8

Library of Congress Control Number: 2007927969

Cover design: Paul Hodgson
Cover illustration: Gérard DuBois
Text design and typesetting: Tannice Goddard

Canada Council
for the Arts

Conseil des Arts
du Canada

ONTARIO ARTS COUNCIL
CONSEIL DES ARTS DE L'ONTARIO

We acknowledge for their financial support of our publishing program the Canada Council for the Arts, the Ontario Arts Council, and the Government of Canada through the Book Publishing Industry Development Program (BPIDP). This book was made possible in part through the Canada Council's Translation Grants Program.

Printed and bound in Canada

For my sister
— G.S.

To the memory of my father,
Hershl Lederhendler (1921–2005)
— L.L.

EXCERPT FROM A DOCUMENT
BY R. COSTADE (HOCHELAGA)
ADDRESSED TO MR. ROGATIEN W. (NEW YORK)

I was there myself. Installed in the back seat of my car with the notepad propped against my thigh, I noted the presumed number of victims and calculated the quotas as the information was brought to me. Every fifteen minutes one of my men would come running and lean into the open car door: five more, good God, another ten!

Soucy, his face in a sweat, was exultant: "There may be around fifty, perhaps more!" I found this beyond belief. He repeated it. Unable to sit still, I got out of the car.

The place was ablaze from the cellar to the rafters. Flames were shooting out the windows with the frenzy of a man possessed. No one could escape from that inferno alive. One could only pray it would not spread to the alley. The shrieks of the victims could be heard quite distinctly. The cries were rather peculiar, like peals of laughter, disenchanted howls. "The cackles of agony," Soucy said to me. The laughter one hears from time to time in hell, I suppose.

Then he said, "Will you look at that — a glacier of blood." It was true. The stones had turned a deep red. Whole sections of them were coming loose from the façade and rolling into the middle of the pavement, like smouldering slag.

"Careful, if ever it collapses, there will be pandemonium."

"I'll be very careful."

I slipped in among the frightened bystanders. It was just like being at the circus. The police strove to keep them at a distance. There were children perched atop shoulders. Hooligans in unpredictable groups threw stones at the windows and then dispersed when they were pursued, mingling with the crowd. Ambulances arrived, others left, laboriously threading their way through with their bells clanging. The fire brigade's horses strained against their harnesses like fish writhing on a hook. A wild-eyed woman in a nightgown whom an officer had pinned against his chest screamed a man's first name and stretched her arms toward the building. Soucy was already walking toward her. The firefighters did what they could to hose down the nearest buildings.

That is when the explosion occurred. I felt the blast singe my face. A fireman was transformed into a living torch, and a horse as well. The poor beast bolted in terror, threatening to spread the flames, and had to be brought down with a rifle. A few seconds later the façade crumbled, blocking the ambulances' way out. The throng in disarray shrank back and I took shelter in the entranceway of a courtyard. The firefighter, I was told, gasped his last breath laid out on a cart.

I was nervously rummaging around in my pockets for my pencil when I saw him. He may have been there for several minutes, I don't know. A stout, squat individual with a narrow forehead overgrown with stiff hair, and the snout of a wild boar. He was standing before me with a witless smile on his lips. The smile of a child guilty of an act whose consequences he had not imagined. I wondered what he wanted of me, why he was looking at me in that way.

"It's me," he said meekly.

I did not understand. He stepped closer and repeated, "It's me," showing me his hands and soiled shirt. My heart stopped. This was too good to be true! There he was, giving himself up, and for a reason that eludes me even now he had confessed to me so that I would turn him over to the police! He added, miserably, "I had too much to drink."

I grabbed him by the collar; I was taller by at least a head and a half. He put up no resistance. I could sense people looking at us. Someone stepped nearer, his voice full of menace: "Is this the one? The arsonist!" I was afraid. But a floor of the building caved in at that very moment, drawing everyone's attention; we were able to continue on our way. My prisoner had been so terrified that he now walked on tiptoes with his legs bowed. He had pissed his pants.

All in all we learned very little about him, quite simply because there was doubtless not much to learn. A farmer, that's all, a habitant, unmarried and what's more covered with pimples. He went through his trial with his head tucked between his shoulders, dazed and docile, just as he had been when he delivered himself up to the police. One day, my brother and I were discussing whether or not we should have our dog put down. Napoléon cocked a worried ear, came toward us, quivering, wagging his tail, shoving his muzzle into the palms of our hands . . . Well, the condemned man put me very much in mind of Napoléon. And when the prosecutor, waving his big sleeves around and choking with indignation, demanded the gallows, the arsonist once again pissed his pants.

As for the motive, my God! It was so clear, so stupid, so candidly stated by the protagonist that the defence was left with almost no latitude, and the young court-appointed lawyer, sweating profusely, incessantly clearing his throat, could do no better in his closing arguments than to stammer two or three inanities which I shall spare you. But here at any rate are the facts. The accused, having despaired of finding himself a wife in his village, where he had been the butt of hilarity since early childhood, had come to the city for the first time in his life. He was not disappointed: on the very first day a lass wrapped her arms around his neck. A room at the hotel, restaurants, shows, nightclubs — this girl would not be denied. After a few days of this regimen they ended up at the Grill aux Alouettes. There, his conquest met some female acquaintances who all had a very merry evening at the pigeon's expense, the latter eventually realizing that his savings of three years had been depleted in three nights. It was time to go back to the village! She pushed him away. He insisted — she slapped him! He hit her, in his own words, "on her big red mouth." Punches were thrown helter-skelter at anything that moved. He was slung headfirst down the stairway.

For a while he wandered the streets. Coming upon an oil dealer, he pawned the watch he had inherited from his great-uncle, a detail that must have affected him powerfully, as he mentioned it to the judge on at least five occasions. He returned to the Grill aux Alouettes, emptied the contents of the cans onto both main stairways, and dropped a match. "Lit?" asked the judge, to be certain. The arsonist found that one rich and slapped his thigh. Among the clients of the Grill, not one survived.

ROGATIEN, I AM not about to forget the night of the fire. It must have been around nine o'clock; I had gone to sleep to restore my strength for the long night of work that I had planned for myself. I was roused by one of my men. Even before I had time to pull on a pair of trousers he brought me up to date. I dispatched three of my people to the site in order to immediately contact the victims' families, if any could be found. Then I went over there myself. The entire parish had gathered in the street. At that point it was believed the number of corpses would not exceed twenty or so. That was already enough to make me break out in hives. "The course of events in this world is such that they rarely turn out for the worst," I complained to you in my last letter. Well, it happens. When the evening was over, all told, the body count stood at seventy-five!

I could do nothing all night, not even sleep, I was feverish. I knew, of course, that we had the best chance, that everything was in our favour. First, the fire took place in our area; also, we were the only ones to have enough space, not to mention our expertise, the touch of refinement that is our hallmark. Furthermore, wasn't I the one who had handed the criminal over to the authorities? Soucy constantly reminded me of this. Yet I remained on edge. Last-minute stumbling blocks might arise, the competition could pull the rug out from under us, I've never wanted for enemies. I paced up and down in my office, altogether obsessed — possessed — as in the first moments of a love affair.

Toward dawn I was finally freed from my anxiety. One of my men called me on the telephone. We had won! We were entitled to the maximum quota! I burst into tears.

Next of kin had to identify the corpses one by one before they could be delivered to us. We expected thirty. With luck that number might go as high as thirty-five. I insisted the bodies be carried down to our cellar as soon as they arrived. Not to boast, but it is the largest in the city, the only one, along with the municipal morgue, worthy of such a hecatomb. Would I be there to receive them, an employee asked me. I told him no, I would wait until they were ready, laid out on the tables, and only then would I go down, quite alone. I gave orders to be called then.

We ultimately obtained thirty-two of them. The last delivery took place at three that afternoon. And so I went down, alone, to the cellar, dressed in a suit and top hat, high collar and red cravat, quite resplendent, as you know I can be. Why is it women have so far not realized how truly handsome I am? They resort to every excuse to deny the truth staring them in the face.

The majority had died of asphyxiation, smothered by the smoke or trampled by the pack trying to escape from the furnace. Some were more disjointed than others, those from the ground floor, I presume, crushed by the weight of the upper floors. "To barely exist and then to exist no more, better not to have existed at all," I repeated quietly over the head of each one, like a blessing. And I inhaled, yes, I whiffed. Blended with the familiar aroma were those of the fire and the intoxicating fragrance of smoked flesh.

My corpses were aligned side by side, hand against hand, on the broad ivory tables. Among them some beautiful women, as yet not too withered, a little swollen at the neck, like sparrows, the way I like them. I recognized certain faces. I walked along the aisle in a dither, there was so much to see. Trying to remain calm, poised. When you are what I am, you mistrust what you are.

That is how I came across Blanchot's remains. In rather bad shape he was, his mouth still open. I mention this because the matter concerns you in a curious way. I had talked to this Blanchot that very afternoon. I had let him have an icon for a song, an icon of the Virgin, to repay a small favour he had done me. Now, this icon, who do you suppose painted it? You'll never guess: you. It must have been a good thirty years ago, when you still regarded yourself as a Christian — we aren't getting any younger, are we? The model was your everlasting love at the time. Tell me, Rogatien, do you remember Justine Vilbroquais?

I can see the wall where when you were seven years old you wrote, I BEELONG TO JUSTINE VILBROQUAIS FORE EVVER. She still lives in the neighbourhood, can you imagine? I saw her the other day from afar. I made some inquiries. She earns her living as a piano player in the movie theatres. If it is any consolation to you Rogatien, her widow's life has been wretched. But physically she has hardly changed at all. I am not joking. Her eyes, I assure you, her famous eyes, are just as they used to be.

Yes, I walked, I had before me all these corpses that we were to transfigure, and I was transported by the prospect of that Masterpiece. And when, that same evening, my team and I set to work, the inside of the human body being the realm of colours, I felt like a horticultural magician, a brilliant gardener awash in light and music, strolling amid his cathedrals of flowers!

R. Costade
Head of Costade & Sons Funeral Home
Undertakers for three generations

(The rest of this document has no bearing on the story.)

I

REMOUALD TREMBLAY, AGE thirty-three, was in the habit of taking his father out three times a week for a stroll in his wheelchair.

Some ten years had passed since Séraphon Tremblay had lost the use of his limbs, the lower as well as the upper. It had come about naturally and without fuss, almost painlessly, in the way flowers dry out in their pots. Invariably wrapped in his purple robe — part housecoat, part bedsheet — Séraphon resembled a hand-puppet: the rag body, the wooden skull, and that obstinate, grinning expression children see in their bad dreams. At first glance, all that showed of the head was the bulging hump of the nose. But, although he was as wrinkled as a raisin, his face was animated, his tongue caustic, and his gaze extraordinarily keen and alive.

Séraphon Tremblay was not much bothered by his handicaps; he knew how to exploit them. He was one of those old men who are, so to speak, born old, who spend a lifetime waiting for the proper age to arrive and then come into their own at the eleventh hour, whereupon they acquire the energy emitted by any thing that has achieved the fullness of its essence. His body required almost nothing of him any more, an achievement in itself and, killing two birds with one stone, it granted him the good fortune of squashing under its crippled mass his son Remouald.

His authority over Remouald was indisputable, uninhibited, austere in its own way, and now his only reason for living. There was, however, a boundary beyond which it could not be exercised. When he saw Remouald contemplating the moon through the window, benumbed by a reverie, Séraphon would have bartered his soul away to enter his son's mind and steer his thoughts from within like a motorist. This kept him in a state of perpetual vexation. Like a man walking with a stone in his shoe. Simmering with rage, Séraphon would invent whims: Could Remouald straighten his under-sheet! Would he mind making less noise when he breathed! Unfazed, phlegmatic, dutiful, Remouald complied with the most extravagant demands. Séraphon would have been glad to hear a complaint from time to time, a sigh of impatience. He found Remouald's obedient forbearance hard to bear.

Like all those who wish things were arranged in accordance with their views, whenever some trifle went awry, Séraphon considered himself forsaken, betrayed, poignantly forlorn. Having married late in life, he had maintained an old bachelor's predilection for self-pity and put it to expert use. He regarded selfishness as the least of the courtesies he owed to himself. When he felt up to it, he would spend entire Sundays whimpering, whining, snivelling, and pausing occasionally to sneak a sidelong glance at the effect this sorrow was having on his son.

Since Célia's death, Séraphon had become in Remouald's eyes increasingly mixed up with her, and, by the same token, Célia's face overlapped in his memories more and more with

Séraphon's. To the point where Remouald could no longer distinguish one from the other — when his father spoke to him it was his mother's voice he heard. Before him, around him, lording it over Remouald's life was this being of indeterminate gender, which he took out in a wheelchair three times a week for a breath of air.

As FATE LIKES to disguise itself in everyday garments, the whole thing began with a walk apparently similar to all those that had preceded it.

They would take Rue Moreau to Ontario, turn right toward Préfontaine, then south to Sainte-Catherine, or even to Rue Notre-Dame on certain bold nights. It was when they were closing the circuit, heading up Moreau from the south, that they would come into the vicinity of the Grill aux Alouettes. Remouald reddened, always afraid of encountering a customer who might say hello to him. Unbeknownst to Séraphon (he believed), Remouald would sometimes come to the Grill aux Alouettes when his father was asleep (he believed), and, ensconced in some dark corner until the early hours, drink a mixture of brown ale and whisky blanc, also known as "lethal weasel." Wherever he might be, Remouald, encumbered by his large body and awkward in both speech and gesture, always had the feeling all eyes were on him, that behind his back he was the subject of whispers and finger-pointing. He was wrong. For though he was a peculiar individual in more ways than one, Remouald was a man who went generally unnoticed.

The way back along Rue Moreau was for Remouald the most depressing leg of their excursion; it was therefore the part Séraphon preferred. They had to go by the freight train station, then the pork factory with its enigmatic chimneys rising up on either side of a badly rutted yard. There was also the reek of the silos intermingled with that of the molasses mill — fit to turn one's stomach — and, finally, there was Séraphon's griping at the level crossing as his chair lurched over the jutting railroad tracks, even though Remould, ever diligent, had thoroughly mastered this manoeuvre.

Across the street, almost directly facing their house, was a building ten storeys high. The windows looked like vacant eyes, the garage doors like mouths, like tombs full of wailing. The building reminded Remould of the primitive totems on some of the stamps in his collection; he saw in it the same expression of spellbound gloom, of fixed transcendence. It stood like a forgotten witness to some cosmic disaster that had in its path swallowed up the very significance of things. What remained was a mummified world, a shell as bereft of memory as the carcass of an animal that has foundered in the desert. A red sign bore the yellow-painted words "ACE BOX." They made cardboard boxes there. And it upset Remould to think about a plant where nothing but empty boxes were produced. "Yet they are necessary, they are necessary," he told himself and tried to imagine everything that could be crammed into those cartons. Still, an empty box stayed an empty box, and all his reasoning could not dispel the sense that a universe once full of secret messages had shut its eyes forever, and that this inscrutable building, mute and blind, blotting out the horizon to the north, was its headstone.

When they arrived again at their door, Remould had to hoist Séraphon in his arms and carry him to the second floor while enduring the rebukes his father never failed to heap on him for his clumsiness. Later, he would reshuffle his stamp collection or fabricate tiny objects, and then have a drink on the sly while Séraphon, having finished reading the newspaper, nodded and eventually fell asleep.

This was how it had been for ages. And, out of an old man's fear of change, which can never be anything but a change for the worse, neither of them would have wanted this existence in any way disturbed.

ONE MONDAY NIGHT in late November, a while after the Grill aux Alouettes had burned down, the notion occurred to Séraphon of going through the ruins on the pretext of ensuring they contained nothing salvageable. Finding the idea perfectly repugnant, Remouald objected. But his opposition only fuelled Séraphon's stubbornness.

"I said we are going through those ruins, so we are going through those ruins," he insisted, with the voice of his deceased wife.

Resigned, Remouald turned his collar up, pulled his hat down, and lifted the cable surrounding the site. They proceeded into the rubble.

"Careful, you fool!"

Remouald struggled to right the chair — the wheels were mired in the gummy, soot-covered ground. The site was strewn with debris. He stopped and looked about. The moonlight spilled a frosty light over the place. Metal skeletons, sections of the framework, corners of walls as black as chimney stones were all that remained of the Grill aux Alouettes. The dance floor had crashed two storeys below and lay there broken apart, like a room whose walls had caved in. The woodwork, columns, handrails, benches, stools with broken legs, ceiling fixtures, shards of dishware, everything had fallen to the ground, into the mud and the all-encompassing stench. Remould buried his face in his scarf.

"Keep going! I said, keep going!"

"But the chair is sure to overturn!"

"If you don't act the fool the chair will not overturn."

Remould reluctantly pushed the chair and continued to advance amid the filth.

"But what if someone sees us? We're not allowed to wander around like this where there's been a fire."

"Tut-tut! Mind where you're stepping, instead. I can feel the chair tilting to the left."

"Our clothes will smell of smoke. Our hair, our skin!"

"Aha! So, there's somebody who takes an interest in the smell of your skin? . . . Wait, hold on. What's that there, on the ground?"

"What? Where?"

Séraphon growled, "There! Right there!"

Remould bent down without letting go of the chair.

"On the other side, you idiot! Here, to my right."

"It's nothing, Dad. An ashtray."

"Pick it up, I tell you. Put it in my lap, between my hands, where I can touch it."

Remould balked, and Séraphon let out an imperious groan. So with his fingertips he dug the ashtray out of the muck and placed it on the plaid blanket covering his father's legs.

While Séraphon was busy inspecting his discovery, Remould let his eyes wander over the rubble. Here lay a bottle twisted by the heat. There, a half-burnt overcoat, and there, too, yes, there was no mistake, a set of dentures . . . Remould felt nauseous. He averted his eyes.

The remnants of a staircase caught his attention; attached to it, part of a wall, still upright though somewhat bulging, stood precariously balanced. He could see a halo, as if tree-branches were burning on the other side of the wall. He had often sat on those stairs waiting for the toilet to be free. He recalled the procession of cockroaches dancing around the urinals, how they scattered as he approached, like thieves caught planning their next heist. Every time, he would muse on the cockroaches, on the original and coherent perception of the world they must have. He shuddered at the thought that, on its own plane, this grotesque reality was surely as valid as the reality he himself perceived. His own reality was no truer, certainly no more complex, than the one experienced by the cockroaches. He sometimes had to keep himself from crying out in horror. They must have perished along with the others, the women, the men, the mice, the rats. Remould tried to brush away this vision. Then he saw something terrible.

"Throw it away."

Behind the wall he could make out silhouettes.

"Throw it away!"

"Eh? What?"

"Get rid of this ashtray!" Séraphon repeated. "Besides, we don't smoke, either of us. So heave-ho!"

Remould gave the ashtray a toss. Séraphon told him to pick it up and pitch it farther. With a hint of exasperation, Remould flung it across the street. He came back to the chair. He pushed it a few paces and stopped behind a mound of garbage. From there, Remould could see without fear of being seen. It was then he understood what the silhouettes were doing behind the wall.

"What is it? What's the matter?"

Remould, stunned, did not respond. His hands had left the chair and dangled at his thighs.

"Will you tell me what is going on?"

Séraphon tried to swing his upper body around. But his too-heavy head dropped on his shoulder. He concentrated, so that his brain began to seethe. He heard Remould's steps growing fainter and after a while, as if from a great distance, what seemed to be the laughter of children. Séraphon was afraid.

"Remould! I'm cold! I tell you I'm cold! Come back!"

A minute crept by in the midst of a disquieting silence. Then, the sound of running feet, shouts, and again the voices of children. A pair of exceptionally strong hands gripped the handles of his chair. A voice, one he did not recognize, spoke into his ear:

"We must leave here right away."

Séraphon felt the joke had gone too far.

"Stop! Right now! Come stand here in front of me. I want to see you, Remould, that's an order! Otherwise, I won't believe it's you! . . ."

He called out for help. The chair jolted over the bumps as it careened toward the exit. They reached the sidewalk, a window opened, a woman's face appeared, she yelled. The chair gathered speed. Séraphon was about to lose his mind. To his right the house fronts flashed by. He felt as though he were tumbling over a cliff.

A wagon drawn by a pair of horses suddenly came into view at the corner of the street. Remould braked by holding back the wheelchair. Ejected by the momentum, Séraphon sailed directly under the wagon. The old man landed flat on the pavement with his neck pressed against the wheel. Another inch would have meant the guillotine.

The horses were so startled by Séraphon's lamentations that the fireman was hard put to control them. He set about berating Remouald, who, breathless and confused, had somehow managed to pick Séraphon off the ground and was doing his best to settle him in his chair. The old man was beside himself, refusing to believe this individual was his son, begging the fireman to save him from the clutches of this impostor!

Remouald shook him roughly, then lifted up his chin and forced him to look at his face.

"Hey! See? It's me! Me, Remouald!"

Speechless for a moment, Séraphon broke into sobs.

"Oh, my little Remouald, my son! Here you are, at last! Someone tried to murder me! To murder me! Where on earth were you? Oh, I guess you'd have been glad, eh!"

And he kept on snivelling: "Nnn . . . nnn . . ."

Remouald gave the fireman a timid wave meaning it would be fine, everything was back to normal. The man lashed his horses furiously and moved off, muttering a firefighter's abuse.

WHEN THEY ARRIVED home, Séraphon, his objections notwithstanding, was parked by the window. A gaggle of youngsters were playing hockey under the lamps of the train station. In front of the Ace Box building some workers were loading a truck.

Remouald had withdrawn to the far end of the flat, near the kitchen counter. His flaxen hair, pasted against his forehead, was sticky with perspiration. From under his coat he pulled out the piece of wood and placed it on the table. His stomach was knotted with anxiety. He felt as though he had just drained a large, icy glass of vinegar. The image of those silhouettes, of what they were doing behind the wall, had left him dazed. He stared at a corner of the ceiling, and their shapes seemed to keep bobbing before his eyes like black spots. He grabbed the flask of caribou from the sideboard and gulped some down.

"Here come the firemen!" Séraphon burst out, with a note of triumph.

Remould rushed to the window. A four-horse wagon had pulled up in front of their door. Half a dozen firemen got out and lined up on the road. The captain rang their doorbell.

"What do those clowns want with us anyway?" Séraphon asked.

Remould hurried back to the kitchen to put the bottle of liquor away. The piece of wood still lay on the table, frightening and peaceful all at once — where to put it, for God's sake? The officer rang a second time. Remould ran to the dresser and thrust his find under a pile of shirts in the middle drawer. Then he went to answer the door.

The captain stomped up the stairs. He sat down at the kitchen table, deposited his cap in front of him, and lit a cigar. Remould diffidently informed him they had no ashtrays.

The captain gestured as if to say, "No matter." He rummaged in the pocket of his uniform and pulled out an ashtray. Remould gagged: it was the same one. There was mud still clinging around the rim.

"Does the sight of an ashtray upset you?"

"No," Remould quickly replied. Wringing his hands, he asked, "Would you like something to drink? Some tea perhaps? . . . Or a morsel of salt pork to eat? We just happen to have some. Are you hungry?"

"I wouldn't mind some pork, now that you mention it," the captain said with just a touch of gentility. "And if your tea is very dark, I won't say no to that either."

Remould never ate meat, but Séraphon, after his meals, liked to suck on a piece of salt pork. There was always a hunk of it in the sideboard. Remould would go through the ritual of slicing it into bits and then handing one to his father whenever he asked. Séraphon sucked on them slowly, savouring them before spitting them out. There were shrivelled scraps of pork rind all around his bed, like fallen flower petals. Remould, on the other hand, maintained a perfectly balanced diet, eating only every other day.

Remould felt he had been too hasty in making this offer to the captain, as the salt pork was stored next to the bottle of caribou. The captain might be offended that he had not been invited to have a drink as well. Remould acted as though nothing was amiss, but his hands were shaking.

The captain, however, was attending exclusively to a padlocked cabinet high on the wall. He winked knowingly, certain of his own cleverness.

"The family fortune?"

"Eh? . . . Oh, that! No. I don't really know what's in that cabinet. My dad is the only one who knows where the key is and he's never told me what's inside."

Remould, who had never taken any interest in the cabinet, was telling the truth though he was aware of the fireman's apparent disbelief. He turned, with a hint of disgust, to slicing the slab of pork. The knife was dull and slid over the fat. To overcome his distaste he concentrated on reading the headlines of the newspaper the pork had been wrapped in.

In the bedroom, Séraphon was absorbed by the events in the street. The children had dropped their game. They were circling the firefighters, their mouths agape in admiration. Some neighbours, who were never seen as a rule, pressed their timorous, shivering noses against the windows. They were old men like Séraphon, or old women; the whole street, every house, was like that — chock-full of old people. Breaking rank, a fireman snatched the hockey stick of one of the boys. With the blade jammed between his thighs and the end pointing upwards, he danced a few steps in a burlesque imitation of a penguin. The little boy laughed.

"Actually," the captain said as Remould poured the ink-black tea, "a witness has declared she saw you and your mother on the site of the Grill aux Alouettes about a half-hour ago. Is that correct?"

"Uh, yes. Yes."

Remould fidgeted incessantly with his shirt collar. The captain, chewing on his wad of salt pork, continued.

"In that case, do you mind if I ask you a few questions? Would you have any objections if your mother took part in the conversation? I think that would be best."

Remould consented and went to get his father. Séraphon protested; he preferred to watch the antics of the firemen and children. Nevertheless, once his son had positioned him in front of the officer, he greeted the man obsequiously.

"Your son and yourself, madam, must realize of course that trespassing on private property, even when it has been razed by fire — indeed, especially when there has been a fire — constitutes an offence, neither more nor less, whose seriousness, I grant you, depends on the circumstances, and in this case we, the officers and I, are willing to turn a blind eye."

The captain, giddy from the convolutions of what he had just said yet relishing every syllable, paused to bask in its echo. Then he tore off another bit of salt pork with his teeth.

"But could you explain to me your reasons for snooping around there?"

Séraphon smiled. Being the son of a schoolteacher, he was not about to squander this opportunity to let the fireman know that in the arena of artful phraseology he had just met his match. He tilted his head condescendingly and cleared his throat as a matter of form.

"Your perspicacity is remarkable, sir, truly remarkable. I would never even dream of attempting to mislead you about anything at all. You called me 'madam' just now, did you not? What astonishing insight! You — how shall I put it — sense others to such a degree! You were able to see the woman in me, the one that the frailty of my constitution, worn down by the years, has ultimately made of me. Yes, the man I've become is nothing but a crone, and your discernment could not lead you astray. I shall therefore answer your question directly, but this old woman's memory plays tricks on me, so I must appeal to your kindness and indulgence as an officer and ask you to repeat it."

Unruffled, the captain repeated his question.

"Well, here it is. My son, here, though somewhat clumsy, is basically a good-hearted man, who takes care of his old woman of a father . . ."

"All right, all right, I get the point."

"As I was saying, my son, at mealtime, said this to me: And what if, in the rubble, there still remained some poor soul? Imagine, a man, a woman — who knows? — miraculously spared perhaps by some mysterious quirk . . . After so many days. Think of it: *after so many days!* It's been known to happen, you know . . . Well, wouldn't it behoove us to go rescue him? An infant, perhaps. One of the Good Lord's little children, Captain."

"I can't see what a baby would have been doing at the Grill aux Alouettes."

Séraphon managed a faint shrug of the shoulders, as if to say, "Oh, but one can never say for sure!"

"If I catch your drift, you ventured into that mess in the hope of finding a survivor."

"Yes, that's right."

The captain turned a questioning eye toward Remouald, whose only response was to lower his head.

"Witnesses say they saw your son pick something up. This, as a matter of fact."

The captain pointed at the ashtray. Planted amid the cigar ashes, unchewable remnants of pork rind sprouted like spider legs. Séraphon was quick to provide a justification.

"Actually, I was the one who asked him to do so. Just think, Captain, what an object of contemplation! Into this ashtray, who knows, an individual like you or me, in a daydream, confidently mulling over plans, imagining his future, had dropped the ashes of his cigar, still believing he had before him many more . . ."

"The ashtray is not the issue, since you left it more or less where you found it. That is not what interests me. But I was told your son had . . . Well, I was told that something happened, that your son did something else. Did he see something? Did he take something else? That is what I would like to have explained."

With his jaws clenched, his pupils burning, Séraphon turned toward his son. Remouald shook his head vigorously.

"I don't know what they're referring to. I didn't take anything. I swear. See anything, do anything, take anything."

"In that case, how do you account for your . . . what's the word I'm looking for . . . your haste when you left the site? One of my men was able to identify you, he saw you coming in here, your house. He was the one, in fact, who almost sliced your father in half with his wagon."

The recollection elicited a pitiful bleat from Séraphon.

Remouald was on his feet. He had absentmindedly grasped the knife, before suddenly realizing this might be perceived as a hostile gesture. He put it down.

"I have nothing to say about that. About the fire. About the Grill aux Alouettes. About anything."

The captain invited Remouald to step into the corridor. Remouald followed him hesitantly. The fireman grabbed him by the collar and shoved him against the wall. He spoke in a low voice so that Séraphon would not hear.

"Now I place you — your name wouldn't be Remouald, by some chance, would it? Well, how about that, little Remouald . . . You know, Remouald, back when we were in grade school together, you already made me sick. Do you remember? You're not such a hotshot these days, by the looks of it. I'm telling you this because I'm not exactly in the mood to act nice to you. I know what you're capable of . . . my memory is pretty good, you know. So, you did nothing, you say, you saw nothing, nothing at all, earlier, at the Grill? That's fine, Remouald, just fine. That's what I like to hear. That's exactly what I like to hear. I'm telling you this for your own good, do we understand each other? Answer me. Do we understand each other?"

Remouald, looking the captain in the eyes, did not say a word.

Yet, quite unexpectedly, the officer did not press the point. He relaxed his grip and with mock graciousness made a show of smoothing Remouald's collar before returning to the kitchen. At Séraphon's insistence he slipped the rest of the salt pork into his pocket. He donned his cap, giving it a pat for good measure.

"Well, show the officer to the door, you fool!" Séraphon whispered.

Remouald followed the captain into the street. Packed together in the wagon, the eight firefighters were dozing with an air of satisfaction. The captain woke them by pounding his fist against the side of the vehicle. They straightened up in a bleary-eyed bustle. Between the hooves of one of the draft horses a hockey stick lay broken in two. The boys were nowhere to be seen. The officer warned Remouald not to start again — next time charges would be brought — and described the penalties he and his father could face. "Do we understand each other, my little man?" Remouald, shaking, answered that he would not start again. The captain nodded and climbed into his seat. The wagon made a cavernous racket as it got underway, rumbled off toward the factories, and, after a few seconds, left the street once again submerged in silence — an audible silence, full of murmurs, the kind an apparition leaves in its wake.

* * *

"Aha! I knew it!" Séraphon exulted. "You've been hiding something from me! What did you pick up over there? You brought it back here, eh? Come on, show me what it is! Do you hear? Hurry up!"

With one elbow resting on the table, Remould stared at the floor. He was content to let his arm swing with the languid jadedness of a cow's tail swatting flies. Séraphon insisted. Getting Remould to own up was his favourite pastime. It was like roasting him on a spit: little by little the rind cracked open, there was a long whistling sound — Remould was about to confess. Séraphon anticipated that joyous moment. What took place, however, was extraordinary. Séraphon was struck dumb. He had never before seen his son like this. Remould had stood up. He stepped toward him, eyes bulging, in a state of unbridled exasperation. Séraphon shrank his head back in terror. His son gathered him up like a sack of potatoes, crossed the corridor, nearly tumbling over the brooms and buckets, and dropped him into bed, furiously yanking the covers over him. The old man, aghast, bounced on the mattress.

Remould returned to the kitchen, panting, stupefied by what he had just done. He turned off the lamp for fear of being watched and went to the sideboard. He groped around for the bottle of alcohol. He was shivering. He sat down again at the table. He could hear Séraphon sobbing in the bedroom. In the end, he blocked his ears with his hands.

That night, he fell asleep very late and had a dream.

Some residents of the neighbourhood had formed a circle around the site of the fire. There was the bank manager, his secretary, the people at the general store. They were looking at Remould in a way that was both jovial and ferocious. Remould was in the company of a little girl who was a stranger to him. The two of them were leaning over a hat, inside of which a genital organ softly wiggled its head like a frail little creature newly born, wounded and eyeless. A fireman arrived blowing on bagpipes. On his belt he wore a game pouch from which the head of a rabbit emerged, speaking in a child's voice. It asked Remould what he was doing with a little girl and what he was hiding in his hat. Remould knew he must answer but he was terrified. Then the fireman burst out laughing and carried off the little girl under his arm. Remould anxiously thought, "He will make her eat the rabbit." Such a thing could not be allowed to happen. The fireman was getting farther and farther away while the rabbit implored Remould with its eyes. The crowd applauded as if they were at the theatre. Remould ran up to the fireman and placed his hand on his shoulder. The fireman would not stop. Remould seized his shock of red hair and stifled a cry of horror: the fireman's grimacing head had come off in his hand. The spectators jeered and threw ashtrays. They clambered down the sides of the hole and closed in on him with threatening looks. The headless body, unperturbed, kept on walking away. Remould awoke, sweating profusely.

He realized he had slept later than usual and that for the first time in fifteen years he might arrive late for work . . . Yet he was not concerned about the time of day. On the other side of the bed they shared Séraphon was mumbling, groaning, having an old man's nightmares. There were large snowflakes slanting across the window.

Remouald kneeled in front of the dresser and painstakingly opened the middle drawer. As he groped under the shirts he glanced over at his father to make sure he was asleep. He drew out the icon of the Virgin that he had hidden there the night before. The wood gave off a burnt odour. He leaned the icon against the wall. Palms pressed together, fingers so tightly entwined that the nails dug into his flesh, Remouald Tremblay prayed with a fervour he thought he had lost. It had been so long, he had forgotten the taste of salt, burnt dreams, and blood that tears had.

2

I AM NOT mad — after all, I did see them. In the event some misfortune should befall me and someone stumbles on this notebook, I would ask the following information to be passed on to the police.

I, Clémentine Clément, teacher at the École Adélard-Langevin, being of sound mind and body, single, and still young, attest that on the night of Monday, November 23, I saw three of my sixth-graders, namely Rocheleau, Bradette, and Guillubart, on the site of the Grill aux Alouettes, recently destroyed by fire. I was able to observe them from my window. They were gathered behind a wall, which unfortunately impeded my view. An individual entered the site and proceeded toward the wall. After a few minutes, possibly two, he retraced his steps carrying something under his coat. I saw him scurry away, showing no regard for his poor mother, whom he was pushing in a wheelchair. I could not restrain myself, so I opened my window and shouted. There, that is all. Rather than contacting the police I thought it preferable to alert the fire brigade. I also took the opportunity to give them the ashtray the suspect had thrown onto the grounds in front of my house. The sight of the ashtray seemed to plunge the captain — who, to speak plainly, is by no means unpleasant to look at — into a vortex of cogitation. Perhaps it was a mistake, but I chose not to mention the children to the firemen.

I am writing this at six-thirty in the morning, Dear Diary that I have so dreadfully neglected. In relating all this, I was hoping to dispel the thoughts that have hounded me through my sleepless night. This is my seventh bout of insomnia in the past three weeks. Sleep is not the thing I will have most enjoyed in this life. When I do manage to drift off, after thirty seconds I start to dream the same dream, the nightmare that has tormented me ever since the fire: I again see the crazed horse galloping in the direction of my house, the horse aflame and heading straight for the yard crammed with oil barrels, if not for a policeman, who brings him down with a rifle . . . In the days that followed, thinking of that poor beast, of the blood bursting from its skull, of its head like a frog turned inside out, many times I all but brought up my food. Sometimes, at night, I am afraid. As though, beyond all control, something were hatching within me, an act whose meaning and implications escape me. An explosion, perhaps? A fall? What's more, I feel tense, vulnerable . . . I look at my face in the mirror and I appear to be on the verge of tears . . . And I know this is the face others see every day.

As for my doubts concerning Bradette, Guillubart, and Rocheleau, I will be satisfied to share them this morning with Brother Gandon — the school principal, at least, should be informed! Once again, he will say I am exaggerating, I'd bet my last dollar on it. It saps my strength to be cast as someone full of suspicion, and it has even occurred to me that Brother Gandon . . . No, I am not going to start nitpicking. We must get back to what's important. The problem is knowing what attitude to adopt toward those three pupils. Since I found those compromising *drawings in Guillubart's binder, they are sure to be on their guard, so it's best not to arouse their mistrust by watching them too openly. Something — I don't know what — is out of kilter with those little boys. It may be nothing more than some harmless conversations, chance encounters, but by the looks of it something fishy is going on. And, if that is the case — I do say if — then last night a crack appeared in their secret. That crack is what I must work on, where I must slip through, but without rushing, otherwise it may seal up again. Even when I was very small, I could not abide mysteries, and I have sworn that I will not be stumped by this one either.*

Enough. I'm going to get some air before my first class. Perhaps I shall put on my new dress. They say it's good for morale. If someone suggested beating myself on the head with a hammer as a way to improve my morale, I'd no doubt do it without any hesitation.

I hope with all my heart my three students are not yet in any danger. I humbly ask God to hear me.

Only, does God exist????????

I love children so much that, at times, I must admit, I almost frighten myself.

THE BRISK MORNING air did Miss Clément good. She gradually regained her composure, and the obsessions of the night faded. Why had she let herself get carried away again? She was not proud of herself. It was about time she learned to rein in her outbursts. Self-control was a virtue she ranked above everything else.

She had been walking for about an hour. She had gone as far as the tobacco factory and, as though drawn by a magnet, had headed north, wandering for a while near the construction sites. She came back along Rue Moreau. She was still far from the school and time was slipping away. Lights came on in the windows, and with the heat emanating from the houses came wafts of fried eggs and porridge. There were birds flying across the sky. Clémentine harked back to the mornings of her childhood.

She was perplexed by the crush on Rue Ontario. Lost in her thoughts, she found it hard to grasp what was happening. Then she recalled that the authorities had announced an official funeral would be held for the fireman who had perished in the blaze at the Grill. The march would proceed to the train station. From there, a special train would transport the deceased to his hometown for burial. Resigned, Clémentine put on a woeful look and waited.

The cortège stretched over a half-dozen streets, from Préfontaine to Davidson. The fireman's remains were to the fore, followed by a municipal delegation including Catholic eminences in full regalia. Various notables tipped their hats at each other and, speaking in low voices, used the occasion to confirm meetings. The grocers, the pensioners, the curious, mourners of all stripes, along with vagrants attracted by the crowd, closed the procession. The wreaths gave off a heavy fragrance of overblown flowers, indolently rich and cloying — the cold, putrid, unmistakable odour of fresh graves. Here and there little coughs of reverence could be heard.

Sitting atop the casket the child wore a fireman's helmet, the one his father was wearing the day of the tragedy. The neck guard, fanning out over his shoulders, gave him the appearance of a droop-eared rabbit. In the wreath that encircled him were the words, written in flowers:

He was one of Miss Robillard's pupils. Well behaved in class, hard-working, perhaps somewhat nondescript; just last year, Clémentine now remembered, he had lost his mother . . . He seemed intimidated by the multitude and, with his head bowed, was blowing into the palm of his hand. Clémentine felt a tremor of revolt. In uneasy groups ageless women advanced with small yet hurried steps; the frailest among them stared intensely at the beads of her rosary, which she fondled like a miser fondling his gold coins. Soon Clémentine recognized the same look of grim gratification on all the faces. She believed she was about to faint, or cry out. She shut her eyes and breathed deeply. Two tears slid down beneath her collar.

She decided it would be better for her to turn back and, though she was pressed for time, to reach the school by making a detour to the north. The bleak expanses of the construction sites did nothing to improve her mood. She had the impression that, even there, the scent of the flowers still clung to her.

THE SNOWFLAKES EXPIRED as they touched the ground, a last sigh, tiny lives. Clémentine was now only two blocks from the school. Some laggards scrambled past her with their chests thrust forward like hens on the run. A blond boy with freckles had halted, legs apart, facing the wall. She stationed herself behind him. Just when he would start to relieve himself she would lay her hand on his shoulder, pinch his ear, as a matter of form, and the rascal would be kept in at recess . . . Clémentine's eyes were shining.

But the schoolboy went on his way again — he had merely re-buttoned his jacket, his back to the wind. She smiled tenderly. He pulled up short to doff his cap at Clémentine. She took the opportunity to plant an eager, amused kiss on his cheek.

Then realized what she had just done.

The child stood there, abashed. Clémentine felt hot around the temples.

"Go on, go on! Run along!"

She motioned as if shooing birds away. The child bolted without a word. She looked around her. No one had witnessed the episode.

THE STUDENTS WERE restive, excited by the sense of reprieve that came with the last minutes before the bell; a riotous clamour rose from the schoolyard. As soon as she walked through the gate a cluster of children grabbed on to her skirt. They began to talk to her all at the same time. Clémentine paid heed all around, answered every question, earnestly gave ear to charming trifles; she settled a dispute over the number of bellies that ants have. When she again crossed paths with the freckled boy, she tried to smile at him but he became flustered and ran away. Clémentine once again felt hot around the temples.

A dark object sailed past her face, obliging her to duck. Some children were gleefully kicking it. A gaunt beanpole of a man skittered pathetically from one youngster to another in the hope of retrieving his hat. Miss Clément recognized him: it was the bank clerk. She thought it strange to see him there, as no one was allowed in the schoolyard aside from the students and the teaching staff — the regulations were very stringent on that point. But that was no reason to tolerate a game of this kind. "Martin!" she shouted, "Gérard! That's enough!" She was about to dispense a few slaps when the bell rang. The tumult collapsed suddenly, like a house of cards. The students streamed back toward the buildings.

They had assembled in lines, and Clémentine, treading slowly, inspected her own; nothing must be allowed to protrude — not a shoulder, nor the top of a head. The bank clerk's hat lay near Guillubart's feet. Clémentine pretended to straighten Pierre Lavallée's bow tie in order to better observe Rocheleau, who was holding something out to Guillubart — a piece of paper he had crushed into a ball. Guillubart stretched out his hand to take it. Clémentine swung around and marched toward them. Guillubart, in a panic, dropped the ball of paper, which rolled inside the hat. Miss Clément moved to pick it up, but a giant silhouette intervened, and she felt a sharp pain: the bank clerk, pushing his way through the ranks of schoolchildren, had stepped on her foot. After sputtering a few words of apology, he bent down to collect his felt hat. Then his eyes met Guillubart's and a look of surprise came over his face; for a long while, he and Guillubart stood facing each other, their lips trembling, pale and petrified as if they had seen a ghost.

"Miss Clément, are you coming?"

It was the voice of the principal, Brother Gandon. Clémentine's class was the only one that had not yet gone inside. She blushed and complied.

As she swung the door closed, she noted that the bank clerk had not moved. He had put his felt hat back on. His face still held the same stunned expression, as if the wind had been knocked out of him. With a shudder, the schoolteacher all at once understood. She had to lean against the doorpost.

BEFORE HE HAD gone three paces Remouald stopped. His hat was giving him the odd, nasty sensation that a bump had grown on his skull. He removed the hat and found the ball of paper. He unfolded it as best he could. Ineptly drawn were a woman's breasts, resembling the eyes of a clown, high-heeled shoes, and a pair of buttocks with hair on them. The paper bore the letterhead of a funeral parlour. There was also an address written in pencil, with a date and time, as for an appointment. Remouald recognized the address of the widow Racicot. She was the nurse who came every day to care for his father. The coincidence intrigued him. He slipped the paper into his pocket and, as he made toward the bank, promised himself to further reflect on this enigma.

The school principal was standing at his office window. The teacher stood next to him. They watched Remouald until he had left the schoolyard.

"I'm certain that is the man," Clémentine said.

The captain of the fire brigade was hiding behind the wall of the laundry. He waited until Remouald had turned up Rue Saint-Germain. Then, lighting a cigar, he fell into step behind him.

* * *

THE CLIENTS AND employees were at the window watching the dwindling outlines of the procession, all that could now be seen. Remouald was able to enter unnoticed by the side door. His desk was narrow and too low for him, but it faced the wall so that he was spared having to return his colleagues' grimaces, for the bank regulations obliged one to smile at everyone at all times. Mr. Judith, the manager, leaned over his shoulder.

"Mr. Tremblay, could you come to my office this morning? As soon as you have a free moment."

Remouald swallowed his saliva. The manager had a way of announcing the worst sort of news by putting on gracious airs. There was not much for Remouald to do that morning, but it took him half an hour to work up the courage to confront his superior. Whenever he was summoned to Mr. Judith's office he found it impossible not to imagine that the scaffold awaited him there. He was certain of being reprimanded for his lateness. He barely grazed the glass door when he knocked on it.

"Come in, come in, my dear fellow! I just need to finish dictating this letter. Do sit down!"

Remouald seated himself near the window. The chair looked like a doll's chair. His height, accentuated by his thinness, was a constant source of discomfort for him (which is why the one place he felt at ease was his kitchen, whose furniture he had built to measure). He heard, without listening, the pat administrative phrases the manager was glibly dictating to his secretary. Through the window, he contemplated the sky, the bell-tower of the church, and tried to think of nothing.

The little girl was staring at him. He had not noticed her at first. She sat engulfed in an overstuffed armchair. Her black eyes were all one could see of her face — everything else was eclipsed by her eyes, deep as wells and wavering between sadness and amazement. She did not smile. Her wool-clad feet, which barely reached past the edge of the seat, rubbed together like kittens at play.

"You may come closer, Mr. Tremblay. And you, too, Sarah. Come now, my child."

Remould obeyed and placed himself before Mr. Judith. Sarah did not deign to leave her armchair. She was content to study their faces.

A Frenchman through and through, and not about to let anyone forget it, Mr. Judith was afflicted with a chronic itch in the eardrum. When conversing, he was in the habit of propping his elbow on the armrest of the chair with his pinky planted in his ear. Fiftyish, plump, and as affable as could be, he spoke with a singsong voice and the smoothness of an oblate.

"Please excuse her, dear friend, she is very shy. But as you will see, she is an affectionate, sensitive child. Sarah is my niece — actually, the daughter of one of my nieces, though it hardly matters. The fact is, her mother had to be hospitalized this week. She will have to remain under medical supervision, I'm afraid, for some time, the poor girl." By way of screening himself from the child he put his hand against the side of his face and whispered, ". . . Tuberculosis."

"How sad," Remould answered, guardedly.

Mr. Judith rolled his big eyes full of commiseration.

"Sarah's mother has been beset by adversity. If you only knew! Her husband suffered a fatal attack last year. I was unaware of it until this morning, when I read her letter. And so she has lost both her mother and her father. Though we have not been able to see each other these last years — you know how it is — I am her closest relation. So, during her convalescence she has entrusted me with the care of the child, little Sarah here. There she was this morning, waiting for me by the door. With this letter in her hand. All alone! Delivered to me like a package!"

Remouald acknowledged this but remained aloof. The manager, whose antennae picked up this reticence, felt that his clerk was not making things any easier for him. He let a few seconds go by, and then, with a slight sigh, promptly resumed.

"You more than anyone, dear Tremblay, know how busy I am here at the Bank." (In Mr. Judith's mind, the institution could not be thought of without a capital B.) "I myself cannot look after the child. As for my wife, she is not well, may God take pity on her, so that, for the time being, I will be obliged to keep Sarah here, where she has been miserable, sitting in her chair all morning."

Mr. Judith, who had just extracted a bit of wax from his furry ear, pretended to focus on the tip of his fingernail. In fact, he was studying the effect his story was having on Remouald. Remouald had wrapped himself in a sullen silence. The manager cleared his throat.

"And so, well, I thought of you."

"Of me?"

"Yes."

"But, in what regard?"

"In regard to the little girl. I am aware that, of late, your workload has not been very heavy. I thought that, given your efficiency, the morning hours could be quite ample for you to complete your tasks for the day . . . Am I mistaken? Would that be possible?"

"Perhaps. What of it?"

"I'm somewhat embarrassed to ask you this. But look at it this way: for the fifteen years you've been employed here your work has always been beyond reproach — you must recall the last meeting of the board, when Mr. Latraverse cited you as a model for the other members of the staff."

Remould, in fact, never attended board meetings. What would he do there?

"I didn't know he said that."

"I can assure you Mr. Latraverse really did say that. If you agree to mind Sarah on certain afternoons, while I make up my mind as to what's best for her, well, it would be a little like a vacation for you, wouldn't it? A token of my confidence in you, at any rate. Think of it, you could take her to the park, the department stores, the movies, or what have you. Needless to say, I would cover the costs. Besides, I am asking you as a friend . . ."

Remould was not fooled: it was not a matter of doing a favour but of toeing the line. What's more, he was fully aware that his work was a model for no one. There was only one thing he knew how to do, and that was to count quickly. Everything else, all those money questions, made no sense to him. He turned toward Sarah, as though she might be of some assistance to him. The little girl slowly lowered and raised her eyelids. It took time for the eyelids to uncover eyes that big. The word "impossible" slipped through Remould's lips.

"How so, dear fellow?"

"Huh? Well, I don't know . . . Why me? Why don't you hire a babysitter?"

The manager was unused to meeting with resistance, especially when the one putting up the resistance was this blockhead Remould. Even though he felt his position to be more delicate than usual, he adopted a somewhat firmer manner.

"A babysitter implies wages — have you considered that? And don't think I'm a wealthy man. Times are hard. Hard for everyone. I would rather not have to bother you with this, but since you leave me no choice I will confess to you that I'm feeling the pinch these days. Financially, that is. I am telling you this in confidence, my good friend. But there is more to it, as well, for who knows whether the babysitter would be someone I could trust? Whereas you . . ." He opened his arms to signify that it went without saying. "At any rate it would be only for a while, as I've already said. Until I find a permanent solution."

Remould smiled incredulously and softly shook his head, no. Mr. Judith looked at him disconcertedly. He wondered if his employee at all understood what he was saying. In his case, one could never be sure. Remould might sometimes appear completely impervious, as airtight as an egg, and the very next moment something would flash across his eyes like a bullet shot from a rifle. Mr. Judith pushed out his stomach, spread his hands, and evinced cordial disapproval.

"Come, come, my good Tremblay, you must admit that you have not had a great deal to do of late! I realize that what I'm asking of you may be a little out of the ordinary, but, come now! It's a favour, between friends: after all these years, haven't we indeed become friends?"

Remould timidly shrugged his shoulders. "That . . ."

"Let's be frank, Remould. You spend half your time twiddling your thumbs — no, no, don't object, we're just having a friendly talk. What about this morning? You arrived late. Now, I understand — it was probably your father — he needs to be cared for . . . But doesn't that prove you can reduce your work hours without it hindering your performance?"

Remould reddened, because if his hours could be diminished so could his wages.

Mr. Judith sensed he had taken the hint and, showing no mercy, added, "I know what you're thinking and I must admit I have had the same thought. You mind the child and I guarantee you your full wages."

Once again, Remould turned toward Sarah, this time under the distinct impression she had just called his name. Yet she had not pronounced a single word. She had put a lock of her hair in her mouth and was sucking on it impassively. Her hair, which was as black as her eyes, seemed to be of a texture so fine that to touch it would surely produce the same sensation as passing one's finger over a candle flame. The more he looked at her the more he realized how beautiful she was. As beautiful as only a seven-year-old girl can be.

He was struck by a sudden bolt of light.

"School! Why not send her to school like other children her age!"

The manager seemed disconcerted. Pulling the finger out of his ear, he straightened up in his chair and folded the panels of his jacket over his stomach.

"That is the touchy part, Mr. Tremblay, that is the touchy part. Sarah is a delightful child, I would even say in some ways a marvellous child, but, well, the fact is, she cannot go to school like other children — there is something special about her."

Ill at ease, Remould pointed to his temple in an inquiring manner . . .

Mr. Judith frowned and shook his head emphatically: no, no, where did you get such an idea? He took a deep breath and, like a man carrying a too-heavy load, let it drop. "You see, she is quite simply unable to talk. Not a word comes out of her mouth. She is mute. There it is."

He hastened to add that she understood everything that was said to her, knew how to read and even showed a gift for music.

"The violin!" he specified, solemnly raising his forefinger. "Her mother wrote all this in her letter."

"I enjoy music," Remouald said, glumly.

He thought of the music one heard on some holiday Sundays in church. Mr. Judith inferred from this that the proposal had been accepted.

"Good, good!" he said as he got up from his chair. "You know, we don't often have the opportunity to say certain things, but I for one have always liked you, Remouald my boy. Yes, it's true. Here, let's shake hands. Sarah will be waiting for you here at lunchtime. I won't keep you any longer. Thank you."

Remouald did not budge.

"If you would be so kind," the manager insisted.

With some effort, the employee stood up. He dragged his feet as he shuffled around the table and over to the door. Sarah followed his slightest movement with her eyes. Judith all at once seemed worried.

"Oh! Remouald, one last thing. I appreciate how difficult your situation must be. I mean, with your father being an invalid and all. So, if you'd like to have an extra half-hour at home in the morning, it's up to you, eh? Please don't thank me, it's my pleasure. All right, see you shortly, my friend. And thanks again!"

Remouald lowered his nose and left the room.

He made for the lavatory, seeking refuge in the tranquillity of the latrines. He went along the service counter where clients were queued up: November faces on a November morning after a funeral. At one wicket stood a woman of about fifty, slender, still beautiful. Remouald stopped dead.

In her gloved hand she clutched some sheet music. For Remouald, who was completely ignorant of musical notation and sang like a horse, there was no design lovelier than a sheet of music. Often, in front of the violin-maker's shop window, he would pause and surrender to the tenderness brought on by those pages covered with indecipherable little wings, as precise as dreams and forever about to fly away. It reminded him of letters sent by angels to the Virgin, which had fallen from Heaven. This image struck him all the more forcefully that morning as, right there, in the bank, at wicket number four, the lady holding the sheets of music in her right hand was the Virgin of the icon.

An apparition, come to withdraw money from the bank!

Remouald stood gawking at her. Tied back with a red ribbon, her hair was deep grey in colour. The grey of gravel in the sun after a shower, when it begins to gleam. Despite the imprint of the passing years, her features — especially her eyes, her lips — were just the same as on the icon. The cashier asked her name and Remouald heard her reply, "Vilbroquais, Justine Vilbroquais." The name, as well, stunned him.

Her eyes met Remouald's, and she gave him a faint smile, but he was incapable of smiling back. He bowed his head, which had all at once begun to throb, and clenched his fists, overcome by a kind of despair. How long this lasted he could not tell. When he once again raised his eyelids the lady was gone, but the manager was holding his arm sympathetically.

"My good fellow, what's the matter?"

Surrounded by employees and clients, he failed to understand. Someone said to apply a compress. Remould leaned against the counter and saw that his hands, shirt, trousers, everything was spotted a blackish red. The secretary arrived with damp cloths; someone brought a chair. It was when he sat down that he realized blood was gushing from his nose.

He felt a hammering in his skull, his chest. There was a foul taste in his mouth. Mr. Judith gave the order to call a doctor. Remould struggled: "It's nothing, I swear!" But they kept him forcibly seated in his chair. Someone dashed to the telephone. Around him everything was astir, as in a bad dream. "You must keep your head tilted back!" Remould was not responding. It was as if he were being addressed in a foreign tongue.

The suddenness with which the blood stopped flowing took everyone aback; the gathering fell silent. Remould gazed blankly before him. The church carillon was all that could be heard and, in the distance, seemingly in answer to this call, the barking of a dog. All of them held their breaths as they watched Remould.

All except Sarah, who was whistling very softly off to the side and to whom no one paid any attention. Remould turned toward her abruptly. Once again, he had the distinct impression she had just called his name. He had heard his name pronounced very close to his ear. There was in her manner the suggestion she apprehended something others did not. With quiet authority she motioned toward the window.

Just then, flecks of sunlight, as mobile as water, appeared on the hardwood floor.

3

AND, THUS BEDIGHT,
   Good Peggy, light —
Her gains already counted —
   Laid out the cash
   At single dash,
Which to a hundred eggs amounted.
   Three nests she made,
   Which, by the aid
Of diligence and care were hatch'd.
   "To raise the chicks,
   I'll easy fix,"
Said she, "beside our cottage thatch'd.
   The fox must get
   More cunning yet,
Or leave enough to buy a pig.
   With little care
   And any fare,
He'll grow quite fat and big;
   And then the price
   Will be so nice,
For which, the pork will sell!

> 'Twill go quite hard
> But in our yard
> I'll bring a cow and calf to dwell —
> A calf to frisk among the flock!"
> The thought made Peggy do the same
> And down at once the milk-pot came,
> And perish'd with the shock.
> Calf, and pig, and chicks, adieu!

"Calf, *cow*, and pig, and chicks," Miss Clément corrected, book in hand.

Thrown off his stride, Rocheleau continued hesitantly: *"Our mistress' face is sad to view . . ."*

"*Your* mistress' face is sad to view," Clementine amended. "The *pronoun* refers to the calf, cow, pig, and chicks."

She wrote the word "pronoun" on the blackboard.

The boy ended in a single breath, without the slightest hint of punctuation: *". . . she gives a tear to fortune spilt then with the downcast look of guilt home to her husband empty goes somewhat in danger of his blows."*

"Good," Clémentine said, "good. You may sit down. Your turn now, Guillubart. Finish the fable."

Guillubart stood up clumsily. His cheeks were the colour of church candles; his pointed tuft of hair shone above his forehead like an orange flame. He sneaked a glance at Rocheleau, who turned his head away. Then he looked toward the window with that air typical of a student who is at a loss for an answer.

"Come now, Guillubart," Clémentine said, and she began herself, with menacing slowness, stressing every syllable:

Who buildeth not, sometimes, in air
His cots, or seats, or castles fair?

What a silly fable, she thought.

Guillubart made a fumbling attempt: *"Purchased on a lofty oak, Sir . . . Fox . . . held a lunch of cheese . . ."*

"Are foxes often purchased in a tree?" the teacher asked in a weary voice. (The class laughed — a complacent, joyless laugh.) "Besides, you've got the wrong fable."

Someone knocked at the door. Guillubart sat down dejectedly. He immediately stood up again, along with the other pupils, on seeing the principal, Brother Gandon, who told them to be seated. Exhausted, Guillubart dropped into his chair. His limbs were leaden. He could hardly hold his head up or keep his eyes open. Evil little beasts were at work in his head right then, armed with complicated devices, twisting steel wires, snipping with cutters. A mass of heat squeezed his chest and his shirt grew damp with sweat that emitted the same sour tang as his sister had when she was stricken with scarlet fever. He saw his hand flipping over on his desk, jerking like a fish at the bottom of the net. His temples ached. He could no longer recall why he was afraid of the teacher; he struggled to remember what it was he had done, but his thoughts collapsed like a bear unable to lift its rump. And the teacher's face — she was at that moment whispering to the principal — prompted no more than a remote apprehension. A soft, transparent screen now hung between him and the others — their gestures, their facial expressions were enmeshed in this glutinous veil. The principal seemed to be turning in his direction. What did that look signify? Guillubart tried to smile at him but was unable. He looked again at Rocheleau but there was no consolation to be had there; rather, that restless snout, those shifty, clever eyes brought home even more his own weakness. *I'm sleeping with my eyes open*, he thought. He had never believed such a thing was possible.

The principal had just asked a question.

"The Dairywoman and the Pail of Milk," Guillubart said.

This time the class burst out in genuine mirth. Why had he said that? He hadn't even heard the question. He was not even sure it was him the principal had addressed! Guillubart batted his eyelids in sheer consternation. Brother Gandon laughed as well, but with solicitude.

"I think you were off somewhere just now. No, I asked: Whom does the Immaculate Conception celebrate?"

He pointed his finger at Rocheleau.

"Mary, Brother Gandon? Mary's purity?"

That was how Rocheleau was. He gave the right answers but always added a question mark at the end. Even when he said hello he made it sound like a question. Brother Gandon repeated the word "purity" with an enigmatic nod of the head, as if a great mystery had been touched upon. He turned toward Bradette.

"What does that signify, 'purity'? I would like you to tell me that."

Bradette had a hard-won reputation to defend. He sensed the class holding its breath: one correct answer would mean dishonour. If ever he was right it was by accident and always to his great surprise. He had a knack for knowing just enough to avoid getting cuffed and having to repeat his year. He looked at the principal, torn between the temptation to utter an inanity of historic proportions and the prospect, if he did so, of taking a clout to the head, for Miss Clément had just moved closer (whereas Brother Gandon, everyone knew, never raised a hand against a pupil). Bradette flashed an affected smile.

"Purity, Brother Gandon?"

The teacher leaned toward him, and he inhaled the womanly scent.

"The Brother has put a question to you, Bradette. Answer," she said.

Bradette would have liked to come up with the words to make the class explode with hilarity, but Miss Clément's warm presence, her hand on his shoulder, had entirely unnerved him. He craved to bite into the flesh of her neck. Clémentine straightened up and patted him on the head. Seeing her move away, he felt a keen stab of disappointment. He glared at her hatefully. *Just another tart*, he told himself.

Brother Gandon launched into a lecture on purity. Guillubart was fond of the principal. He enjoyed hearing him speak. Just then, though, the meaning of the sentences eluded him. He grasped only a few isolated words, which sank into him like stones dropping into mud. He was fond, too, of Miss Clément; she, however, was severe and she frightened him. All at once, he remembered the drawings. *Yes, that was it! It came back to him now: she had found the drawings! That was why he was afraid!* How could he have forgotten! His teeth started to chatter. He had the impression Miss Clément, who stood by the window scratching the back of her hand, was preparing to strangle him. Brother Gandon was referring to the purity of the body and the purity of the soul. Guillubart felt insects crawling inside his limbs, nibbling at his bones like ants beneath the bark of a tree. The janitor was walking down the corridor ringing the bell for recess. The students rose en masse and began to line up. Guillubart wondered whether his legs could carry him that far. Miss Clément cast him an angry frown. Pushing himself up from his desk with his fists, he rose to his feet and pretended that all was well. His hands were shaking, so he buried them in his pockets. He managed to read what the teacher had written on the board:

Impurity is a disease for which you are responsible.

***

As Brother Gandon filled his pipe, Miss Clément could not help but admire his long, lean, very masculine hands, the fingers always a little stained, due to the principal's avocation as a Sunday painter. It was with a forbearance born of familiarity that Miss Clément breathed in the stale air of the room. The office, which was never aired out, was permeated with the smell of musty tobacco and old whisky (of which — it was hardly a secret — Gandon partook regularly, but as he did not overindulge, everyone turned a blind eye). He must have been thirty-six or thirty-seven years old — Clémentine had never succeeded, though not for lack of scheming, in ascertaining his exact age. Slim, greying at the temples, a perfectly triangular face with a high, rather handsome forehead and sloping, heavy-lidded, slightly wistful eyes. He was reputed to be a highly intelligent man. And it was for that very reason Miss Clément was so often annoyed with him. So great was his intelligence that he understood nothing at all; everything needed to be explained to him, for he had the remarkably infuriating gift of being unable to admit the existence of wickedness or foolishness though it might be staring him in the face. He was quick to excuse everything and to attribute to everyone the best of intentions. For Clémentine, one had only to open one's eyes to realize that the evidence against such delusions was legion, and she took this Franciscan benevolence as a personal affront. Furthermore, Brother Gandon was extremely adept at taking no notice whatsoever when Miss Clément appeared before him in a new dress.

But she believed she had at last managed to rattle his quietude. She saw this in the contemplative way he packed the tobacco into the bowl of his pipe, and she could not suppress a quiver of delight. She waited; her palms were moist. He struck the match on the back of his thigh, and while he sucked on the tip of his pipe to ignite the tobacco a smile emerged at the corners of his mouth. Clémentine realized she had been too quick to cry victory. It was the kind of smile she knew all too well, the kind they exchanged in the midst of the little boys when they scolded them, telling them it was dangerous to throw snowballs. She saw that the Brother, once again, did not take very seriously the fears she had confided in him.

"But, Brother Gandon, did you see how they reacted? Especially Guillubart, who looked so unsettled? Aren't those signs?"

"Signs, perhaps, but not proof. Listen, Miss Clément. A teacher must not, of course, let her pupils pull the wool over her eyes. I know you have the insight needed to avoid this. But it is wrong to be constantly mistrustful, to always suspect something is amiss. Suspicion is a passion and, like all passions, it can turn into a vice."

"Thank you," Clémentine said, "that's very kind of you."

The principal chuckled graciously.

"Come, come, please don't take it that way: I am not judging you. It was an altogether general observation, one that may just as well apply to me some day. You know, in fact, that I resist the temptation to judge people, to classify them, to wrap them in labelled packages, as if God created them on an assembly line and had only a small number of moulds to choose from. One never acquires enough life experience to make unerring assessments of individuals — that's one lesson that comes with age. Having said that — and, believe me, I speak as a friend — it seems to me you are inclined sometimes to lend too much weight to events that ultimately prove to be rather harmless. What those pupils did, in my view at any rate, amounts to so much childish foolishness. Culpable, certainly, and to be prohibited, but still childish foolishness. Particularly when one considers that the fear of punishment has no doubt already dissuaded them from continuing. They are aware that you suspect something; they are not idiots. They will be doubly cautious, believe me. They'll behave like perfect little gentlemen."

Clémentine would have liked for a witness to be there, so that she might have the bitter pleasure of saying, "Look! Just look at how this man thinks!"

"If they abstain from such behaviour, Brother Gandon, it should not be out of fear of chastisement. They should abstain from such behaviour because they *understand* that what they did is evil."

Touché! she thought. It was discouraging, all the same, to have to reiterate such basic principles. For an instant, she worried that he might leap at the chance to hold forth on a point of theology. This was one of the principal's manias: If you let him broach such questions you were in for an excursion to another planet. When it came to educating children, Clémentine, on the other hand, preferred to keep her feet on the ground and fancied herself a practitioner of Anglo-Saxon pragmatism.

She knew that at bottom all Brother Gandon wanted was to spare himself the chore of castigating the students; he was not at all inclined to lecturing. He loved the children as comrades and tended to treat them as such. Clémentine studied him more attentively. The principal was stroking the leather border of his desk. His eyes lingered absent-mindedly on the teacher's legs; he realized this and immediately looked away. Then he yawned. A shiver ran through Clémentine's body.

She asked gruffly, "Am I to understand you find this affair irksome? If you are indifferent to the path our pupils follow, well then, perhaps you should find another occupation."

Gandon looked like a man whose nap has been rudely interrupted.

"Not at all, I assure you. Where did you get such an idea?"

He shrank in his chair as if she were waving a revolver under his nose. *I frighten him*, Clémentine thought with a twinge. She bowed her head in dismay. Well, she had sought to wound him and she had succeeded, but the blow had boomeranged and now she was the one who was hurt. It was just like her to step on the rake.

"I didn't mean what I said, Brother Gandon. Please accept my apologies. Yet I am telling you these are the same boys I spotted on the site of the fire last night. Rocheleau, Guillubart, Bradette! I saw them from my window. Saw them with my own two eyes!"

"That is dangerous — no question — they could have been injured. And I do intend to scold them, today, if that is what you expect of me. But you must allow that it's all quite natural. So many died in the fire, I suppose they believed there might be ghosts or something of that sort, out of a taste for adventure, for something terrifying. Such feelings are so new to a child that he relishes them all, even the most disagreeable. They were not able to forego the thrill of going down there for a good scare. That's all there is to it!"

"You are forgetting that man who also went down there!"

"But you told me yourself he was hidden by a wall; you don't actually know what took place. And suppose something did take place. You don't even know if the man was able to talk to the children."

"I saw this individual walk away with an object concealed under his coat, something he seemed bent on hiding from his very own mother, a poor old lady in a wheelchair! You don't find that suspect? I even telephoned the fire hall to inform them — the captain is a very fine person."

She caught herself thinking about the captain of the fire brigade longer than she had intended.

Gandon appeared to mull this over. "And you say that this is the man you saw this morning in the schoolyard?"

"The same — he is employed at the bank. I did not recognize him at once without his hat, because yesterday, at the Grill, he was wearing one. I saw Guillubart drop a piece of paper into the hat, earlier, when the students were lining up. The man had come for it; otherwise, what would he be doing in the schoolyard? So you may call me suspicious if it pleases you, but if you put that together with the obscene drawings I found yesterday in Guillubard's binder and

Bradette's very obvious discomfort when you spoke of purity, you must acknowledge that I have good reason to fear there is something very . . . well, you understand, Brother Gandon."

The principal responded with a pensive yes. It all seemed far-fetched to him. But could one ever know for certain? He had often noticed the individual in question, around the neighbourhood or at Sunday mass. What set him apart was that he never took Communion. He prayed with enormous fervour — that was obvious. Yet, even at Christmas, even at Easter, he would leave the church hurriedly at the moment of the Elevation. This intrigued the principal and he had raised it with Father Cadorette, who seemed to know the young man very well; but the aging priest had looked uneasy and quickly changed the subject. Since then, the principal had not actually thought about it again.

Brother Gandon had stepped over to the window; he held his pipe between his teeth and crossed his hands behind his back. He was watching the students at recess. Mechanically, he followed the dodge-ball teams moving about. He regretted not knowing the children better, one by one, the way one knows one's brothers and sisters. But year after year, they came, they left — it was all so swift.

Clémentine had joined him by the window. She found it comforting to stand beside him like this. She followed his gaze. Rocheleau and Bradette were not taking part in the game. Always together, always apart from the others. They seemed to be engaged in a lively discussion. It was a mystery what those two boys had in common. Bradette was a perfect dolt, something Miss Clément complained about constantly, whereas Rocheleau, with his edgy little fox-like face, was one of those children who grasp everything — arithmetic, grammar, geography — before one has even finished explaining.

"They are called the twin birds," Clémentine said. "There's no accounting for the affinities that little boys develop."

"Which is all to the good. This school has a mixture of everything: sons of notaries and poor children, intelligence and stupidity, the impatient ones and the dreamers, those who spit on the ground out of conviction and those who eat their snot when no one is looking, future politicians and future criminals, too. And all of them are nourished by this and steeped in it, like sponges thrown into the water. Later on each of them will go off to his own place, shut himself off in a world that resembles him. An adult sometimes knows less about people, about their diversity, than the child he once was."

"That is true," Clémentine said. It was not the first time she had heard the principal voicing one of her own thoughts. She told herself this could not be merely a matter of coincidence. She raised her hand.

"Look!"

Guillubart had just been knocked down by a schoolmate carried along by the game. He stayed prostrate and immobile. Gandon struggled to open the window. He leaned out and shouted that recess was over. They were relieved to see the frail Guillubart get to his feet.

Miss Clément hobbled to the door, due to her clubfoot. She asked the principal what he proposed to do.

After a pause, Gandon said, "Tell those three scamps to come see me in one hour. That should be enough time to give them a good fright."

Clémentine took this as a jibe, one she felt may have been coming to her. The principal gave her a sad little smile; she left the room without a word. No reference had been made to her new dress.

* * *

I TOLD HER today it was not my aim to judge others, which is true, but I do not think it conceited of me to affirm that I have a better than fair understanding of people. I have no illusions as to what she thinks of me; I am well aware she considers me a dreamer, a harmless idealist easily duped by all and sundry, but nothing, or so little, can be done about the opinion people have of us . . . If you consciously base your behaviour on kindness and consideration for others, you are regarded as a fool, as someone completely ignorant of the remorseless rules of life (you will even be called weak or, worse, a hypocrite). These so-called remorseless rules, if they exist, are vulgar, and it seems to me that it is incumbent upon us, first and foremost, to fend off vulgarity. Take, for example, these suspicions of hers. I, more than anyone, am in a position to appreciate the extent of our exclusion from the world of children. Childhood is a freemasonry that no adult can penetrate except through deceit. And then he is liable to bring his personal hell along with him. As educators we must never let our guard down, obviously. But to infer on the basis of some absurd coincidences that the bank clerk's intentions were bad, Good Lord! That is something altogether different. And Miss Clément's suspicion, when taken to such extremes, becomes unwholesome in my view, even grounds for concern. My impression is that the woman has never lived through any truly dramatic events. Her existence, as far as I can surmise, has not been very exciting. Consequently, her experience of the world must be, in short, quite limited. I had an aunt who was a hypochondriac, one of the "outlive-us-all" variety; having never been afflicted by any serious illness, she would make mountains out of molehills — a pimple on her lip or a pain in her fingers. My sense is that Miss Clément is like that. For goodness' sake! Torturing herself over some obscene drawings? How can she have so little insight into the mentality of young boys, especially after dealing with them as a teacher for fifteen years? (I won't go so far as to say this is typical of women.). Among my acquaintances, Miss Clément is the only person I have never seen laugh. It's as if she finds the very idea of laughter repulsive. Having known her for five years, I am sure this is no exaggeration. She is a passionate person — clearly — a person subject to strange outbursts. But at times I am afraid (afraid for her) that she is incapable of feeling true affection for someone. Not because she is heartless but for another reason which I am unable to pinpoint. I must add, however, that at other times I find myself wondering if I might not be mistaken on this score.

As for the bank clerk, I spoke to him once at one of the bank's charity functions. He struck me as a gentle individual. Self-conscious about his size (he must be at least six and a half feet tall), shy to the point of being sullen, and, to look at him, somewhat of a blockhead, to be quite frank. He would not have made any particular impression on me had it not been for a peculiar incident. We were having a conversation: I asked a few routine questions, he answered in kind, using as few words as possible. Then suddenly I glimpsed, in the space of a heartbeat, deep in his eyes, a flash of intelligence; it was unexpected, utterly intense, astonishing. The best way to express what I felt would be to imagine that a corpse, for just a split second, had blinked: it was as weird, as ghastly, as that.

One day I went to the zoo with some students. A raccoon had gotten its paw stuck in the mesh of its cage. I tried to free it, and while I was handling its paw the creature watched me, and that look disturbed me profoundly. What was it? I had the distinct feeling that behind that gaze there was someone. *I stood up and was unable to continue. The raccoon implored me with its eyes. My heart ached with pity for him, but there was nothing more I could do — I was paralyzed.*

It seems to me that the bank clerk troubled me in much the same way. He had gone off in a corner by himself to drain his glass of punch. For an instant (as I said, the space of a heartbeat) that imbecile's face evinced more intelligence than I have ever encountered in my entire life — a light, a lucidity *fit to make your blood run cold. What am I to make of him now, after what Miss Clément has told me?*

Brother Gandon paused. While lifting his flask out of the drawer, he thought he heard the sound of scuffling coming from the upper floor. He cocked his ears . . . No, it was nothing: his mind had played a trick on him. Having poured himself a generous glass of whisky, he turned the page of his notebook and found a note written the night before last: *"Above all, remember to put on a clean soutane on Wednesday."* After sucking on his pencil for a long while, he set to writing again.

That said, please be advised, Mr. School Commissioner, that I deem Miss Clément to be a distinguished teacher, and nothing written here bespeaks the slightest intention to denigrate her. If ever someone were to disparage her work as an educator, I would be the first to come to her defence, even if it meant putting my own position at risk, so absolute is my confidence in her dedication and integrity.

He reread with satisfaction what he had written and then was shocked when he glanced at the clock: he had not seen the time go by. What would his lecture be to those three ne'er-do-wells? He would have to extemporize. He emptied his glass of whisky in a single draft.

Once again a commotion arose in the corridor, a row in the stairway, the same noise of scuffling he'd thought he had heard earlier. He stood up. The door nearly struck him full in the forehead. There was Miss Clément in such a state that he believed she had lost her mind. Little Guillubart had been taken to the infirmary and might have to be transferred to the hospital emergency ward. He had just returned to the classroom, she explained, when he was overcome by convulsions.

4

Remould sauntered along Rue Notre-Dame toward the park called Dézéry (which people pronounced *Dézyré*), alive to the strange sensation of holding in his hand the trusting hand of a little girl. His overcoat, buttoned to the top, concealed his bloodstained clothes.

He did not quite know what to do with Sarah; he considered taking her to the movie theatre, a form of entertainment suitable for a young mute girl, it seemed to him. Sarah, meanwhile, was moderately attentive to her surroundings, which she observed with both patience and detachment. If he halted at a display window full of toys, she would halt as well, then both of them waited, Remould believing this pleased the little girl, and the little girl believing it pleased Remould. A sure sign they were beginning to get along.

In front of a café, a cardboard chef with a toque and fleshy cheeks proffered handfuls of soda pop bottles. He had a jovial air and a handlebar moustache. Remould hesitated momentarily before going in. Sarah accepted a glass of strawberry milk but hardly tasted it. She preferred to make bubbles by blowing into the straw. Remould looked through the window distractedly, his chin resting in the palm of his hand.

He thought about the slip of paper he had found in his hat that morning. Chance had just dealt him some strange cards pell-mell — a knave, a queen, a king perhaps, a two of clubs, and a two of spades — and with these he had to put together a hand, though he failed to see how. Sarah scissored her legs under the table, giving him an occasional kick. He let her. Whatever their origin, Remouald always had the impression the blows he received were warranted. When Sarah realized what she was doing she put her hand over her mouth and apologized with her eyes. This was the first time she smiled at him. And it stirred Remouald as though someone had lit a firecracker under his rear end: he dropped some money on the table and they left.

Remouald pretended not to have seen the captain of the fire brigade. Two passersby had approached him to ask for directions and, looking down from his mount, the officer had instructed them with administrative earnestness. The lady idiotically repeated the names of the streets as they were spoken to her; the young girl sank her head in shame. Remouald led Sarah down a cross street.

It was a winding, baffling street that went on forever. Remouald was unsure where it would take them. They walked for a long time. Finally they emerged, altogether unexpectedly, in the Faubourg à Mélasse (which people pronounced *Faubourg à Menaces*). Remouald, who had never set foot there, recognized it from something in the air — he could not say what — something that one breathed in. His heart contracted. He placed his hand on Sarah's shoulder. They had not gone twenty paces when on their left there appeared a sort of piano stool, a living tripod lurching toward them. It was a woman. Her head did not reach past Remouald's knee.

She planted herself before them and pointed one of her crutches at Remouald, but he could not determine whether this was a threat or a plea for pity. Tears ran down her cheeks. Her face, her skull, her neck were covered with lumps. Remouald walked on. Sarah turned back toward the invalid: a nervous, scrawny dog had joined her, and the woman was kissing him on the muzzle. An old man leaned out of his window hurling insults. The dog scuttled away and the tripod disappeared under a porch.

Remouald continued on his way. He wished at all costs to leave this place behind, but after a few minutes he found himself again confronted by the invalid, weeping in the doorway. Propped on her crutch, she held out her hand and repeated the word "Love," which in her mouth had a chilling ring to it. "*Luhhhhph? Luhhhhhph?*" Remouald felt a knot in his throat. "Madam . . ." he said. At this she emitted a hideous cackle. Remouald stepped back, pulling Sarah by the sleeve, but as Sarah did not want to go he had to hoist her in his arms. Sarah waved a tiny goodbye to the woman. Remouald wanted to scream for help. Flung from a balcony, a piece of fur landed slap at his feet and let out a horrific wail before bolting like an arrow beneath a verandah. Remouald was beginning to panic. He had been haunted his whole life by the fear of getting lost, of never again finding his way home. His thoughts turned anxiously to Séraphon: what would he do without his son? The paving stones in the lane were loose, and they twisted their ankles at every step. He breathed the exhalations of cabbage soup, of boiled rutabaga, of shabby interiors, of peels, of heating oil, of rot. He heard the bawling of a domestic dispute, the mewing, the snivelling, and through a door left ajar the intolerable braying of an infant, which was answered by the hoarse screeching of a crone, as obnoxious as a fingernail raking a slate. As he walked, Remouald's eyes flitted in every direction.

Behind them, suddenly, horse hooves. Remouald dared not turn around. He headed up another side street, then still another, haphazardly, borne along by his distress. The horse continued to pursue them. Remouald put Sarah down and crouched. He pretended to tie his bootlaces and snuck a glance over his shoulder. The captain of the fire brigade observed him with the haughtiness of a vigilante; he puffed on his cigar scornfully. Remouald once again took Sarah in his arms. They made off through the entrance of a courtyard, stole their way among the houses, skirted the walls, strode over fences, walked again for a while longer. Eventually they found themselves on Rue Sainte-Catherine. The crowd moved along in peaceful normality. Remouald leaned his back against a wall and breathed, his fist pressed against his chest. *Thank you, Lord*, he thought. He was sweating heavily, as if in midsummer.

Sarah, meanwhile, beat her mittens together for joy.

POWERFUL AND STOUT, head lowered like a battering ram, the priest, wrestling with the wind, almost collided with them as he turned the corner of Rue Darling. Father Cadorette had been ministering to the Nativité parish, souls and tithes alike, for close to thirty years. In an uncertain voice Remouald asked, "How are you, Father?" Cadorette had reached the age when one no longer feels obliged to answer such questions.

"What are you up to, out on the street at this time of day? Why aren't you at the bank?"

It seemed to Remould that an explanation would take hours. He thought it sufficient to say that Mr. Judith had entrusted him with his niece for the afternoon.

The priest's inquisitive eyes shifted from the little girl to Remould, as though he were searching for blackheads on their cheeks. He leaned down toward the child.

"And you? At your age? How is it you're not in school?"

Remould informed the priest that she was unable to speak. Sarah observed the priest with an air of supreme indifference, which vexed and troubled him at the same time.

"Does she at least understand what I'm saying?"

Without giving Remould time to answer he again bent down toward Sarah. Now, even her gaze went mute.

"What about Jesus, tell me, do you know who He is, Little Jesus?"

Sarah paused for a few seconds before nodding yes. Cadorette smiled with relief. With a roguish wink in Remould's direction, he let the crucifix that hung from his neck swing under the girl's nose.

"And do you know where Little Jesus is? Can you show me?"

With a solemn gesture, and no hesitation, Sarah pointed at Remould.

The priest recoiled.

"Who on earth has been putting such ideas into her head? She obviously doesn't understand a jot of what I've said to her. Without a doubt."

He uttered a peculiar chuckle, an appalled titter. But at the sight of Remould, whose face had turned stone grey, his laughter broke off, leaving behind a pitiful echo.

"I don't understand. I only met her this morning. I'm not the one who . . . Come now, Father . . . You don't actually believe . . ."

Remouald had removed his hat and was holding it meekly against his chest. With his jaws clenched, the priest left without saying goodbye. Remouald took a few steps in the opposite direction. Then he swung around and saw that Cadorette had also stopped and was looking at him. After a time, the priest walked away.

A gentle snowfall had started and Sarah pointed a finger skyward. Some birds, maybe pigeons or seagulls, were circling the church tower. She watched them, her face beaming. Remouald began to feel the cold.

"Coming?"

She did not budge, so he said, "Come, Sarah . . ."

She finally complied but walked with her head turned back so as not to lose sight of the bell-tower. She smiled at the bell-tower the way one smiles at an accomplice.

Remouald just then realized that was the first time he had spoken her name.

THEY ARRIVED AT the vegetable market, where the throng was denser. There were the shouts of the vendors and of warehouse workers unloading the crates. The trolley cars trundled along the rails, slowed to a stop, then rumbled away again amid the clang of bells. Remouald headed toward the music stand.

Some women had taken shelter there and were chatting, having set their shopping bags down by their feet. In their laps they held babies who drivelled and gummed their fists. Preschoolers played around them, rolling marbles, running after hoops or balls. Police officers on patrol came and went, hands clasped behind their backs, looking stolid and protective.

At times, from behind a gruff mask, a policeman would flash the children a conspiratorial wink.

It was at this point that Remould received a visit from his mother.

These meetings with her took place from time to time, quite by chance (although the priest had explained to him that it was only something he imagined). She had just stepped out from behind the stand, she was walking toward him, or rather, since her purple dress did not touch the ground, she floated toward him, like mist over a lake. Her hair was adorned with faded flowers. Remould saw her bearing down on him, her eyes brimming with anger and threats. He squeezed his eyelids shut just as the phantom passed through him. He felt a cruel twinge where his heart was . . . Then he opened his eyes; his mother had vanished.

Remould set off again, exhausted. He felt overwhelmed, drained, for the phantom had absorbed a portion of his blood. "It's nothing, it's only in my head," he repeated to himself, and harked back to the events of that morning — the lady with the sheet music. Now, *she* may have been a genuine apparition.

HE LET HIMSELF drift with the flow of the crowd. His hold on the little girl's hand had become flaccid. They walked along the stalls; the dampness dug into them bone-deep, but the next moment their faces were seared by a blast of heat from a brazier. Remould feared the little girl would catch a fever. Around them people bustled, shouted, bargained; the odour of vegetables and fruit was enough to make one's head spin. Remould had to summon all his self-control to keep from going to pieces and running amok like a dog.

Sarah snuggled closer to him. She laid her cheek on his hand and her hair grazed his wrist. A nun, very short and wide at the hips, was filling her shopping bag with canned goods as hurriedly as a burglar. Buzzing like a fly from counter to counter, she pivoted on her heels and, without realizing, knocked Sarah squarely in the face with her bag. The child collapsed. Her skull struck the ground and pink saliva spurted from her mouth. Remould gathered her in his arms and rushed straight ahead. Elbowing his way through the crowd, nearly upsetting some stalls, he dashed blindly to the far end of the market. He stood Sarah on her feet and kneeled down. Wild with worry, he examined her bruises. Sarah laughed. Her gums were draped with blood, her swollen right eye was half-closed and turning purple. Remould caught himself laughing too, nervously. But at the thought of having to account for the incident to Mr. Judith, his face clouded over. Sarah sensed his anxiety and in turn left off laughing.

All around people were looking at them suspiciously. Addressing no one in particular, Remould said, "How stupid! An accident! That's all!"

An old woman, leaning on a cane, eyed him reproachfully and muttered between her rotting teeth.

Sarah seized Remould's hand and pressed her wounded lips to it. Remould understood this was intended to ward off any suspicions; his eyes welled up. He wanted to thank her, to say a kind word to her. He wanted to tell her he thought she was beautiful. But the words stayed trapped in his throat. Besides, Sarah had already started on her way again and was marching boldly toward Rue Sainte-Catherine; he had to run to catch up with her. From then on, she was the one who decided which route to take, and Remould fell into line.

NEAR THE EXIT of the market stood a hut resembling a birdhouse. The roof tiles looked like cake, as in the story of Hansel and Gretel. There was an oval opening in the middle of the façade, green shutters on either side, but instead of the cuckoo there was a child: Maurice Bergeron, the little orphan firefighter.

He had on a helmet, the one he had worn the morning of his father's funeral. He was flanked by two charitable ladies who had organized a lottery to raise funds for the child. It was their duty to smile, as sadly as possible, while Maurice's was to hand the tickets to the buyers. One could see how seriously he took this role — he was as tense as a knife-thrower's assistant. Without giving it much thought, Remouald, towed along by Sarah, bought a ticket and, unsure what to do with it, offered it to the little girl, who ignored it. She was studying Maurice with a look that said, "So that is what an orphan looks like?" The boy turned his head away piteously; he was too well trained not to feel, in the presence of another child, that he was betraying childhood. After a while, he put on a faint smile. Sarah made a face and shrugged her shoulders. Remouald stuffed the lottery ticket into his pocket, where it was quickly forgotten, and they once again set out for nowhere in particular. He was so careless of the contents of his pockets that he would carry that ticket with him for the rest of his life.

TOWARD THE END of the afternoon, they climbed the stairway leading to the viaduct. Remouald noticed that Sarah did not stomp on the stairs as children are wont to do, for the same reason they never close a door without slamming it, because they enjoy the proof that noise provides. Sarah, on the contrary, set her foot down on each step, resting her weight on it, which gave Remuald the impression she trusted things and shared with them a secret that must not be disclosed.

From the top of the overpass they could view the neighbourhood stretching all the way to the river. It was strange. Remuald was unaccustomed to wandering this far from home. He sought his house amid the dark warren of streets, but his vision was blurred by the snow shower. One could barely make out the Ace Box building and the church of the Nativité d'Hochelaga, whose intricate forms, dominated by a too tall bell-tower, put one in mind of a sleeping swan fluffing its wings in a dream.

The sky was much as it had been the day Célia, his mother, passed away. Remuald was then in his early twenties, and Séraphon had already begun to be incapable of moving his limbs, which deserted him one by one like candles going out. Contrary to her habit of getting up first, Célia had remained in bed that morning. Remuald and his father sat silently at the kitchen table. They waited timorously for their breakfast, as if the best way to parry the blows of fate was still to cling to that good fairy, Routine. But time passed, neither of them daring to venture toward the bed to enquire after Célia, and their disquiet grew. Their fear, as well, a fear that dared not speak its name. Unable to bear it any longer, Remuald proposed to his father to take him for a stroll in the wheelchair.

At the time, the itinerary of their excursion had not yet been finalized. They had advanced as far the church, where, surprised by a sudden flurry, they took shelter under the portico. When the beadle noticed them shivering in the wind he went to advise the priest. Puzzled to find them there so early in the morning, Cadorette asked what the matter was. They were evasive. Séraphon said, "We've come to sing the praises of Our Lord!" Cadorette was not amused: "Stop fooling around; something's happened to Célia, is that it?" Séraphon moaned, but it was impossible for the priest to draw him out. In the end he told the beadle, "All right, I'm going to see for myself." All along the way he was irritated by the squeaking wheels of Séraphon's chair, following behind.

When they arrived at the door Remould refused to go in, and the priest was obliged to wrest the keys from his hand. Father and son waited in the snow. Cadorette entered the house and found the poor thing in her bed; there was nothing to be done except acknowledge that her life had been lived out. The undertakers were called, and, it being Sunday, Mr. Costade himself came to pick up the remains, which he loaded onto his back and carried to his automobile. Remould and Séraphon stayed huddled in the kitchen until nightfall. Cadorette had to take care of all the formalities: they were too terrified to sign anything. There was no choice but to bury Célia in the paupers' common grave. And it was twenty days before Séraphon agreed to return to sleep in his bed. During that whole time they slept in Remould's bunk, hugging each other like orphans.

Sarah had let go of his hand and was drawing on the parapet with the tip of her mitten. The snow kept erasing what she had doodled. Remould scarcely realized she was moving farther away. When she had gone some twenty paces she clapped her hands. He stifled a cry: Sarah was standing on the parapet sticking her tongue out at him. To her right was a chasm seventy-five feet deep.

Remould took a step, and she took a step back. He tried to rush her; she began to run. He stopped and yelled for her to come down from there, at first commanding and then imploring her. To no avail. She danced on the parapet and, out of mischief, at his slightest gesture, threatened to jump off. She removed her toque and threw it into the void.

"Why are you doing this? Why are you being so wicked?"

Sarah screwed her face up in that grimace of exertion a child makes when pinching someone with the intention of causing pain. She set to stamping the snow frenetically and, wielding her finger like a knife, slashed her arms, her thighs, her trunk, her cheeks — mouth agape, eyes shut, as if she wished to scream. Remould buried his face in his hands and wept.

Sarah stopped immediately. She came back all contrite and touched his arm three times: she needed for him to look at her, to see her smiling at him. Remould grabbed her and made her climb down from the parapet. She offered no resistance. She clasped his fingers, held them tightly against her cheek, then she pulled him along behind her.

The snow was falling as though the sky had split open under the weight of limbo. The flakes clung to Sarah's hair. They formed figures, signs perhaps. Remould tried to cover her head with his hat, but she would not hear of it. She shook her hair to rid it of the snow, newly ensnared, as in a trap. He thought she was sulking and this saddened him. He marched behind her, blinded, letting her guide him. But Sarah was not angry. With her nose hidden in her woollen scarf she smiled to her court of invisible elves, forever prancing around her, whose secret sorrows she knew by heart, together with each of their given names.

5

RIVETED TO HIS pillow and prevented from sliding out of the bed by an ingenious system of straps, Séraphon Tremblay waited for the widow Racicot to arrive at ten o'clock sharp. As a rule, she began her rounds with him. She would stay a half-hour, making certain nothing was wrong — in other words, that nothing was going on — then go off to visit another invalid. Her life was spent in this way, ranging from one old person to the next. She was the cheapest nurse in the neighbourhood, and he who pays for biscuit should not expect cake. A few coins a week for each patient allowed her to buy her porter, and that was all she asked. She daily imbibed about two and half gallons of it.

The widow Racicot shared her house with some ten cats, which, through a calling for carelessness, she by and large neglected to feed. There trailed after her everywhere an aura-like effluvium of dry turds and sand-covered piss. Speech was not her strong suit, but when she did speak it was exclusively about her kitties; she spoke of them as a mother does of her offspring, indifferent to whether anyone listened and confusing all their names. She was the joy of the neighbourhood children. When she walked down the street in wintertime they hurled so many snowballs at her, she could have opened a shop.

She stopped at Séraphon's house every two hours and stayed longer than with her other patients. Many times she would even wait until Remould returned from the bank before pulling up stakes. Remould was entitled to special consideration because he went to work in a white shirt. As for Séraphon, who was confined to his bed, he was the least demanding of her clients, and tranquility was what the widow cherished above all else.

The day would begin to drag, and Mrs. Racicot treaded more and more heavily. The clinking of bottles would announce her arrival, the stairs would boom as though pounded by a sledgehammer, and toward the late afternoon it was not uncommon for her to topple over as she stepped into the flat. In spite of Séraphon's many supplications, she never locked the door upon leaving, because she inevitably got snarled up in her keychain and patience was not her chief virtue.

She installed herself in her rocking chair, set a bottle of porter down at her feet, and pulled her knitting out from her shoulder bag. Séraphon never managed to ascertain what exactly she was trying to knit. It resembled the web of a spider gone mad. Not to mention the wool she used and reused, which must have been purchased at least twenty years ago. That was the widow Racicot, mother to no living child.

And she scared the living daylights out of Séraphon.

No sooner had she come in than she would bend over him and ask, mincingly, "How are we today, Mr. Tremblay?" Séraphon, holding his breath, was astounded that a person could convey so many odours. She fussed a little with his blankets to put her mind at ease, and patted his pillow. Then — but only if it occurred to her, which it did not always do — she tossed that day's newspaper into his lap.

His whole life long, Séraphon had always been an inveterate newspaper reader. Generally speaking, the tribulations of others, announced in large headlines, gave him a jubilant sense of superiority; he was comfortably out of harm's way — misfortune is good for something. The story of an ill-treated dog or of some *Canadien errant* was enough to bring tears to his eyes and, hence, afforded him the opportunity to delight in himself: he remained in bliss for a few moments, piously enthralled by his own fine sensibilities, like the little match-girl at the apparition of her grandmother. Politics left him cold, he felt nothing but contempt for athletic prowess, and so far as he was concerned foreign affairs, regardless of geographic particularities, took place on another planet. Everything else, however, he read voraciously. First the human interest stories, an inexhaustible wealth of inanity, then the local news, which he analyzed with a demented zeal. The residents of the neighbourhood may well have had no recollection of him, but Seraphon's knowledge of their private scandals was encyclopedic.

Because his eyes had survived the wreckage of his body, Séraphon Tremblay had no difficulty reading even the finest print. Nor did the classified ads escape his scrutiny. Alas, for some years his infirmity had prevented him from sending anonymous letters, but he continued nevertheless to imagine them as he scanned the addresses in the obituaries. Finally, he was not above examining the advertisements and never passed up the chance to be shocked by the prices. And, having received his share of education (his mother had been a schoolteacher), he would rage at the sight of the least spelling mistake.

Once he had read a page of the newspaper, he had no way of turning it on his own. He said nothing; he waited. Should the widow Racicot notice — "Finished your page, have yous, Mr. Tremblay?" — he would answer a diminutive, "Yes." At times, in the jumble of paper sheets, she was apt to place a page upside down on the old man's plaid blanket, quite unaware, for her illiteracy was ironclad. Séraphon would smile wanly but dared not point out the error.

She scared the living daylights out of him because she sometimes — oh, without meaning any harm — mistreated him.

When she was properly in her cups, she was liable to leave her chair and, staggering, let herself get carried away on a wave of generosity, of a primal desire to do good.

"Will yous take some nice hot tea, Mr. Tremblay?"

Although he pleaded with her not to go to all that trouble, she bumped her way to the kitchen, where she proceeded to ransack the cupboards, sometimes crashing down amid the pots and pans, and to wreak general havoc while jiggling all over with a belly laugh that filled Séraphon with terror. She came back with the bowl of tea wobbling on the tray. Séraphon could not repress an anguished whimper ("No! No!"), but she assured him:

"I don't mind givin' yous a hand, Mr. Tremblay."

Then she shoved his nose into the scalding drink. Séraphon gagged and struggled, but she insisted, and the tea spilled over everything. She then felt obliged to rap him on the skull in order to calm him. She pried open his jaws by jamming her fist against his chin and poured the tea down his throat.

Ordinarily, this put an end to her fit of goodness. She motioned with her arm for him to go to the devil and, finally, to the valetudinarian's great relief, returned dourly to her rocker-porter-knitting routine. Séraphon snivelled and spluttered: he felt as though he had gargled with tobacco juice. When Remouald came home from work Séraphon could spend hours reproaching him for not earning enough at the bank to be able to provide his old father with something better than that gorilla.

SINCE THE DAY before — actually, ever since the visit to the site of the fire — Séraphon had been in a peculiar mood. He had had bizarre dreams during the night and his disquiet had only increased since morning. He looked around him and the familiar surroundings of his room suddenly appeared strange. Everything was as it always had been, yet something had changed. He could sense it in the air, like a drop in the temperature. As of yesterday the world had begun to exist without taking him into account. Yes, that was it. He felt himself departing; he had the impression he was lighter. He floated in the midst of things, and his own body seemed to him to be a thing abandoned among other things. The minutes filed past him like pedestrians who walk by without seeing you. Being Séraphon no longer meant the same thing, no longer meant anything, perhaps. He dozed off, and when he awoke he peered at the Racicot woman at some length before recognizing her. He was not certain of being in the same room as her. He saw her the way a clairvoyant perceives things in her crystal ball. His newspaper was spread out on his lap; he tried to read the headlines. The letters were possessed of an indefinable stubbornness and refused to yield up their meaning. They clutched the page, huddled together, as inflexible as the entwined fingers of a corpse.

The malaise was temporary, but it left him in a state of utter mental exhaustion. His head could retain nothing, his thoughts slipped away. He began to regard the dresser drawer with curiosity. That morning, as he was waking up, he had surprised Remould in the process of closing it. Afterwards, Remould had seemed abnormally nervous. Séraphon inferred from this that Remould had indeed brought something back from the Grill the previous night and that he had hidden the object in the drawer. He felt convinced that that object was somehow involved in the metamorphosis he had observed in and around himself. What if it were some sort of talisman designed to addle his brain?

It was a chore for him to address the widow, but he summoned his courage. He asked her if she would be so kind as to open the dresser drawer. The Racicot woman checked the rocking of her chair and pondered for a moment, not sure if she would comply. Then she stood up, adjusting her ample bosom with both hands, and went to open the drawer. She went back to her knitting. Séraphon uttered a disheartened little chuckle.

He took counsel with himself, weighed the risks, and in his most affable voice said, "I wonder if you could tell me what there is *inside* the drawer."

The widow scowled at him. Séraphon forced a smile. She stood up again, grumbling, and sloppily withdrew some rags from the drawer: Remould's shirts. This was not a great discovery for Séraphon. He wanted to know if there was out to them, "Don't leave. . . !" Objects, too, have a soul — an almost nonexistent, warm, invisible vibration that makes them familiar. That secret soul was dissipating. Whole segments of the room were becoming inert; he no longer received anything from them, neither shape, nor colour. Like candles that have been snuffed, things were going out around him, sinking one by one into *absolute coldness*. There were his old shoes, which for years had not moved from their shelf, and Séraphon, in anguish, repeated to himself, "My boots, those are my boots!" But they as well eventually faded away. Séraphon felt the icy coldness working its way inside him. When sensations reached him now, they were muted, weakened by the hard journey. The universe was shrivelling around his body, shrinking away. All that was left inside him was a flickering, tremulous flame, overawed by the surrounding void. He turned his face toward the still-open drawer. The dresser seemed to be sticking its tongue out at him. Séraphon wanted to hold on to that grimace, which did, after all, offer him a little warmth, but the dresser, too, sank — he no longer existed for it and it could do nothing more for him.

Séraphon had not prepared himself for the idea of his own death; he had never concerned himself with it. He could imagine neither the world coming to an end nor the universe going on without him, so serenely certain was he of being its centre. Each time his thoughts had ventured into the hereafter, that unthinkable time when he himself would no longer be, they had plummeted back to earth, onto the terrain of life, so that such efforts appeared puerile to him, as futile as trying to hit the moon with an arrow. He would invariably say to himself, "There will be time enough to think about it." Even when he had reached a more than venerable age he continued to believe, due to some unexplored proclivity, that he still had at least twenty years ahead of him.

Those twenty years had just dwindled down to the scale of a few weeks, a few days perhaps — all it had taken was for him to see the icon. The message was clear, with no possible ambiguity, as portentous as an annunciation. And death suddenly appeared to him in the guise of something horrendous: a long, cold wakefulness at the bottom of a pit. He saw being dead as though it were to *feel* oneself dead: to wake up dead, entombed for all eternity. His imagination was racing. The worms pierced the skin, passed through the bones like a turd through the anus. He wished to drown his anguish in this vision, he wallowed in it, hoping to convince himself that this was the ultimate horror. But he divined that there was worse still. For one never stopped disappearing; nothingness was a never-ending spiral — even reduced to the state of rotten soil, blind, deaf, henceforth *insensate*, less than a dog, less than a plant, less than a stone, still the tremulous flame endured: the awareness of being in the grave. So that was Hell? To no longer experience anything and yet to continue to be? Imprisoned like a fly in honey, trapped in the glue-pot of night and death? Everlasting absolute coldness? "I don't want to go!" he screamed. The picture of the vast Côte-des-Neiges cemetery foisted itself on his consciousness. "Remouald!" he called out.

A desperate notion took hold of him: "But, then, why should *I* go to Hell?" And in answer to his question he heard plainly, in the depths of his heart, a cruel snicker. Séraphon was seized by violent shivering. He was mortally afraid of having to pay. The memories the icon had aroused jostled within him, came into sharper focus, spewed forth like wellsprings, burst out like flower buds. He felt hounded by them and tried to appease them: "How could I have known? I wasn't responsible," he pleaded, attempting to convince himself of his innocence. By way of diversion, he admitted to older misdeeds, innocuous little-boy sins, which cost him nothing. It was like trying to placate wild beasts with a few crumbs of bread. He immediately realized he would have to confess his true transgressions — where? to whom? — and he saw a curtain of fire rise up before him. Séraphon fainted.

A sound of footsteps on the stairs, the door opening: it was Remould. Séraphon regained his wits. Near his son stood the widow Racicot, teetering. She craned her neck, looked with apprehensive curiosity in the old man's direction, appeared at last reassured. Séraphon let out a heart-rending cry: "Remould!"

His head resting on his son's bosom, Séraphon began to weep. Remould silently stroked the fine, sticky hair, as frail as a spiderweb. "I don't want to die," Séraphon moaned. Rémould needed no further explanations.

The widow Racicot had waited for Remould by the front door, not daring to go up by herself — she was terrified of corpses. She did, however, very much wish to retrieve the bottles that in her haste she had forgotten upon leaving. This she attended to in a disjointed manner. Remould wondered if he had paid her her wages. On her own initiative Mrs. Racicot would not ask for them; if someone omitted to pay her she would simply forget to show up. She mumbled something he interpreted as a yes. She finally left, and Séraphon finally stopped weeping. Remould closed the dresser drawer and without saying a word withdrew to the kitchen.

REMOUALD FIXED HIS eyes on the soup simmering in the pot. While taking Sarah back to the bank, had he not decided to stand his ground, that he would not take care of her, that he was not a babysitter, nor paid to be one? He had mentally prepared his speech down to the last comma and rehearsed it twenty times. Yet when the time came, he said nothing. Was it Mr. Judith's hysterics at the sight of the child's bruises? Was it the fear of losing his job? The fear of standing up to his employer? Remouald was afraid of everything — he made no bones about that. But he was no coward. So what was it that had kept him from speaking up?

He turned on the lamp and extracted from his pocket the paper he had found in his hat that morning. How could such a thing have ended up in his hands? He studied it at length. The address written there was indeed that of the widow Racicot. He mulled over the events he had witnessed the day before at the site of the fire. What did it all add up to? What sort of message was he being sent?

His father's sobs drew him out of his cogitation. He rushed to the bedroom like a valet, forgetting that he was holding a bottle of caribou in his hand. Séraphon was aware of his son's bad habits, but they had an unspoken agreement not to let on. His stupefaction interrupted his tears. Remouald followed his father's gaze. He put the bottle down on the pedestal table. Both of them refrained from commenting.

"Number two? Number one?"

Séraphon exhaled through pursed lips.

"One."

Remouald lifted the blankets and set about changing his father's newsprint diaper. When touched on the belly Séraphon was as ticklish as a monkey, and this evening task was usually tinged with mirth; Remouald would at times get caught up in the amusement and, as he was closing the safety pin, tease his father with his fingers. Both would laugh the same laugh, something that never happened otherwise.

But now Séraphon gazed at the ceiling gloomily, and Remouald registered with a frown that, for the first time, his father was mistaken and had also served up some devil's food cake.

The whole package was wrapped and tossed out the window.

"It's seven o'clock, Dad. Time for your soup."

Remouald took him in his arms and carried him to the kitchen. He sat him in his high chair, tied the strings of his bib behind his neck, and turned toward the pots. Most of the time they ate purée. If there were raw vegetables — carrots or potatoes — Remouald would chew them up first, and Séraphon, head tilted back, received the beakful of food from the lips of his son. That night he spat back whatever Remouald put in his mouth; everything had a vile taste. He even refused to suck on the salt pork. Remouald took him back to his room and returned to the kitchen.

No, what had really kept Remouald from telling Mr. Judith that he no longer wanted to mind his niece was that he had never before felt himself becoming attached to someone as, after just one afternoon, he felt he was to Sarah. On leaving the bank a little earlier, he had not gone ten paces when he'd realized he missed her already. He'd whispered, "After just one afternoon." It had left him amazed and alarmed.

He tried to think of something else. Since the previous day his mind had been toying with a plan. It was a modest undertaking, no doubt, but he was convinced it would be the most important one of his life. He saw the whole thing with crystal clarity: the location, the dimensions, the material he would use. In the shed there was some wood of excellent quality; he had put it aside for a worthwhile project. If he started on Saturday, everything would be ready for the appointed date. Remouald stepped up to the stove in a more peaceful state of mind, his heart untroubled by memories.

Provided I am still alive on Saturday, he thought as he dipped the ladle into the pot.

6

WHEN WEDNESDAY NIGHT came around, Rocheleau had to lie to his father once again. It was easy, almost too easy, and depressing. As he was packing books into his schoolbag, he explained that he was going over to his friend Bradette's to review his arithmetic lesson, he would not loiter on the way, and he would be back no later than nine o'clock. The clock already showed a quarter to seven. His father did not notice the tremor in his voice.

The only son of an only daughter, Mr. Rocheleau became a doctor to please his widowed mother. He had a slow, methodical, thorough mind, and he absorbed science with the digestive patience of quicksand. He was renowned among his comrades for the care he took of his socks, which he hung in his window each night, with no comic intent, to air them out for the next morning. His love for his textbooks and everything in them was genuine. He would secretly whiff their fore-edges. He would grow fond of certain diseases, marvel at their etiology, at what he called their dramatic escalation, without giving too much thought to the flesh-and-blood individual who might be stricken by them. Each night between eleven o'clock and midnight he wrote to his mother; the drafts of sonnets intended for her would be found among his papers. He fainted three times during his first autopsy class, which earned him a good deal of fame. He was named the Princess of the Pea. And he became the butt of the most time-honoured university jokes.

After graduating, Dr. Rocheleau turned out to be a rather poor practitioner. That he was capable, furthermore, of compassion did nothing to improve matters. He was weighed down by the demands of the profession, and diseases, in all their brutality, left him breathless. The anxious hope that he read in the eyes of his patients left him helpless. He moved to the country, in part because he was ashamed of himself and also to avoid prying eyes, but was obliged to change towns every six months due to his blunders. Some twenty years had passed since his coming to this neighbourhood in the middle of the city, believing that, lost among the multitude, he would have a better chance of going unnoticed. Then one night, while mending a father's leg, he met the woman whom in his heart he immediately called the Apparition. With his gentle manners, his somewhat more than pleasing features, and his sort of manly thickness, a wink and a smile were sufficient to conquer the young woman. Mrs. Rocheleau received the news, predictably, with admirable self-denial and muted resentment. She nevertheless consented and the lovebirds were married.

The effect of this union on his existence all but felled the doctor. Happiness descended upon him like an avalanche. It took him some time to recover. The heavens, as if struck by madness, unleashed hurricanes of delight on earth, archangels contended to enter their house. He was so caught up in his conjugal bliss that tumors were imbued with something ineffably cheerful, and the misery of his patients affected him less; Dr. Rocheleau thus became a more or less acceptable doctor.

He succumbed only once, and only after three years of matrimony. Gnawed by remorse almost to the point of falling ill, he promised, swore, crossed his heart that he would never start again. His wife took pity and forgave him. But too late — the harm was already done. After two months the Apparition began to vomit every morning, to go from laughter to tears, to string together garlands of craving, to eat raw onions with jam. There was no room left for doubt: Mrs. Rocheleau the elder was going to be a grandmother. The fit of amorous frenzy that had carried away the husband on that celebrated night, and left the Apparition half-dead with surprise, now took on a new meaning! The Offence contained a Blessing! God was sending them a child! The seraphs bellowed with enthusiasm.

She expired giving life to a son; she was about to turn eighteen. She would have died even without the ineptitude of her doctor of a husband, but he could not forgive himself. Thereafter a survivor to himself, Dr. Rocheleau sank into despondency. And he began to adorn with capitals anything related to her. The Departed became the object of a cult. Little by little he withdrew from the medical profession until he had abandoned it altogether, in part because he felt less and less able to deliver babies and then not able at all. In the groans of birthing he heard, to the point of fairly losing his mind, the groans his wife had uttered.

With early retirement came poverty. His only income derived from two small farms he had inherited. Actually, his finances would not have fared so poorly had he not been so roundly chiselled by his tenant farmers, for he never went to the farms to check the ledgers himself, nor did he delegate anyone else to do so. At all events, his was a sweet poverty, just as everything had become sweet since the passing of the Deceased — the stale sweetness of an old sorrow that was no longer a pain.

He was the lone minister of his cult, but every priest needs a flock, and Dr. Rocheleau believed he had found his faithful in the perfectly suited person of his son.

Alone with a morose father and a declining grandmother, the little boy did not meet children of his own age before going to school. Until then he had grown up in a museum of sorts, where the rules dictated that every window be smothered by curtains as heavy as bibles, and that in this dusty dungeon only the rays that *Maman* sent from Heaven be entitled to shine. No matter what he did, she was present and knew the thoughts that surfaced in his little heart, even the most fleeting. She especially knew her little boy's love for her, and from her Paradise, that eternal summer of grace, she repaid it a hundredfold. Never, in truth, had a little boy been so loved by his mother — he had better not forget it for a single moment — loved to the extent of dying to give him life.

Rocheleau knew it was easy to lie to his father, because his father believed his child would never dare to lie beneath the heavenly gaze of his *Maman*.

Dr. Rocheleau rose laboriously from his chair: his ennui had given him a bad heart. He bent down to plant a pensive kiss on his son's forehead. He asked him to kiss his grand-mother as well. Despite all the evidence to the contrary, he maintained that the poor woman still appreciated these displays of tenderness, that in her own way she was conscious of them. Rocheleau went over to his grandparent, who looked straight ahead with the eyes of a fish forgotten at the bottom of the boat. He brushed his lips against the sagging cheek that tasted of plaster. In a flat voice he said, "Goodbye, Grandmother," but she was not aware of it. Had a firecracker exploded in her face her reaction would have been no different.

Rocheleau left without taking his schoolbag, but this detail was unlikely to dent his father's trust. It was getting late. He crossed the garden and came out on the street, not running like a child in a hurry, but making haste, like a child tormented.

* * *

THEY HAD AGREED to meet at the intersection of Adam and Dézéry. Bradette had not yet arrived. It was much colder than the day before, and it had snowed. Rocheleau passed the time by twisting the laces of his hood. He mused on the tracery of a tree against the sky. It resembled the illustrations of brain sections in his father's books, which he perused in secret.

He thought about Guillubart. The image of Guillubart had stayed with him constantly, ever since he had crashed to the floor in class, frenzied, eyes rolled up. The idea that he was at that very moment in a hospital room terrified him. He was shocked that his schoolmates could be so detached when talking about him. Hey! The word was he might die! . . . When Rocheleau heard that he thought he would faint.

A pair of claws grabbed him from behind just below the ribs. He let out a yelp of surprise.

"Quiet, you dumbbell! It's me."

Cheeks aflame, Rocheleau looked at his companion's nervous, gleeful face without recognizing it. He was ashamed to have reacted so sharply.

"As chicken as an Anglo!"

Rocheleau half-heartedly protested that he had not seen him coming, but Bradette had a knack for not listening to Rocheleau's excuses. Instead, he took the cigarette he had been carrying behind his ear. It was badly crumpled. He snapped his fingers for Rocheleau to give him a light. Rocheleau pretended to rummage through his pockets before admitting he had none. His friend sighed heavily.

"I've got to take care of everything, eh? Haven't I told you to always have some on you?"

Bradette unfolded his matchbook. The flame flared up like two hands joined together, and he took a long, expert, voluptuous puff. Then, after hawking right down to his tonsils, he spat a wad of phlegm deep into the snow.

Rocheleau watched him with respect.

When it came to spitting, Bradette outshone them all. And he knew how to smoke, too! His movements, his pose: just right! Others would hunch over and cross their eyes as they sucked on the cigarette. But Bradette smoked with all his heart, with his whole being. He let the cigarette rise to his lips, half closed one eye, and inhaled with tranquil gusto while gazing aloft, like a man reflecting on manly things. Discouraged by his second-rate results, Rocheleau had long ago given up on imitating him.

"Will you let me have the butt?"

Bradette made a reassuring gesture and spat out a speck of tobacco.

"By the way, we didn't fare too badly, I'd say, yesterday, what do you think?"

Rocheleau hesitated. "You mean in Brother Gandon's office?"

He coveted the cigarette that was burning down. It was humiliating to always wait for someone else's cigarette butt, but he had resigned himself to that humiliation. Bradette ignored the question.

"Guillubart is a chicken. He was worried for nothing. Did you see him collapse yesterday? Humph . . . what Guillubart wouldn't do to stay away from the principal!"

Rocheleau looked at his shoes. He had the feeling no one had the right to say things like that about Guillubart. He answered, "Me too, I was scared."

"Because you're as much of a candy-ass as he is. Besides, what's so terrible about spending a half-hour in Gandonella's office? He lectured us for strolling around the Grill property, and he made us stay behind for an hour because of a dirty picture, so what? Brother Gandon is a sap, you know that just as well as I do, and I'm not afraid of saps."

Bradette spat into the snow once again — a young boy's affectation.

"Bradette . . . Do you think . . . do you think Guillubart will talk?"

Bradette shrugged his shoulders cockily. But Rocheleau was expecting an answer, which was not forthcoming. Bradette sensed his impatience. After a pause, he issued his diagnosis.

"He won't talk. When you don't have the guts to go through with something, you don't have the guts to snitch either."

He spoke with the tone of someone who had learned a great deal about people, and this carried weight with his companion.

"Anyway, if you want my opinion, being rid of Guillubart is, well, just fine. When you really think about it, don't you find he was a bit of a fairy? We've got no use for fairies. Want some?"

He held out the cigarette butt, shivering. Rocheleau pinched it clumsily between his thumb and forefinger, like something venomous. He felt a slight burn as he held it to his lips. An acrid juice filled his mouth and nearly choked him. He batted his eyes but managed nevertheless to keep from coughing.

"Okay, I guess it's time," Bradette announced. "O, Love, when you've got us in your clutches! . . ."

Rocheleau chuckled, which made him feel like crying.

HE FOLLOWED BRADETTE, who was in a whistling mood, and advanced into the darkness of the alley with his hands in his pockets. Rocheleau was sorry he had come. He thought of his room, of the warmth of his bed — how good it was to lie on his stomach under the lamp, with the door locked, and read the adventures of Claude Lightfoot. So what prevented him, at that very moment, from turning around? Nothing, he told himself. It was not too late. And yet he felt compelled to follow.

They arrived at the wooden gate. Bradette put his finger to his lips. Once again, in a flash, Rocheleau thought of fleeing to the warmth of his bedroom.

They entered the courtyard. The snow mixed with gravel crunched underfoot. To Rocheleau's ears, the noise of their footsteps ripped the night as if it were a sheet of canvas. The shed door was open, just as they had hoped. They climbed the stairs to the gallery, where the window was.

"It won't be much longer," Bradette murmured.

From his pocket he had pulled out the watch purloined from his uncle. In the glimmer of a nightlight they could just barely make out the hands of the watch under the cracked crystal. It said eight o'clock. Through the walls they could hear sporadic, shrill mewing that rose and fell.

"Well, at least you can be sure there are no mice in this dump!" said Bradette.

They were sitting on the floor, swathed in the woollen blanket Bradette had brought. Their heads were touching. Rocheleau breathed in his companion's vaguely sour breath. He could not believe that everything would take place as planned. The waiting seemed endless to him and, he expected, altogether in vain. Their eyes were glued to the window.

Then the bedroom door opened and the lamp went on.

"There it is!" Bradette said hoarsely.

The widow Racicot took a few unsteady steps, then tumbled onto the bed. Two of her cats joined her, their tails upright like exclamation marks. She sat up ponderously. From her mouth a strand of saliva dribbled between her breasts and swung there like a spider at the end of its thread. A pair of boxer-style underpants stained with large red splotches were the only clothes she wore.

Behind her the man stood immobile in the doorway. His muscular chest was carpeted with tightly coiled hair. There was something feral in the curvature of his legs. He studied the back of the widow's neck with a hard intensity, as if he were about to strike it. He stepped toward the bed, impelled by a cold anger, and grasping the cats by the tail flung them out of the room. He popped loose his trouser buttons. Then, turning her over on her back, he tore off the widow's underpants. He limbered up a little before climbing into the bed with her, kneeling on the bare mattress, his member erect. The Racicot woman fell into a fit of laughter. With the tautness of a gymnast, he stretched out on top of her. The bedsprings began to creak.

The widow continued to guffaw like a big brute being tickled. She had wrapped her arms around the man's trunk, but as he plied, the expression on her face changed, and she looked somewhat appalled.

It was not long, however, before the widow fell asleep. Her partner managed to wake her now and then only by accentuating his thrusts, at which point she would open wide a pair of agonized eyes, utter a long, lowing sound, and then let her eyelids fall shut again. The man paused. His lips were quivering; one could see the sweat dripping from his hair. He flipped the widow over like a pancake and, hiking her haunches up as best he could, ardently took her again. The bed swayed. The man swore under his breath and slapped the woman's buttocks.

The tremors of the bed spread as far as the gallery, where, under the blanket, Bradette was so aroused that he repeatedly jostled his comrade. Rocheleau took these knocks without saying a word; he was dizzy, foggy-eyed, gripped by a kind of seasickness. He could not tear his gaze away from the face of the Racicot woman, who mumbled out of a dream, her nose crushed against the pillow.

Three cats slipped into the room and bounded onto the bed. The man hit out at them in an attempt to drive them away. But soon more cats arrived, mewing. The man got down from the bed. He bent his arm in a vulgar salute addressed to the widow. The woman collapsed on her side like a tent when the centre post is removed. The cats were kicked out of the room. The man grabbed one of them by the scruff of the neck and hurled it to the far end of the kitchen. Finally, he came to the window and opened it. A warm aroma of cat litter drifted out of the room. He peered into the shadows.

"Hey kids, you there?"

Bradette, his cheeks flushed, stepped into the light.

"To a man, Roger!"

"Keep your hands still, and come in. Are you alone? Who's there with you?"

Rocheleau approached shyly, wrapped in the blanket.

"It's me, Big Roger."

The fellow lifted him by the armpits and brought him inside.

"You sure no one has seen you?"

"That's for sure!" Bradette replied.

"And where's Guillubart?"

"Couldn't make it."

Rocheleau raised his hand and wanted to say that Guillubart had fallen ill, but, disheartened, he did not breathe a word. Big Roger spat on the floor.

"The whore! She fell asleep right from the start."

Emboldened by his high spirits, Bradette gave Roger a virile slap on the back.

"The way I see it, with you, women prefer to go to sleep!"

The two swift smacks to the face left Bradette completely stunned. Rocheleau took a step back. The man seemed to regret what he had done, which might have been taken as a sign of weakness, and endeavored to regain his composure.

"No," he said. "I must have overdone the drug dose, that's all. Anyway, it's not surprising, given the amount of porter she knocks back. Besides, it was on purpose — if she hadn't dozed off, you wouldn't have been able to get in here. She just went under too soon. Will you look at that. Puts you in mind a pile of shit."

Rocheleau stood with his back propped against the wall. Slumped on her side, the widow slept on; the volume and monotony of her snoring were reminiscent of a steamship's foghorn. Rocheleau tried not to look at her, but in spite of himself his eyes turned back to the swollen ankles streaked with purple runnels. They looked for all the world like his grandmother's ankles.

Big Roger buttoned his trousers and briskly scratched his scrotum. He walked around the bed and lit a cigarette. Rocheleau was surprised to recognize Bradette's gestures when he smoked.

Bradette had placed his hands on the mattress and was brazenly ogling the slumbering body. Big Roger watched him, the lit cigarette wedged between his lips.

"You like her, eh, you little lecher? Admit it."

Now at a fever pitch, Bradette began to circle the bed while fondling his groin. Roger stopped him, grabbing him by the hair and forcing his head back. Bradette at once became very earnest. He gazed at Roger's face hovering over his. He sniffed.

"You have my permission to touch, okay? Careful, though! Just the upper part."

Rocheleau was crouched in a corner of the room. His legs had buckled and, without him realizing, his back had slid down the wall.

The breasts lay one on top of the other and Bradette hesitated, frozen by lust. He seized one, and the breast took the shape of his grasp. He held it for a long time between the palms of his hands, as one holds the head of an animal, and he stared hotly at the big brown eye of the nipple. A shadow swept over his face. What next? He turned toward Rocheleau, but Rocheleau was not laughing. He began to knead the breast, then to twist it, even managing, with a giggle, to fold it in half. Here, he studied the enchanted, incomprehensible object. Roger sniggered. Finally, with a kind of growl, mouth wide open, the child flung himself on the teat and bit it. The widow moaned in her sleep.

Roger yanked him away from the nipple. Suspended by the collar, a wild look in his eyes, Bradette flapped his arms like a panicked swimmer. He appeared terrified.

"Don't touch!" Roger said, laughing.

Then, setting him down again, he turned toward Rocheleau. "You, come here!"

"I can see just fine from here."

Bradette broke out in laughter.

"Come on! I told you to get over here."

This time Roger was as serious as a prefect. Bradette chimed in, "Come on, damn it!"

Rocheleau approached with tiny steps. He remained enveloped in his blanket. Roger tapped the edge of the mattress.

"Closer! Right here!"

The boy obeyed.

Roger stretched out his arm and snatched up his shirt, which was hanging on the bars of the bed frame. He pulled out a loaf of bread.

Rocheleau heard himself say idiotically, "I just ate."

Roger let out an admiring whistle. "He really takes good care of his sonny boy, Doc Rocheleau does!"

Rocheleau found himself responding even more idiotically, yes. Bradette let loose another outburst of laughter.

Leaning against the bed, Rocheleau received the widow's breath full in the face; the odour reminded him of a blend of boiled cabbage and molasses. Each time she snored, her ribs lifted and vibrated. She suddenly snorted, which gave him a start.

Big Roger tore off a piece of bread that he rolled into a ball and slipped between his lips. He turned it around his tongue. He looked at Rocheleau mischievously.

"Here, this is for you."

He held out the ball of bread he had just removed from his mouth. Rocheleau looked down and did not move. They stayed like that for a long while. Then Big Roger slowly rotated his hand. The bread ball fell to the floor.

"Pick it up."

Rocheleau scratched the tip of his nose.

"Go ahead and pick it up like you were told," Bradette said in a strangely affectionate tone of voice that rattled his friend.

Roger put his hand on Rocheleau's shoulder and forced him to kneel. The child kept his arms crossed over his chest, holding the blanket over his shoulders with his fingertips. The man placed his heel on his head and pressed down.

Rocheleau stood up again. He chewed, looking straight ahead. Roger scanned his face anxiously, his black hair, his big grey eyes always full of tangled questions and surprises. Then Roger relaxed and let out a sigh of relief. He placed his lips close to the child's ear.

"You know you almost frighten me?" he whispered.

The boy looked him squarely in the eyes.

Breathing slowly, as though he were running out of oxygen, Roger brought his trembling hand near the child's cheek. But Rocheleau pulled his head away.

Big Roger slowly clenched his fist. He had turned livid. His forehead had broken out in sweat. It was Bradette's turn now to step back. Rocheleau lowered his eyelids, preparing to receive the blow. But the man grasped the widow's legs and bent them brutally against her belly. It gaped like a wound.

"Who do you bloody think you are? Look at where you come from, look! Everybody comes from there, you the same as everyone else, even the Little Jesus! Who do you think you are, with your princess airs? Go ahead, answer me! Did you know that's where we come from?"

Rocheleau said yes. There were bits of bread stuck to his gums. Roger's voice became softer, and icier as well. He told him to take a better look, to not look down at the floor. He grabbed him by the hair.

"Look at the Racicot woman, doesn't she look dead? Shouldn't it remind you of something? Didn't you, by some chance, come out of the belly of a dead woman? There's not much difference between two dead women, and it's your Uncle Roger who says so!"

He shook Rocheleau's head like a bell.

"Admit it, you'd like to kiss her right there, eh, admit it! And what if I were to go and tell your father afterwards? You know your father believes everything I say! Eh? Answer me! Answer me when I'm talking to you!"

Rocheleau was snivelling, his chin against his chest. He held the blanket tightly around him. Roger dropped the widow's legs. Taking some coins from his pocket, he pried open Rocheleau's fist and placed them in the palm of his hand. The child's fingers closed over them. This time he did not shy away from the stroke on his cheek.

"You're pretty, you know, little princess. And it's because I love you that I'm letting you know all this. Some day you'll understand, you're too young now. You'll understand that I loved you and you'll thank me."

Roger had spoken gently, but his features expressed something else: intense desire, and distress. The nerves in his neck twitched visibly. He blinked as he looked about him, seeming to no longer recognize his surroundings. He frowned and lowered his forehead, as though someone had just shouted in his ear. He rose with difficulty; moving unsteadily and leaning on the furniture, he went to sit off to the side, where the light from the lamp did not breach the darkness.

Rocheleau had not raised his head. The Racicot woman's snoring had stopped, and the cats' lamentations in the kitchen only heightened the silence.

"We'll have to get going."

Bradette cast a glance at the shadows where Roger was.

"I'm not leaving," he said.

Rocheleau's face crumpled.

"But we agreed . . ."

"You go. Me, I'm staying."

They heard Roger's quiet laughter. Rocheleau stayed rooted in the middle of the room. Bradette approached him and shook his arm. He looked terrified himself.

"I'm telling you to go! I'm staying here. Do you hear? *I'm staying!*"

It came out like a cry. The widow began to laugh mournfully. For an instant the three of them remained on the alert. But the Racicot woman broke off, flung her body sideways, a corpse turning over in the grave. Their hearts began to beat again.

Rocheleau mumbled, "It's over, I'm not coming back any more." After a moment of silence he added, "It's not like before. It was never like this before. Now he's bringing us in, he made you touch. She's . . . I'm not coming back any more."

"Yes," said Bradette, "you'll come back, and you'll stay, you too."

He had injected just the right note of complicity into his sentence, and Rocheleau felt the pain. He stepped to the window, which he had trouble opening. Again, Bradette halted him.

"The blanket. It's mine."

The two boys looked at each other.

"I'm staying," Bradette repeated.

"The window! We're freezing!" Roger yelled irately.

Bradette gave him a shove in the backside and Rocheleau found himself on the gallery. The window closed behind him. Under his feet, the snow was dry, like flour. Rocheleau shivered. It was as cold as Hell.

* * *

IT WAS TIME to go back home; in fact, it was long past that time. This was certain to incur a punishment: dry bread for two days, a ban on reading, a tightening of the Pin . . . Rocheleau would have to submit to his father a written request to be punished, for his father dispensed justice out of charity, as one grants a favour. Asking to be punished, out of a passion for fairness, was part of the punishment. "Dear Father, your guilty son humbly asks you to tighten the Pin . . ." Rocheleau would have vastly preferred shouting, raging, and blows to the indulgent, rigid kindness with which his father carried out his sentences. That a person could detest what he most cherished, with a hate torn by pity, tortured Rocheleau sometimes the whole night through. This, he felt, proved his wickedness. It was on his mind whenever he hugged his father, so that he hugged him even tighter, buried his face in that rough cheek and wanted to weep. At times he would be awakened during the night by the sensation that his body was covered in vermin.

He went down the top stairs cautiously, testing each of them as one tests bathwater with a toe, and then stood still. He scanned the darkness around him. He felt a quiver run up his back and slowly lift his hair as a hand might have done. An overpowering certainty had just taken hold of him: *he was not alone in the yard.*

He held his breath.

The individual must have been at the bottom of the stair-case. It seemed he could hear him breathing. A new, even more terrible thought overtook him: *they had been spied on the whole time.* Rocheleau considered warning the others, but the prospect of seeing Roger again held him back. He considered asking, "Who's there?" But he was afraid the blare of his own voice would frighten him even more. The thoughts in his head became blurred. It was pitch-dark. His heart pounded all the way to his throat. He felt he could not bear it another instant. He rushed forward, charging down the last steps, dashed to the gate of the yard and screamed — an arm had grabbed him and thrown him to the ground. In the semi-darkness he glimpsed a silhouette, which appeared gigantic to him. A single phrase was pronounced, a sort of moan, "Have pity!" perhaps, he was not sure he had heard correctly. The gate to the yard flew open. Rocheleau stood back up, looked around him. There was no one now.

For a long time he stayed there, not knowing what to do. But the cold was setting in, and he began to lose the feeling in his toes. He hazarded a step into the alley. The individual was standing a few paces away, observing him. Rocheleau recognized him: *yesterday morning, in the schoolyard, the man with the hat.* He quaked as he thought, *He's going to jump me. I've got to defend myself.* But in the time it took to bend down and pick up a stone, the silhouette had disappeared.

AND WHAT IF that man had seen and was going to tell his father everything? Going up Rue Dézéry, Rocheleau stopped. At night, when everything was silent, if one listened closely one could hear the murmur of the river. For a moment, Rocheleau thought of throwing himself into it. How black, how cold the water must be, and thick as oil. He imagined himself sinking down, and it sent a terrible shiver through him. "I don't want to die," he said to himself with conviction. Earlier, despite his patent desire to turn around, what had he done? He had followed Bradette. Rocheleau experienced an anguish he had never known. What if he went ahead all the same and threw himself into the river? What if something more powerful than him drove him there, his mother for instance, from the depths of her grave? But what if *he did not want to* throw himself into the water, what if he *refused* to do so with all his might? Oh, why was everything so complicated? He began to walk again; his teeth were chattering.

The snow fell down his collar and every flake stung like a needle. He felt an insane desire to start running. To turn on his heels and flee, to purify his body, to intoxicate it with fatigue, to hurtle forward no matter where.

Yes, to run all night, until the ends of the earth if need be, to the glaciers and ice floes, so long as he could at last be alone, be free and never again hear about the Mortal Wound of the World — love. The very word made him want to vomit. His soul was expiring under the blows of love. His father's love and Big Roger's, the love in whose name everyone claimed to act — Jesus, the priests and the teachers, the Love that was God and that granted the right to inflict suffering. But Rocheleau was unable to run; he was barely able to walk, the Pin hurt him so much right then. He went along, sniffing the air like a lost dog. The church tower seemed to be planted in the clouds like a stake in a vampire's breast. Memories of horror stories he had read bobbed around in his mind; he heard whispering, and the windows had a menacing look. It took courage simply not to think about it. The wind drove away the clouds and unveiled the sky. He passed by Guillubart's house and it wrung his heart.

No, he would not go back; it had gotten ugly. With his whole being whipped by an urge to revolt, he took the coins from his pocket and raised his arm, resolved to hurl them into the night. But there was Bradette's voice in his head, repeating, "You'll come back, you'll come back. And you'll stay, you too," and he did not have the strength. The cold froze the tears at the rims of his eyes, and as he looked at the firmament the stars were multiplied.

The Pin was a small metal device that, on his eleventh birthday, his father had fit between his thighs to obstruct those masculine tensions to which young boys are given and whose sight would have been unbearable for a *Maman* who, from her Heaven on high, loved her son with such Magnificent Love.

7

Saturday being his day to visit those whom, despite his own seventy-four years, he persisted in calling "his old-timers," Father Cadorette started up Rue Moreau, which overflowed with them.

He left Mémille's house and headed toward the Crampons'. Mémille confused the priest with his own grandfather, with whom he had scores to settle going back almost eighty years, and had berated him relentlessly. However understanding and sympathetic Cadorette might be, it was nonetheless unpleasant. He felt it was in the Crampons' best interests to behave affably, otherwise he would not fail to remind those old guzzlers of their past transgressions and scold them in turn, in keeping with the universal principle of communicating vessels.

Some children were playing at trying to hit the top of a pole with snowballs, which smashed on the pavement like exploding shells. Cadorette had nothing against this sort of game; his indulgence, however, did not go as far as tempting the devil, for experience had taught him that his hat, which did not easily stay put on his bald wrestler's skull, was a choice target. He decided to reach the lane by way of the courtyard passage.

"I BEELONG TO JUSTINE VILBROQUAIS FORE EVVER" . . . The priest wondered what had become of the "Rogatien" who had signed this monument to orthography. It was written in red letters on the walls of the passageway. He was incapable of going by it without pausing for a moment, and each time his heart twinged tenderly, bitterly. It was impossible to write such a thing without one day somehow regretting having written it. Life takes pleasure in giving the lie to this sort of poisonous pledge. Who was the child that could have scrawled it, and for what strange reason? In all his thirty years in the parish the priest had not been able to solve this enigma. Remouald, when he was small, had often questioned Cadorette about it. The priest had been content to reply with a vague shrug. "Still, it's odd, the name Vilbroquais," Remouald said as he slowly, dreamily traced with his finger the curves of the signature. "It sounds a little like Bilboquain."

The priest started on his way again and arrived at the courtyard. He nearly collided with a backside, and when the backside turned around he recognized Remouald Tremblay. (It had been confirmed a hundred times over: whenever the priest thought of him, he never failed to stumble on Remouald.) He was sawing a board, but he blushed as though he had been caught doing some unseemly thing. By way of greeting he doffed his hat.

"You're building a shed?"

Remouald was nailing the board to two posts. The priest barely reached his elbow.

"It's not a shed," he replied.

He seemed to want the conversation to end there. The priest was about to continue on his way none the wiser but changed his mind. Using his toque he brushed away the snow and sat down on one of the stairs.

The priest was sentimental about handicrafts and could not resist the pleasure of watching a craftsman at work. As a child, he had dreamed of plying the cobbler's trade, like his grandfather, so that he might measure himself against the honesty of things, and also for the peace of mind it afforded, but as there had to be a priest in the family . . . Remouald, at any rate, was just the ticket. This bank clerk was by far the best woodworker and carpenter Cadorette had ever known. His movements were sparing, without needless waste, and his face shone with a calm clarity such that one might expect him to levitate like a saint. But as soon as he set down his tools it was as if a magic wand had been waved, and the big bank clerk reappeared, with his air of a beaten spaniel; Cinderella clothed in light became Cinderella clothed in rags. Cadorette could not comprehend why Remouald refused to earn his living with this talent.

Remouald watched the priest out of the corner of his eye and kept on planing without saying a word. After a while, feeling intimidated, he paused. Cadorette jumped at the chance.

"So, what exactly are you making, Remouald my boy, if it's not a shed?"

Remouald carefully examined his closed hand. He seemed to be listening to the question hover around him, to be waiting for it to land on his fist like a fly before answering.

"A chapel," he finally said.

"A chapel?"

"Yes."

He set to work again. Cadorette wiped his forehead. He sensed that what would ensue was certain to give him a headache.

"A chapel, just like that, in the middle of your yard?"

"Yes, a votive chapel, a shelter for the Holy Virgin — I have an icon I'm going to put in it." He added very softly, "An icon saved by a miracle."

The priest used his toque as a fan: it was worse than he had feared. He took a few moments to reflect.

"Isn't this a strange place for the Holy Virgin? Propped against the wall of a factory? What's all this about a miraculously saved icon?"

"Why strange?"

The priest pouted. He knew that Remouald, when faced with someone defending a point of view contrary to his own, had a peculiar way of manoeuvring that consisted of frowning, flaring his nostrils, and looking as though he had not understood a single word.

"Seems to me you might at least have talked to me about it."

Remouald shrugged. His mouth was full of nails, which emerged from his lips one by one, and which he drove in with mechanical regularity. The priest observed him with the admiration of a little boy. Then he began glumly to scratch the palm of his hand. Things were so much simpler with the other parishioners. Cadorette spoke the same language they did, sensed their concerns; true, he sometimes had to make the Holy Spirit fly very low to the ground, but at least you knew where you were headed. But with Remouald . . . Aside from Justice Lacroix, Dr. Rocheleau, Séraphon of course, perhaps the chief of police, Cadorette was probably the only one in the neighbourhood who knew the bank clerk's secret. Yet it was one of those secrets that cannot be shared, that do not bring people closer together. There remained between them only an awkward sympathy comprised of silent embarrassment and lowered gazes. At times it occurred to the priest that Remouald had died when he was thirteen; at times he wished this were true and that nothing had survived in the adult but a carcass devoid of memory, devoid of anything within that might suffer. But how could one be sure without asking terrible questions, without running the risk precisely of rekindling memories? It was akin to verifying whether a man was dead or asleep by prodding him with a red-hot iron rod.

Remouald stepped toward him and handed him a folded sheet of paper.

"I received this yesterday at the bank."

The priest unfolded it. It was a poison-pen letter. It contained the foulest terms, the vilest verbs; it referred to certain acts, to the involvement of children. The letter concluded with a litany of insults. The writer called Remouald a "goddamn game eater!"

Cadorette was completely dumbfounded. He reread the letter carefully, scrutinized the paper for a clue to the offender's identity. Remouald seemed to have forgotten him. He was smiling as he petted a mouse that he had nearly crushed underfoot. The mouse trembled in the palm of his hand like a financier suspected of tax evasion. He put it back down; it etched faint lines in the snow as it zigzagged away. It disappeared among the planks, shimmying like a tadpole.

"When you get letters like this," the priest said, revolted, "you immediately chuck them in the fire! They're not worth holding on to!"

Remouald took the letter and put it back in his pocket.

"In any case, what does it matter? I'm going to die anyway."

The priest leapt to his feet.

"What are you talking about, you fool? Why do you say you're going to die? Are you ill? Go on, answer me!"

"I was just talking, Father. What I was trying to say was that such things aren't important for anyone, since we're going to die no matter what, each and every one of us, and it doesn't amount to anything, isn't that right, Father?"

The priest hesitated a moment, his chest puffed out as though he were about to bite — coming from anyone else such words would have been taken as a provocation! But in the end he sighed. With heavy-hearted slowness, he picked up his toque, which had slipped off his skull.

He distractedly inquired about Séraphon, a priestly reflex. Remouald made no answer. He had just filled his mouth again with a handful of nails.

The priest checked his watch and realized he was running late. He stepped toward Remouald with only the foggiest idea of what he would say, though he was brimming over with the solemnity of the moment. Just when he parted his lips he had a strange hiccough that resounded to his very temples with a cartilaginous crunch. He leaned softly against Remouald and hung there a few seconds, dazed and giddy. He had the impression this was a warning. But of what? Cadorette straightened up, shaking off the faintness as one might dismiss some bad thoughts. Remouald placidly hammered his nails. The priest finally spoke.

"You know, son, you could start taking Communion again."

The statement came out almost in spite of him. He had not raised the subject for fifteen years and he braced himself for Remouald's reaction.

Remouald spat out his last nail and replied simply, "No."

Cadorette placed his hand on his shoulder. "God has forgiven you, Remouald. He forgave you a long time ago. Look at me."

Remouald looked at him obediently. His eyes were blank, his face expressionless: a snowman melting at springtime. Cadorette sadly shook his head.

"All right, then," he said with a friendly pat. (He put his toque back on and held it down.) "But make your little chapel nice and pretty for me."

The priest moved off with an uneasy gait. Remouald called him back.

"Father! Look how beautiful she is!"

He held the icon in his hands. Above the Virgin, the cherubs were unfurling a banner with musical notes dancing on it. The bottom part had been damaged by the fire and the hands were no longer visible. Remouald grinned. Cadorette thought that if donkeys could smile they would look like that. He answered with a dejected smile, "Yes, she is beautiful." These were the smiles of farewell. The priest left. He went by way of the alley toward the Crampons' house. He was definitely not feeling well. The air entered his lungs with difficulty and at times he felt he was about to throw up. Was it the shrimp he had eaten the night before? he wondered. Or the over-rich cretons of that morning's breakfast?

Those were the first signs of the heart attack that would strike him down ten minutes later in the Crampons' stairway.

* * *

As it was getting close to noon, Remould decided to take a break. He went up to see if there was anything his father might need. Séraphon was sleeping with his tongue protruding, like an infant who has just stopped sucking its thumb. He brewed himself some strong tea, went back downstairs, lit a fire to warm himself, and surrounded it with bricks; then he sat down on the stair where the priest had been earlier.

He tore up the anonymous letter and used it to feed the flames. He knew it had been penned by the captain of the fire brigade. That way of writing — "Eh, my little Remould? Do we unnerstan each other?" — left no room for doubt. The paper closed like a hand as it burned. A plume of soot swirled up and was dispersed by the wind; the residue embedded itself in the surrounding snow.

The mouse returned, attracted by the heat. It resembled a young girl who has run away with her lover only to be betrayed by him: it advanced in spurts along the wall, stopped, stabbed the air with its snout, then went on, forlorn, since every mouse knows it will die a violent death, expects it at any moment, and trembles. Should the mouse come near him, Remould would slip it into his shirt pocket and keep it warm for half a day. He was about to set to work again when a cat arrived in the courtyard with its whiskers twitching and that predatory Mona Lisa smile. Remould pitched a stone at it. The cat hopped sideways in three elastic bounds and let out a wail. Remould pitched more stones at it. The cat retreated a little. Then it approached again. It described an arc like a wrestler who, having missed his hold, comes back to circle his opponent. Remould had to charge at it to drive it away. As soon as it was far enough, the animal adopted a jaunty demeanour, occasionally looking back with a contemptuous air and showing its rear end as if to say, "Why bother, you fool? You know I will be back."

For a brief moment, Remould looked for the mouse, but the mewing had frightened it back into hiding. He doused the flames with some mud. A column of steam went up like the belch of a volcano. He stamped out the embers with his boot. A very fine snow began to fall.

As Remould bent down to pick up his hammer he was overwhelmed by the odour of wet ashes. A tremor welled up from the depths of the ground and overtook his legs. He felt himself reeling. "My God, not now," he thought. He cocked his ear, his heart filled with apprehension. It was still nothing more than a faint buzz, quivering on the surface of things, but the hum grew louder, became a rumbling, and this phantom, grimacing drone, where clamouring and sniggering intermingled, rose up to assault the world like a savage army surging over the horizon in a tumult of dust, and making the earth reverberate like a drum. Remould put his hand to his forehead and joyfully believed he was on the verge of fainting — he hoped he would lose consciousness. But he realized that this mercy would not be granted him. He would have to endure the coming attack — which he recognized as one recognizes a face — through to the very end.

He cast a worried glance about him. He wanted to be sure that everything continued to be there, that there was nothing around him but the present. But things slipped away, seemed to turn their backs on him, and he had the heart-rending sensation they were betraying him, handing him over to demons. He looked to the icon for help. The

Virgin was looking somewhere else, over his head; she, too, was forsaking him. Remouald summoned his courage.

Then it began, the attack. The feeling, when one first falls asleep, of losing one's footing, of missing the step, this is what Remouald felt at that instant. He swung around, ready for a face-to-face confrontation. There was no one. He waited for another assault. The din had died away. All he heard were the hoarse gasps of his own breathing. But the din rose again, this time within his skull. Like a ferocious beast whose cage has been unlocked, it had pounced inside him. Remouald felt abysses opening up and he stepped back. Maws assailed him on all sides. His arms thrashed the air, his head shook furiously, but each of his movements ensnared him even further. He began to climb up the stairway backwards, dragging his back over the stairs. His strength was draining away. He finally stopped in the middle of the staircase with dread in his eyes, at the mercy of Memory, as sovereign as a spider at the centre of its web.

REMOUALD WAS THIRTEEN years old when Séraphon's wood yard was destroyed by fire. The details of this affair were kept carefully hidden from the public by order of the Court. It was thought sufficient to declare that the fire had been lit by a madman.

Strangers had agreed to take Remouald in for a while: the Costade family, of the funeral parlour. Laid low by a brain fever, he was locked in a bedroom where it was forbidden for anyone to enter, aside from the doctor and nurse. He was prohibited from seeing even his mother.

Actually, it was all the same to him: he no longer had

anything to do with anyone and expected nothing at all. Had he been stood on a table with his arms stretched out and one foot in the air he would have stayed like that for hours without so much as a frown. He wallowed in indifference, saw nothing, heard nothing, felt nothing. Whatever was fed to him he swallowed with a blank expression. Once the fever subsided a decision had to be made as to what should be done with him. Father Cadorette argued that the child should be returned to his mother; Dr. Rocheleau said that, given the state she was in, this was out of the question. A judge came down with a ruling. And a week later, two men in cassocks took Remouald away.

The Collège Saint-Aldor-de-la-Crucifixion was separated from the rest of the world by a kilometre of woodland. This was not a minor change of scenery for a child who had never in his whole life left the neighbourhood where he was born, nor seen either countryside or lakes, and for whom the woods had been merely the setting of fairy tales. Most of the children who landed there, had they landed elsewhere, would have found their way to prison, for there was no one under the sun who cared about them. The administration accepted all the applicants that were brought to them, so long as there was room. Among them were parricides, the mentally retarded, vagrants, and abandoned children. It was a charitable institution, and democratic besides, in that all the residents were treated equally, the same punishments applied to all, from the murderer to the orphan.

Remouald turned out to be a model inmate. He arrived at the college already broken. To be awakened by the bell in the middle of the night in order to shake out his sheets did not seem excessive to him, any more than the clouts to the back of the head or the ice-cold showers in the morning. His docility was disarming. On the other hand, he had to be forced into the chapel, and everything that resembled a church plunged him into a state of terror: he collapsed in front of the door, put his arms up to shield his forehead, began to bleed from the nose. He was taken in hand and the results were astounding: the directors watched in bewilderment as Remouald threw himself into devotion and became the most pious child in the community.

As the mission of Saint-Aldor was not to train the elite, the cult practised there was that of learning by rote. In this, once again, Remouald shone. Having arrived at the college with an empty memory, he could store anything in it. Standing in the middle of the classroom, he would reel off in a monotone the capitals of the entire world, whose names brought to mind not the slightest image for him, then sit down again. He earned a measure of notoriety, as well as the affectionate regard of the geography teacher, a stooped and hairy man who did not smell very good and did not always realize when the students were making fun of him. (One day, he gave Remouald an album containing a few stamps, which, out of inertia, Remouald held on to his whole life and which Seraphon ironically called his "collection.") Then there were the catechism, the rules of grammar to recite, and the square roots to derive, three times a week, in the late afternoon. Remouald did it all, ingurgitated it all, indiscriminately.

Meanwhile, his body was the scene of all manner of strange phenomena. This body of his had turned into a bizarre thing, fairly teeming with a life of its own whose meaning he was unable to grasp; powerless, he witnessed these metamorphoses as if they were the materialization of a fable. He had always been small — being small was for him part of the order of things, like being a boy — but now, in less than a year, he had reached the height of six feet, six inches. The change was so abrupt it left him bedridden. The administration was worried. Stretched out on his bed, Remouald looked like a boiled leek and at times felt like one. When he was feverish, he had the impression that extraordinary transformations were at work within him, that he would grow breasts, become a woman. If it were possible to no longer be small then it ought to be just as possible to no longer be a boy, to no longer be human, perhaps, to turn into a fly or a spider. The geography teacher spent entire nights at his bedside. In September, Remouald was at last able to get up. He understood that nothing had happened to him besides growing up and he was somewhat disappointed by the results. "In a few months, he'll fill out," the directors said, relieved. Spring came and he was still as thin as ever.

Over the course of his three years at the college, Remouald took no part whatsoever in the games of his schoolmates. He spent his free time strolling by himself. He gathered pieces of wood, three or four nails, disappeared for a few hours with a pocket knife, and the following day, near the grounds, one would come upon some astonishing unfinished projects. The directors decided to take advantage of these talents. There was always a roof, a window, a table to repair. Remouald did not balk. This situation gave rise, of course, to jealousies. Yet his appearance was so disturbing that the residents refrained from harassing him. With his stooped back and his arms held tight against his sides, his bearing brought to mind a large bird of prey, wild and wounded, prevented by adversity from returning to its natural habitat. At night, upon his return from the chapel, some of them would pull the covers over their heads when they saw him passing.

Nor would it have occurred to his schoolmates to make friends with him. They would scuffle in the dining hall to avoid sitting beside him. As for the geography teacher, Remouald never expressed the least gratitude toward him. There was gossip in the corridors that on Sundays he would hide behind a column and weep as he watched Remouald in prayer.

At age sixteen, on a Holy Friday, he was called to the principal's office. As he made his way there, Remouald quaked with animal fear. Quite unexpectedly, the principal showed him a great deal of consideration. He held forth on certain grand principles, spoke of Christ, explained to Remouald that the college had acted only in his best interests, all of this in a solemn tone of voice, and Remouald, taken aback, acquiesced. The principal was reassured. "Good," he said, and left his office.

The geography teacher was also in the room, sitting off to the side near the window. Teary-eyed, with the gracelessness of a soft-hearted, suppliant bear, he flashed an adoring, toothy smile at Remouald. Remouald observed him with indifference.

The principal returned and presented the resident with a valise bearing a name. This is how Remouald learned he was no longer called Remouald Bilboquain, but Remouald Tremblay. "Your mother has remarried," the principal said. "You will go back to live with her." Remouald was stunned and did not notice the hand that was held out to him. The principal did not press the matter. Through the window of his office, he pointed to the carriage waiting outside.

The sky was so blue, the snow so dazzling, that his eyes hurt as if he were staring at the sun. The students had scrambled up to the windows to watch him go by; their faces, without warmth, tempered to a sullen hardness, always apparently on the verge of crying out, yet — he well knew — never doing so, those faces conveyed nothing but a frozen sorrow, like wolves in a pack coldly considering the dead body of one of their own. Not a single wave, not a single grimace. The transparency of a window erected an infinite thickness between them and him. To have gone through the door was all that was needed for him to no longer be part of their world.

Remould stopped a few steps away from the carriage.

A woman was seated there. She wore a hat festooned with a sprig of holly. It was his mother. He did not recognize her. However, he did recognize Séraphon, who sat beside her. She addressed Remould in a trembling voice.

"You have brought my son's valise?"

Remould placed his baggage in the back of the carriage and climbed in next to her.

"Your son, Ma'am?" he said.

Séraphon snickered and cracked his whip at the horses.

THE FIRST FEW days were hardly cheerful; Célia wept constantly. Her memories were of a little fellow with bright eyes, blond hair, a laugh as fresh as a bunch of daisies; she had been handed back this spent giant, already in danger of going bald, who hunkered in a corner of the kitchen, guilty of existing, emaciated, and haggard. Célia would plant herself in front of Remould, pull his chin up, scrutinize him sarcastically, and then recoil and flutter her hands in horror, as if at death's door. "This is not him! This is not my son!" she cried. She took to drinking with a vengeance. Stroking his nostrils, Séraphon chuckled and said she was crazy.

Célia eventually grew accustomed to the presence of this individual and in time brought herself to call him by the name of her child. She was no longer even certain that she had ever had a child named Remouald. She would make up bizarre stories on the subject, which she would rattle off in a hollow voice while gazing straight ahead of her. These stories amused her husband no end. In those days Séraphon was a spry old man who still moved his arms and walked up and down the stairs. He would pretend to be busy because if she became aware that he was listening she would leave off. Apparently, she was talking to herself. To Remouald as well, perhaps.

Otherwise, she seemed to take an interest in Remouald only when giving him orders. She had gone back to doing housework for the affluent residents of the neighbourhood, and she often obliged him to come along. It vexed her to see Remouald idle, and when she could no longer think of something for him to do Séraphon would take over. Remouald never complained, even when they were at cross purposes, which was often the case. It was as though Célia and Séraphon were playing a game of chess. Remouald was all at sea. To the point where, at night, in his dreams, he sometimes confused their voices.

Célia was prone to inexplicable fits of anger, which prompted Séraphon to bolt. Most of the time, however, she displayed a docile disposition. She prepared and served the meals, darned their socks, made sure their clothes were always spotless, and beneath the visible ravages of drugs and alcohol there survived the quiet sweetness of the loving young girl she had been, before the wreckage. Yet she could spend whole days wandering from one room to another, mute and lost in reveries. Even on afternoons of frenzied activity, she might on occasion stop her dusting for no obvious reason and, with a look full of regret and startled tenderness, examine the bauble she was holding. Remouald hardly dared come near. "Mom . . ." he said. She would stiffen and curtly order him to go sweep the front porch.

"I just swept it."

"Well, go sweep it again."

At other times she seemed to become suddenly aware of Remouald's existence. She gazed at him in amazement, as if she were witnessing an apparition. She went up to him, sniffed his neck, his ears, his armpits, stepped back, the better to study him. She sat down and took a gulp of caribou without taking her eyes off him. Remouald, leaning over the potatoes he was peeling, did not have the nerve to look at her. He watched her out of the corner of his eye, saw her hand reach out and stroke his hair. He heard her aching, horrified voice whisper, "What on earth have they done to you, my poor little boy?" Remouald took the risk of reaching out hesitantly for her hand. She immediately brushed him off. Once she even slapped him.

The months went by, and the years. The repeated gestures and ritual habits fixed each hour of the day, each day of the week, within an ever more definite recommencement. Remouald let himself coast from one day to the next; he pushed his life along from hour to hour without venturing to look farther afield. Each yesterday fell into the very nothingness where today would be swallowed up tomorrow. The earthworm crosses a stretch of sand by ingesting the earth through one orifice and discharging it from the other: this is how Remould moved through time. He retained nothing of his days; he voided his memory as he went along. He lived under the dictates of a single voice, which issued its orders at times through Séraphon's mouth, at times through his mother's: he made no distinction, there was no distinction to be made. Obedience was a perpetual state of grace, as it kept him on a leash outside of himself. He knew that any other life would have been a hell for him. He eagerly rushed to satisfy his parents' wishes.

One night Célia woke him, lay down beside him, and, with her mouth next to his ear, told Remould in a low, breathy voice, so that Séraphon would not hear, that she was pregnant with a little girl who would never exist. It had taken her a long time to understand that the little girl was also a little boy, and since one cannot be both a little girl and a little boy, the little girl was not able to exist on earth, which of course was no reason not to exist anywhere at all. The little girl's soul had escaped from Limbo. She passed through things, she began to come to life through a bauble, she hid in a padlocked cabinet, she sometimes found her way right to Célia's entrails, and Célia said the name of her little girl, who was also a little boy, was Joceline and that, being both dead and alive at the same time, she was her own grandmother, because she was pregnant with the Christ. Remould fled from the house with the housekeeping money, went on his first bender, rambled in the streets with the feeling he was being followed, and returned home only forty-eight hours later when he could not abide himself any longer. The moment he stepped into the kitchen, distraught and covered in filth, Célia leapt from her chair and, weeping, flung her arms around his neck. Séraphon wept too, and kissed whatever money Remouald had brought back. Remouald had found a bat along the way, and he held it out to his mother. The thrashing she gave him kept him bedridden for two weeks.

Following the fire, the wood yard had been rebuilt only in part and shoddily. Remouald, who had no head for commerce, practically gave the wood away, and with the business floundering Séraphon found himself obliged to sell off his houses at a loss. Ultimately, he was forced to shut down. It was at this juncture that, through the priest's intervention, Remouald was hired at the bank. The position brought in only a modest stipend, but together with his mother's odd jobs it allowed them to survive. Remouald was eighteen at the time.

Célia never admitted that Remouald was her true son, even on her deathbed, for she was spared the marathon of agony that facilitates repentance. She died without a comment, just a sigh as she slept not fit to blow out so much as a match.

* * *

REMOUALD SAT UP; he was livid. The attack seemed to have run its course. He leaned on the handrail as he went down the stairs, knowing an attack could set off aftershocks, a final tremor, like the debris a shipwreck sends up from the ocean floor, breaking the surface in a burst akin to a cry. Such bouts usually occurred at night, and they were what drove Remouald to the watering places. He never drank for pleasure, oh no. When a nail juts out, it must be hammered down. And the same goes for memories.

He looked at the votive chapel. The framework was almost done. This meant he would be able to finish the project for the Feast of the Immaculate Conception! He wiped the icon with the back of his sleeve. There was the Virgin, smiling at him. Remouald savoured a moment of forgetting, sweet forgetting, merciful forgetting, and he thanked Heaven for it. Behind him he heard the voice of a child.

"But what is it you're supposed to have forgotten?"

Remouald swung around. A young boy of about twelve was standing before him. This had never happened to him. This child was none other than *himself*. Remouald swept the air in front of him.

"It's not real. Go away."

The child disappeared. Remouald tidied up his boards, ready to set to work again. The little boy was sitting atop the factory chimney, nonchalantly dangling his legs in the air.

"What do you want? Go back to where you came from."

The child went out like a candle flame.

Remouald went at the job with fevered concentration. In his head he heard the sound of crackling embers. The little boy's body was swinging from the main beam of the framework. Remouald recoiled, dropping his hammer. He was hanged and he was smiling at him.

"What is it you're not supposed to remember?" he asked him again.

Remouald shook his head. The little boy began to speak softly. He spoke about life *before* the college, *before the wood yard fire*. Remouald placed his fists over his ears. Then he began to scream.

"You don't exist. Go back to where you came from!"

The child vanished. Remouald made the sign of the cross and, trembling, kissed the rabbit's foot he had pulled out of his pocket. A layer of snow had once more covered the icon. Remouald took a few drunken steps. He heard a whistling and raised his eyes. A name streaked across the sky and exploded in his head. Remouald froze. He mumbled, "Joceline . . .?" Again he pressed his hands against his ears. Would it never stop? Here came the memories of the time before the college, before the wood yard fire, pouring forth in horribly vivid images. He saw everything again, remembered everything, and lived through it again in the present. The impression of plummeting into a chasm was so real that he searched about for an object to hold on to. He seized his hammer, grabbed some boards and nails, and began to strike, to strike, but it was howling inside his skull. Beside himself, he threw himself down on his knees in the snow.

"Have pity!" he pleaded, his face turned skyward.

God, apparently, was busy with something else.

8

Talking to herself in the mirror: Clémentine Clément called it "being alone and a half." What she wanted above all was to laugh, to laugh for the sake of laughing, because to laugh is to be alive. But as it is impossible — barring insanity — to laugh on one's own, she arranged these evening tête-à-têtes with herself.

Yet laugh about what? Her fellow teachers? Mrs. Baril's dresses? The hairdos of Lucienne Robillard, who passed her faulty grammar on to her third-graders ("I explains to them how it weren't right to . . ." and so on)? Such things could not draw so much as a smirk from her; in fact, they enraged her. Clémentine tried something else. She partly undid her nightgown and looked for something to laugh at in herself. Her diminutive breasts, with their large, hard tips going off in different directions — the left breast was named Over Here, the right breast Over There. She tried to laugh at this. But all that came out was a nervous yelp, and suddenly the face in the mirror, this Clémentine-and-a-half, looked at her with the utmost gravity. She tried to smile at her, but the results were even more dismal; she turned away in horror and went back to pacing up and down in her apartment.

No, she wanted to laugh as she had when she was eighteen and Ducharme would put her down on the straw mattress and tickle her belly with his mouth. One Sunday, she had fallen as she was leaving the church; he helped her up and from the first glance he was able to fill, say, her soul, with a delicious torment. A handsome lad, six feet tall, thirty-four years old, sturdy as a tree and gentle as a kitten. They courted for almost six months. With him, she forgot she was the lame girl of the village; she even managed to joke about her deformed left foot! "Thanks to my club foot," she would say, "I've joined the club of those who always get off on the right foot." Together they dreamed of raising a family, a houseful of boys. They could already hear them laughing, and the thought of it made them both laugh, too. He turned this into ballads that he would sing at night to his comrades at the logging camp. He accompanied himself on the accordion. His voice was cheerful, clear, mellifluent. "My darling's named Miss Twinkletoes." He was respected by his companions because he had won the heart of a young woman with an education. His teeth were a dazzling white. His curly hair smelled of fir tree resin. He died a week before the wedding.

A log had slipped off a stack and dropped on his skull. It was said repeatedly that Réjean had not had the time to feel anything. The same could not be said of Clémentine. She was pregnant. Due to the shock, she lost blood, and something else resembling eyeball preserves. She wept for over a week, and in the middle of the night before the appointed wedding day she disappeared from town. She absconded with her meagre savings after relieving her mother of the contents of the shop cash register. She spent three months holed up in a seedy hotel in the big city — the city terrified her — obsessed by her lack of money and the idea she would have to give up her child. Finally, one day in December, with the assistance of some nuns who treated her like a harlot, she gave birth. A boy like Réjean was what she desired more than anything in the world, and she prayed to God for this throughout her thirty hours of labour. She realized she would be incapable of abandoning this life that she felt coming out of her; it was an injunction against which she was powerless, as unshakable and imperious as her pain. "Come, come! My love. Mommy's waiting for you!" she repeated as she pushed. The heavens granted her a boy.

Her stillborn child. Thinking of him again, seventeen years later, Miss Clément still writhed in her bed, lying in the fetal position, her fists digging into her belly.

For a few months Clémentine eked out a living as a nurse in the hospital where she had given birth. Her behaviour was beyond reproach, as was her dedication, and the nuns came to appreciate her. Her education was acknowledged and the fact she had a good head on her shoulders, so that one thing led to another and Miss Clément ended up a teacher. Everything seemed to be going well, but inside she felt wilted. Persuaded by the books she had read that a heart could be given only once, she believed the light within her had gone out forever. She decided to sacrifice her heart on the altar of Memory and swore everlasting faithfulness to her betrothed. She was moreover convinced that, in terms of her interior life, this sacrifice suited her perfectly.

In time, however, the loneliness became hard to bear. Each night she would renew her vow, recognizing in her persistence the expression not of an inalterable and lasting love, but of the absurd pride that had always bedevilled her. At times she was able to rekindle her ardour by contemplating the portrait of her betrothed. But photographs get worn out if looked at too often. Her passion became mummified. When, like someone opening the doors of an abandoned house, Clémentine finally released her heart from its vow, she saw there was nothing left inside but dust and ruin, and her solitude from then on became a disease, aggravated by the hope of ending it.

To top things off, in her early thirties she fell in love. And, what is more, with a "constrained" man! Her shrivelled heart became suddenly gorged with blood, swelled like a balloon, and lifted Clémentine to heights of suffering, veritable seventh heavens from which she tumbled exhausted and all at sea. This passion harried her for five years. She then joined a lonely-hearts correspondence club and received, via general delivery (she still had her pride), a periodical titled *The Rubicon of Lonely Souls*. Since the man she loved could not have her, she sought another outlet for everything this passion had aroused within her, for if she were to keep it inside she would surely go insane, as she sometimes felt she might at certain critical hours of the night when, emerging from sleep as from a house on fire, she leapt wildly from her bed and, groping her way along the corridor walls, imprisoned in a dream from which there was no exit, pursued by a faceless enemy, she would finish her flight crouching in the corner of a closet, her knees pressed against her forehead and her arms wrapped around her whole body, like a little girl who has just been raped.

ON HER WAY home from buying her groceries, she was insulted by a boor. Clémentine ignored him in a dignified way. He then called her a tart and for the better part of a block hurled abuse at her with a verve and range of vocabulary that surprised her. "A flat-chested woman is a cripple!" he shouted three times. There were children, children from the École Langevin, playing nearby. When she arrived home, Clémentine sat down at the kitchen table; she began to empty her shopping bag; her hands started to tremble and she broke down sobbing. *Contempt and vulgarity always prevail in this land*, she thought.

It should be added that it was Saturday and her frame of mind on Saturday mornings was especially fragile. She looked at the clock. It was time to visit her mother at the rest home.

After her forced departure from the town of Saint-Aldor, Clémentine wrote about forty letters to her mother — tortured, pleading letters that comprised a sort of vindicating autobiography detailed to the point of eccentricity, which Mrs. Clément, in her role as the majestic shopkeeper, refused to open but, in full view of the entire village, returned to the post office one by one. When she stopped receiving them, she concluded that children were ingrates; she began to leave her shop as often as possible and personally deliver the flowers so that everyone might see how red her eyes were. As if it were not enough to marry a lumberjack, become an unwed mother, run away, have an abortion no doubt, and then write her letters, her daughter had now added the affront of no longer writing at all! Gnawed by guilt, Clémentine continued to deposit money into her mother's bank account from time to time. Theoretically, the deposits were anonymous, but Mrs. Clément was well aware of their source. She moreover felt this was the least a child who had caused her so much pain could do. For years, this was how things stood between the widow Clément and her only daughter. Then, one morning, Clémentine received a missive from the accountant in Saint-Aldor addressed to "The Widow's Benefactor."

Madam, or Miss, or Sir,
Dear Benefactor,

I do not know who you are, but I have nevertheless taken the liberty of writing you. As you seem to take an interest in the welfare of the widow Mrs. Clément, based on the sums deposited in her account at your behest, I feel it is my duty to inform you of an event that has taken place of late. For several weeks, indeed a few months, some of us in the village had noticed what appeared to be an alteration in Mrs. Clément's health, an alteration, if I may say so, of an unfortunate nature. It has to do with an illness — the matter is not an easy one to broach — one that compromises the dignity of the affected individual. This affliction, I must point out, causes the individual to commit certain acts, to behave in a way that she would, I am altogether certain, be the first to repudiate if she were entirely aware of it, which evidently is not the case. Until quite recently it was still possible to speak in terms of mere eccentricities. Alas, things have deteriorated to such an extent that it seems to me impossible, for her own good, to allow the lady to conduct her own affairs. Believe me when I say that I am truly loath to relate the following incident; I do so only to show you how far matters have gone, and to persuade you, if that is still necessary, of how grievous the situation has become. Last Sunday, during the noon service, Mrs. Clément came to church with her backside exposed, clad in a nightshirt, innocent as a baby, and (please forgive me for having to write this) with both kinds of excrement, dried excrement covering her legs . . . In this sad attire, she began to rail against those present and, needless to say, her speech was incoherent. What could we do, I ask you? For the moment, some charitable ladies are taking turns minding her. But what is the appropriate course to follow in the long term? That is why, in the name of my fellow townspeople, I am turning to you, in the belief that you are concerned for this poor soul. Should you be ready to concretely act on her behalf, would you be so kind as to advise the notary, Mr. B . . . ? I can assure you this would come as an immense relief to all the villagers.

Concerning her flower business, I am personally quite up to date and can therefore pledge my wholehearted . . .

Etc.

Clémentine could not help wondering what an accountant who wrote this way might look like. She arranged to meet him on the pretext of discussing the shop. She put on her powder-blue dress and a little eyeliner. He was a little old man, potbellied and crabby. She left his office as quickly as she could. She also visited Mr. B., the notary, and settled the issues of title and liability. Mrs. Clément, it turned out, was worth a tidy sum, one that left her daughter somewhat reeling. Finally, she was relieved to leave behind the village of Saint-Aldor; what remained was for her to deal with the Maison Sainte-Rose-Idarène-de-la-Miséricorde-du-Christ-Roi, where the care bestowed on Mrs. Clément turned out to be adequate and expensive, as was to be expected from an institution located on the banks of the St. Lawrence.

Nothing was as free of germs as a resident of the Maison Sainte-Rose ("Not even a scalpel!" the head nurse said categorically). But cleanliness did not amount to mental health. The old lady, who was washed, scrubbed, polished, and who glistened like a bar of soap, spent most of her time smiling at no one and looked as though she were about to wave goodbye with a handkerchief. Clémentine had to accept this as the living outcome of what her mother had once been. "You know, she probably doesn't recognize you," the head nurse asserted at her very first visit. Still . . . Whenever Clémentine, who always held her mother's hand, lowered her head due to fatigue or boredom, she felt her mother's sidelong gaze on the nape of her neck, a sharp, annoyed gaze that seemed to be a specialty of Mrs. Clément's, a gaze where disdain and worried disapproval, frustration and injured pride, fought it out. It was, in sum, just how her mother would have looked at her had she actually known that Clémentine was Clémentine.

The schoolteacher would spend an hour or an hour and a half in this way, sporadically sharing with her mother a few inconsequential and rather incoherent remarks; then she would be off. Clémentine was of the opinion that this was, after all, pretty much the average relationship between a daughter and her mother.

CLÉMENTINE HAD JUST left the rest home. The clock chimed the half hour. She sat in the trolley car reading a novel by Victor Hugo, her favourite author, and reflected that she, too, would have been able to love Gwynplaine. Certain sentences arrested her, like thunderclaps, leaving her stunned and shot through with an unfathomable shiver. Oh, how deep he was! How she would have liked to write like that! Reading him, she felt a youthful sense of security, as though a very pure, very chaste old man, who moreover bore a vague resemblance to God, was leaning affectionately over her shoulder and speaking to her in a kind, paternal voice. On her night table there was a photograph of him at Guernsey.

She closed her book and cast a glance outside. The trolley could have taken her to within a stone's throw of the Guillubarts', yet she decided to alight at Rue Orléans, which added at least a kilometre to her route.

Nevertheless, she was set on going by the fire hall.

There was one chance in a thousand he would at that very moment be standing at the window, but a chance in a thousand represents acceptable odds to someone with nothing to lose. She sauntered under the caress of this unlikely gaze. Over the years she had learned to adopt a dignified deportment when she walked; with her slow, thoughtful gait, her forearm on her stomach, she did in fact bring to mind a wounded general reviewing his troops. It moreover seemed to her that that gaze improved her altogether, made her more beautiful because it was beautiful, and this is what kept her warm, whether the gaze was real or not, for such things, she well knew, were essentially figments of the mind. She turned her eyes skyward, as though musing on the poetry of Lamartine. Then she stepped into a pile of chance.

The dog was still a few paces away, its tail pointed down, its muzzle abashed, ready to bolt. Clémentine hurried to a park bench and set about repairing the damage using a piece of newspaper. Fortunately, only the sole of her good foot had been affected. The odour rose from underneath the boot with a kind of enthusiasm. For the first time in a long time she caught herself laughing heartily. And this laughter roused her, uplifted her, to the point of reassuring even the dog, which wagged its tail. Clémentine stood up with renewed aplomb. Coming across the park attendant, she winked at him naughtily, stirring distant memories in the old man, and continued on her way with a bearing that would no doubt have been less brazen had she known that all along the captain had indeed been standing at his window in the fire hall.

* * *

IT WAS MRS. GUILLUBART who opened the door. When she entered the vestibule, Clémentine found herself standing amid a welter of boots, of which ten or so were unpaired. She spent a long time wiping her feet on the edge of a rug. Then she removed her coat, which she preferred to keep on her arm. However, she finally parted with it at Mrs. Guillubart's insistence.

The embarrassed housewife apologized for the untidiness of the place and cleared a path for the schoolteacher, hastily kicking aside a jumble of objects that littered the floor: rolled-up socks, a fishing rod, newspapers dating from the previous week. She was constantly rubbing her hands on her apron or wringing them, like someone inclined to touch people who has been taught it is not polite to do so.

"He's better, I trust?"

Mrs. Guillubart smiled timidly. She had the feeling she was behaving improperly when she admitted that Eugène was not better. Arriving in the kitchen, Clémentine had to repress a jolt of surprise. Brother Gandon sat at the table holding a one-year-old on his knees. To his left stood a cradle, which Clémentine was drawn to.

"My eldest daughter's baby," the woman said.

Clémentine bent over the cradle. All one could see of the infant were its tiny, wondering eyes, and a snout protruding between its fists, like a weasel in the springtime. "How lovely," Clémentine mumbled. Then, realizing that Gandon was watching her, she straightened up. There was another child in the room: Lorèthe, who must have been ten. Mrs. Guillubart offered Clémentine some tea.

"Please, don't go to all the bother."

But Mrs. Guillubart wanted to show that she was a capable housekeeper. She told Lorèthe to warm up the teapot. As the little girl stepped near her, she grasped her by the neck and planted a big kiss on her cheek. Lorèthe wearily squirmed her way past.

Clémentine took a seat at the table and questioned Brother Gandon with her eyes.

"He's still in bed. But I was able to see him earlier for a little while." He cast a glance at Mrs. Guillubart. "The two doctors who have examined him cannot agree on the diagnosis. One says epilepsy, the other says it may be a tumor or a blood clot. Because a scar has been found on his scalp."

He pointed to the back of his head.

Miss Clément's shoulders sank, and she smiled at the mother in dismay. Lowering her eyes, Mrs. Guillubart smiled back in kind.

"You have a very pretty face," Lorèthe said abruptly. "It's exactly like the face of Jeanne d'Arc."

The cup and saucer rattled in the schoolteacher's hands. She set them down on the table.

"Well, you are the only one who has noticed."

She turned completely red.

"Out of the mouths of babes and sucklings," the brother said.

There was an awkward pause. To break the silence Mrs. Guillubart declared that as soon as the little guy felt better, she would scold him for what he had done. Lorèthe burst out laughing.

"You're going to give him a slap on the wrist and then you'll give him thirty thousand kisses."

"You're asking for it, my little tramp!" the mother said, showing her a threatening hand.

Lorèthe did not flinch. She looked at her mother from under her lowered eyelids with a fierce little smile.

"Oh no, you must not scold him," Clémentine insisted. "What he did does not amount to much, and he was without a doubt egged on by his friends — one of them, at any rate."

She was thinking of Rocheleau, *the little hypocrite*.

"I was the one who was overly strict, and suspicious . . ."

Mrs. Guillubart, her head tilted sideways, smoothed out the hem of her apron.

"It's true, he's not a bad boy," she acknowledged.

Holding a hockey stick as if it were a patriarch's staff, the eldest son came in through the door at the back of the kitchen. He remained standing, intimidated by the presence of visitors.

"You don't say hello to our guests, Marcel?"

Marcel nodded hastily and addressed a how-do-you-do to the woman who had been his teacher five years before.

Brother Gandon, who liked to catch up with his former students, questioned him about his new job at MacDonald Tobacco. The boy answered in monosyllables. Mrs. Guillubart took the opportunity to invite Clémentine to look in on Eugène.

CLÉMENTINE FOLLOWED MRS. GUILLUBART. It was strange, almost painful, to consider that such a frail woman could have given birth five times. She walked with an almost comic wiggle, as though her exceedingly short legs had trouble bending. Her dirty, poorly knotted chignon exposed a few bald spots on her skull.

Miss Clément would have preferred to beg off this visit. She had that feeling of indecency one sometimes experiences when in the midst of a family to whom fate has dealt a harsh blow. She pitied Mrs. Guillubart and was unable to banish entirely the thought that by tormenting the child she had made him ill. And what if Eugène actually denounced her cruelty in his mother's presence?

Mrs. Guillubart took the schoolteacher's icy fingers in her hand. She softly opened the bedroom door. The room was damp. Through the lace curtains the pallid winter light bathed the room in a milky glow that muted the colours and outlines of things. Eugène, whose features could barely be made out, was lying in his bed with the blankets drawn up to his armpits. His carrot-coloured hair was all there was to add a little lustre to his pillow.

"Look who's here."

Clémentine sat down at his bedside.

"You don't say hello?"

The child cast a long, apathetic gaze on the schoolteacher. Clémentine, fighting back the tremor in her voice, asked how he was. He made no reply. From her handbag she drew out a greeting card signed by his classmates; she unfolded it under his nose. Eugène examined it glumly, then turned his face toward the wall.

Clémentine stood up, resolved to leave the room. Mrs. Guillubart held her back, her fingers clasping her wrist like claws.

"No, I beg you, he needs you."

The schoolteacher tried gently to free her hand. But the woman squeezed harder.

"Stay!"

"But you are hurting me."

She said this with the pleading voice of a little girl. The face Mrs. Guillubart turned toward her suddenly frightened her. It was like that of a witch who has been splashed with holy water. Then, without the slightest movement of the muscles but only by virtue of the shifting shadows, the facial expression was transmogrified. Clémentine realized the woman was smiling at her. It was a humble, beseeching smile, one the schoolteacher could not abide another instant. She again attempted to free her hand, when Eugène let out a moan; the grasp was released. Clémentine stepped back toward the door. The woman's fingers had left burning marks on her wrist.

She could hear smatterings of their whispered exchange: the child voiced a request, and the mother hesitated. "No, not right away, darling." The child insisted.

Mrs. Guillubart lit the oil lamp and a yellowish light trembled into the air. She placed the lamp on the table near the bed. Clémentine saw the woman take up the knife. She saw her spread her fingers, slowly lick the palm of her hand, and then slide the blade into the quick: the skin opened pliantly, as when the pages of a bible are opened. She brought her son's lips close to her bleeding hand.

Clémentine rushed out of the bedroom. Mrs. Guillubart joined her almost immediately and, seeing her in tears, began to weep as well.

"You ought not to get worked up like this, Miss. He's going to get well, I know he's going to get well. I know better than the doctors."

From under the strap of her brassiere she pulled out an old handkerchief and offered it to Clémentine, who, after considering it a moment, declined. Mrs. Guillubart used it herself. When she saw Brother Gandon coming toward them she hid her wounded hand behind her back.

"Isn't that so, Brother, he's going to get well?"

The principal tried to console her but it was no use: the schoolteacher's nervous sobs made him chafe. She was one of those women who turn ugly when they cry. Her sniffling reminded him of the grunts of a pig.

"Miss Clément, please . . ." he said.

In spite of himself some of his irritation came through in his voice. He instantly tried to make up for this and, in his turn, proffered his handkerchief.

"Here, my friend."

Clémentine's sobs halted at once. With wide-eyed amazement she uttered a barely audible thank-you. *He had called her "my friend."* Ill at ease, Brother Gandon looked away. Here, Mr. Guillubart burst into the house and slammed the door behind him. He wavered slightly upon seeing them. Then he crossed the hall without a word of greeting.

This was the signal that it was time to leave. Clémentine and Gandon went to collect their coats in the kitchen. Lorèthe was in the process of setting the table. She roughly jostled her father, who sat before a bottle of cider, elbows propped on the table. Staring at his glass, Mr. Guillubart ignored the visitors. His son Marcel eyed him as though drawing a bead on him, his gaze so full of hate it made Clémentine shudder.

"You could be polite with people, Hector, eh?" Mrs. Guillubart snapped at her husband.

The brother looked at the woman as if to say, "Oh, no, it's nothing, you already have enough trouble as it is." But Mrs. Guillubart insisted, speaking loudly, as one does to the hard of hearing.

"He's not a priest, Totor. He's the school principal and this is Eugène's teacher. They've come to ask after him."

Hector lifted a buttock to let a noise pass.

"Well, we'll be leaving now," Clémentine said tactfully.

Without pausing to button her coat she stepped toward the door. Gandon, a man of the cloth, lingered a while. The youngest sat on the floor amusing himself by jiggling his hand in front of him. Mrs. Guillubart laughed.

"He's trying to catch angels by the tips of their wings, and then he blows on the feathers that are left between his fingers."

Mrs. Guillubart saw them to the doorstep. Miss Clément asked to be called should Eugène's condition change. Mrs. Guillubart promised. Before shutting the door she took Clémentine's hand and put her lips to it.

In the bathroom, she dressed her wound with a rag and then returned to the kitchen. As she went by his bedroom she resisted the urge to look in on Eugène for fear of waking him.

"A priest! A crow!" her husband sputtered. "Letting black robes come in here!"

He waited for his wife to be within reach, then seized her by the arm and shoved her as hard as he could against the wall. Marcel shouted threateningly. But his mother soothed him with her gaze.

She went to the cabinets where the rice for soup was kept. Without letting on, as if it were a secret she wished to share with him alone, she stroked the cheek of her youngest in passing, and from the tips of her fingers — "via fairy-mail" she would say — she blew him a kiss.

The infant clapped with joy, completely enchanted to be living in paradise.

* * *

CLÉMENTINE PROSECUTED HERSELF with the obstinacy, the dark ferocity she at times summoned up to disparage herself before the principal. A ferocity, he knew, that in the end she invariably directed at him. She had almost reached the point of despising him for respecting someone as unworthy as herself. And the more he defended her against herself, the more vexed she became with him.

"You must stop repenting like this," he said. "After all, it's not your fault the boy is ill. You acted in good faith, you believed you were doing the right thing."

"But I *harassed* Eugène, like the mistrustful old maid that I am! You don't understand! I knew he would be the first to betray himself because he was the most vulnerable. Don't you see? *I played on that!* Oh, those damned drawings . . . If you had only seen the way he looked at me the morning of his attack! Imploring me! And I . . . I thought, 'That's it, he's going to cave in, I'll find out at last!' How stupid I am!"

She got so carried away that she spluttered. She wiped her lips with her fingers.

Night was falling and the wind grew stronger and keener. Here and there, windows lighted up. For a long while they walked in silence.

"Would you mind very much if I were to accompany you to your door, Miss Clément?"

Clémentine shrugged indifferently. In spite of her leg, she advanced quickly, as if she wished to keep ahead of him, so that he would appear to be clinging to her. She ostentatiously looked all around her, showing an interest in everything, anything, but him.

Brother Gandon felt hurt and sad. As when he was fifteen, walking along the shore at dusk and skipping stones on Lac Brome while reciting lines from Virgil. A wild and merry noise reached them — the cries of children. There was the banging of sticks and the clatter of blades on the ground. They turned the corner of the building: some boys were playing hockey in the schoolyard.

The two teams comprised a single, intricate cluster whose movements followed the hops of the puck. Snatching the stick from a dumbfounded youngster, Gandon grabbed the puck, elbowed his way ahead, dribbled nicely, slipped between two defencemen, and finally burst out in front of the net, cassock billowing in the wind, to let go his shot: the goaltender did the splits and with the tip of his glove made the stop, which was greeted with a roar of enthusiasm.

The principal came back to the teacher, cheeks aflame, brimming with the pleasure of having loosened up in the cold.

He looked youthful — this was to some degree intended — and amiable. Yet he sensed something cruel and penetrating in the way she observed him; he felt he had been caught *in flagrante delicto* of puerility. She turned on her heels and continued on her way. He had to run to catch up with her.

Gandon had noticed a change in her over the past few days. She appeared distracted and gave him the impression he was disturbing her. He wondered what he might have said, or done, to have elicited such a shift. Until now, it seemed to him, their relationship had been natural, unmarred, and free of dissembling, and although he had become accustomed to her mood swings, he saw these as nothing more than the outbursts of a slightly peculiar sensibility . . . Why this sudden coldness? Gandon saw nothing blameworthy in his behaviour. Perhaps he should more often note the excellence of her work as a teacher? But under that head there were the reports he wrote about her, where, as she was well aware, he always expressed his utmost satisfaction. What more could she expect from him? After all, he was not about to compliment her on her new dress, which, to be perfectly objective, he had to admit was supremely becoming. That Miss Clément might be the least bit vain about such matters seemed to him inconceivable.

They walked along the railroad track in a silence that apparently he alone found embarrassing. He would have liked to ask plainly, "What do you have against me?" But he was afraid of betraying himself by doing so, of conceding an advantage. He tried whistling. The results were so pathetic that he gave it up after a couple of bars.

They came across some policemen on patrol, unusual for that part of the neigbourhood. The schoolteacher halted;

Gandon followed her eyes and recognized the captain of the fire brigade. The officer saluted by clicking his boot heels. He bowed and, holding his cap over his breast, said, "Miss Clément." He straightened up and offered an explanation.

"Some people have complained about the presence of a prowler. It seems he may have lit some fires here and there in the alleys."

"Good Lord."

"Nothing to be afraid of, Miss! There is no indication this individual meant to set fire to any houses. Some paper set alight in the middle of the road, that's all. A madman, no doubt. To be on the safe side I've come to assess the situation myself. Everything is under control."

Brother Gandon offered to accompany the teacher to the nuns' residence, where they would surely agree to take her in for the night. Clémentine tried to catch the captain's eye, and succeeded. She turned to Gandon.

"No, that will be fine, I am not afraid. After all, the captain assures us we are in no danger. Isn't that so, Captain?"

"Everything is under control," the officer repeated.

The schoolteacher lowered her head and batted her eyes. They stood there, stiff as fence posts, not saying a word. Miss Clément was as tall as the two men, and this disturbed her. During the silence, which lingered on, the captain and Gandon sized each other up out of the corners of their eyes. Had they been dogs they would have sniffed each other's hindquarters. The firefighter abruptly eyed the principal's robe, and the principal registered the irony in his gaze. Had they been little boys Gandon would have punched him in the nose.

The principal had the vague, nagging impression of being dressed like a woman. During the war, one night, he had dreamed of a dinner attended by military officers and magistrates. Everyone was in formal attire and he, in high spirits, danced in, perched on one foot, waving his hand over his head like a crest. "I'm wearing a dress!" he sang softly. "I'm wearing a dress!"

The principal shook off this memory.

Meanwhile, the fireman cast a questioning glance in the teacher's direction, as if to ask, "Can I speak in his presence?" Clémentine hesitated, then nodded yes. The captain waited a few moments, for the pleasure of seeing them hanging on his words. Gandon clucked with impatience.

"I'm sharing this with you because of who you are. I have some news concerning your kids, though I can't vouch for it. Nothing has been confirmed. I heard it today from the police inspector, a personal friend of mine, you see, who trusts me implicitly."

"Well?"

"Well, the night that you, Miss Clément, contacted us to express your fears about the bank employee being on the site of the fire, that same night, a witness stated that he saw a man . . . a man who . . . Actually, it's a rather touchy subject to mention in the presence of a lady."

He took a deep breath and spewed it all out at once, like one long word.

"A man who dropped his pants in front of some kids and did things to himself in front of them."

"Ha!" Clémentine exclaimed. And then repeated, "Ha!" like someone who has discovered a dead rat in her bedsheets. She turned to Gandon.

"I told you so! I told you so!"

Alarmed by the rage she directed at him, the brother took

a sideways step, as though looking to the captain for aid. The captain was unfazed.

"I can't tell you any more for now, as I myself have no further details."

The schoolteacher was shocked.

"Why hasn't anyone yet taken action!"

"Well, there is still nothing official. The information came in an unsigned letter sent to the police station. They get tons of letters like that — can't very well believe every one of them, you know. At any rate, I wanted to tell you in person."

"Did the witness identify the man?" Gandon inquired.

"Who else could it be?" said Clémentine.

"The letter doesn't mention any names," said the officer, speaking impartially and in a superior, professional tone of voice. Turning to the schoolteacher, he added, "Which, needless to say, doesn't prevent us from having certain suspicions."

Brother Gandon's face crumpled.

"All this must of course remain confidential. In the meantime, you must excuse me; I have to complete my inspection."

The officer walked away, with the principal offering no response to his goodbye.

"We must do something, Brother, we *must* do something!"

"I need to think all this through with a clear head. We can talk about it again on Monday. Please excuse me."

Clémentine clutched furiously at his sleeve. The principal was outraged. *Does she take me for her dog?* he thought. He was the very epitome of gentleness and patience, but he could not tolerate being touched.

The schoolteacher was beside herself. He brutally shook free of her grip.

"I must ask you to remain calm. You look like an ostrich. Nothing has been confirmed yet."

Gandon dropped his head in disbelief. God, what had he just said! Clémentine stood there, arms hanging at her sides, mouth gaping. Her eyebrows were raised very high and she stared at the principal incredulously. There was a hesitant smile on her face, at once amused and suppliant. Gandon was frozen with mortification. He had merely wanted to impress upon her that there was no point in overdramatizing. The word he had had in mind was "actress"! The other had slipped out on its own.

Clémentine turned on her heels. She waited a moment, hesitating, as though she were giving him one last chance to retract. Gandon said nothing. She charged toward her house with a groan, climbed the stairs almost on her hands and knees, pushing herself along using her elbows and hands, unmindful of her dignity, with the alarmed haste of an ostrich.

Brother Gandon had not budged. It was as if a Chinese vase had just fallen from his hands and smashed on the floor. He stupidly contemplated the irreparable shards. He felt that between him and Miss Clément nothing would ever be the same again.

The principal set off again toward the school. Their footsteps in the snow were still fresh. He imagined that he might never do that again with her — walk in step, side by side, simply as friends — and it wrung his heart.

When they were leaving the home of the Guillubarts, in the confined space of the hall, she had been obliged to lean on him for a moment, and his nostrils had been surprised by a subtle perfume, like the fragrance of flowers after a rain shower. *You could have told her her new perfume smelled good, you fool, it wouldn't have been a sin, after all!* Gandon quickened his pace.

But it was no perfume. It was Clémentine's natural scent.

* * *

THE CAPTAIN WATCHED the principal until he was out of sight. Then he took the alley, so as not to be seen entering her house by the front stairway. The lamp in the kitchen was burning in the window — that was the signal he could go up. He knocked on her door. There was no answer. Perplexed, he tried again. Still no answer. The captain hesitated. Was he to go in without Miss Clément's permission? As he had only known her for a few days, he was unsure how she might react.

Still, if she were to reprimand him for it he could always argue that he had been worried. He looked left, then right, and twisted the doorknob: it was not locked. Clémentine was not in the kitchen. He called — no reply. He advanced farther inside the house.

He found her in the corridor, standing in her overcoat, still holding the telephone. She looked devastated.

"Little Guillubart," she sighed.

That was all she could say.

9

EIGHTEEN YEARS OF patience, of backroom manoeuvring, of secret pacts with creditors had allowed Séraphon to wrest the wood yard from his great-granduncle. Uncle Anselme was tough, but Séraphon was born to bide his time, and the old man eventually loosened his grip. On his deathbed, he shouted, "You finally got the best of me, you rascal!" And Séraphon answered, "The best, indeed, Uncle. I made my selection and kept the only part that interested me." He said this while dangling the keys to the wood yard under the nose of the dying man. His great-aunt wept.

At its most flourishing, before the fire that destroyed everything, the business employed no fewer than six men, who might be asked to work up to three nights a week. But during the day the yard stayed empty, steeped in an atmosphere of desolation, and the craving to give orders nagged at Séraphon until dusk. He entertained the prospect of hiring someone to maintain the premises and help him in the day-to-day operations, since he had no great appetite for work and liked it less and less as old age set in. One morning a young man carrying a knapsack introduced himself. He was twenty years old, he was sturdy, he had no family. He said his name was Wilson.

"Wilson what? Wilson who?"

"Wilson."

Séraphon looked him up and down, from his bushy red hair to his feet, which were as huge as his hands. He decided to try him out.

The idea was to house him in the shed near the railroad track. Séraphon promised him firewood, one meal a day, blankets, and sheets; for anything else, the apprentice would have to fend for himself. Wilson agreed. Besides, he said, he preferred to prepare his own meals as much as possible, for he considered himself a peerless cook. His only condition was that Séraphon must never enter the shed in his absence; he wanted the place to be exclusively his own. Séraphon said he found this perfectly natural. He proposed a wage, the lowest he could imagine that would not elicit a howl of laughter and, miraculously, Wilson deemed it acceptable. The bargain was sealed. The boy started that very same day.

Wilson proved to be the recruit Séraphon had dreamed of. He was adroit with the saw and axe, could haul large loads of wood, and readily caught on to the petty frauds of retailing and to matters of money and organization. He was hard-nosed in his handling of widows and orphans (a considerable boon in that parish), could instantly sniff out a welsher, and was always good for a laugh, especially at the expense of the client who had just left the shop.

The only drawback was the odour he gave off. Séraphon was not himself a paragon of personal hygiene, yet their respective lacks of cleanliness were not compatible and clashed in the way a barbarian's might with that of the confirmed bachelor. Séraphon changed his underpants only once a year, on the pretext that he hardly perspired. He let the dust gather in his wrinkles, on his furniture, between his toes, avaricious even on these points, and liked to find himself in his bedclothes in the morning, alone, with his sour little smell. But he found the smell of other people revolting. He went so far as to hold his breath when someone came within three paces. The presence of Wilson, who reeked of gamy fish, was a veritable ordeal for him. The apprentice picked his teeth at the table, wiped his hands on his hair, his clothes were covered with grease stains, and when sated he would flex his chest muscles and make no bones about belching with stentorian pride. There were times when Séraphon would disdainfully push his plate away. "You've made me lose my appetite," he would say. And Wilson would explode with laughter and a shower of spittle.

During the first weeks Séraphon never missed an opportunity to spy on Wilson. He double-checked the cash register each night and, forgetting his keys there, pretended to have fallen asleep with the door of the safe ajar. Wilson sidestepped all these traps. Séraphon began to wonder what sort of weirdo he had stumbled upon. He regarded honesty as something bizarre and instinctively mistrusted it. He would ponder the situation on nights when sleep eluded him. "He must be waiting for his chance," he would tell himself. One day a client let a dollar fall out of his pocket, and the apprentice ran three blocks, to Rue Dézéry, just to hand it back to him. Séraphon could not believe his eyes. Was Wilson sick, or what? The apprentice had continued sawing planks as though nothing was amiss.

As he grew accustomed to his presence, Séraphon became more and more consumed with the urge to know more about Wilson's past. He failed to squeeze the slightest confidence out of him. Occasionally he surprised Wilson in the act of writing, and straight away Wilson would shut his notebook and slip it inside his shirt. Séraphon questioned the other employees. Wilson treated them with brutal contempt, and they were not exactly fond of him. "One too many horses in the stable . . ." they insinuated. Séraphon would turn away with a shrug.

Wilson would occasionally give himself leave to take some time off, apparently without the proprietor voicing any objections. He would disappear for a weekend; Séraphon had no idea where but took advantage of his absence to comb his hut in search of his notebook. He came away empty-handed every time.

Upon Wilson's return his backpack would be full of small animals, still alive. He relished wild game, he said, and when there was none left he simply did without meat. When Séraphon questioned him about this, he answered that he could not eat what he had not killed himself. He said this as a joke, and began to laugh his peculiar, throaty laugh, which made his shoulders shake. Be that as it may, on further examination this turned out to be precisely the case.

"Actually, that's also why I never take Communion," he added.

Then he stopped laughing.

It was nearly the middle of April. Séraphon shivered as he crossed the yard. He passed by the apprentice, who had almost finished stacking the wood, and without bothering to stop invited him to come discuss some urgent business.

"Hey, apprentice, I'm talking to you! I thought I told you to come along."

Wilson stood there, motionless, just like a statue.

"What are you gawking at like that?"

Séraphon retraced his steps. A little boy was scrambling down the knoll. He must have been about twelve years old. He held a sheet of paper out in front of him at chest level, like a choirboy carrying a candle. He stopped near the hill. His hair was the colour of the setting sun on freshly cut boards. Séraphon told him to go play somewhere else. The child answered that he was delivering a message.

"Slip it under my door and I'll take a look later on."

The child walked away softly.

Séraphon said, "I just hired that kid as a messenger. His name is Remouald, Remouald Bilboquin."

Wilson's eyes followed the blond head as it receded.

"Anyway, when you're through musing on angels you can come see me."

"Shut up," Wilson retorted.

Séraphon returned to his kitchen.

SITTING NEXT TO the stove, Séraphon waited. As he chewed over how he was going to chastise his apprentice for his insolence, he rocked his chair at a furious tempo. Little by little, as the warmth enveloped him, the cadence slackened, and he eventually drifted off. In his dream there was a turmoil of animals, commotions and chases in which images from his childhood were jumbled together. He surfaced peevishly from his slumber, with his mind in a fog and set on one thing only. It was dark now. The embers in the stove sent blood-red streaks of light dancing on the furniture. With the single-mindedness of a sleepwalker Séraphon donned his toque and overcoat, seized a lamp, and, forgetting to shut the door, plunged into the night.

His legs took him to the stable. With the dampness, the cold, the smell of the horses, he was now fully awake. He approached the stallions. When Séraphon was a child, Uncle Anselme had taught him to rouse the male so as to impress the customers. He had become quite adept at this trick. On dull nights he would revive his boyhood and, with the same amusement, marvel as the apparatus swelled to clownish proportions.

Séraphon began by arousing it with a duster. The beast stirred and knocked him down with a twitch of its rump. Séraphon stayed on the ground for a moment, laughing uncontrollably. Then he grasped a panel to lever himself onto his feet. But the panel swung away and there fell out a notebook. Séraphon brought the oil lamp closer. On the cover were the words "Confessions of a Monster." The writing was unmistakably that of his apprentice — uneven, messy, chaotic. Séraphon started to read at random; his heart was thumping.

. . . *AND THOUGH AMÉDÉE was the very embodiment of the grace, the beauty, the charm of childhood, while I, Jean-Baptiste, was misshapen in both heart and countenance, we complemented each other as the night complements the day. Yet, for the Mare, I was the devil.*

All the details concerning my first weeks in this world —
I mean to say: my first weeks in the form of Jean-Baptiste —
were divulged to me the day I discovered, hidden behind a shelf
in the library, my father's diary. Indeed, "divulged" is not the
right word. *This account, which I read until I knew it by heart,*
in fact only served to confirm my recollections. *I revisited*
certain scenes with the precision of the most distinct memory.

Himself a doctor, my father insisted on being present at the
birthing. The pangs started in the middle of the night. It was
winter. The dawn, apparently, was magnificent. At noon, the
top of the infant's head emerged at last; all was well. Out came
the head, the shoulders, the trunk — the baby seemed to have
all its parts. Then, just as the seat was about to pass, when all
believed the labour was nearly done, there was a standstill.
Something was stuck inside. They began to worry. No matter
how the Mare pushed, it was to no avail. The baby started to
cry feebly, and then to pant. "There's something else in my belly,"
my mother said. Within her she felt a foreign body, "squirming
all over," torturing her. Her deliverance arrived only six hours
later, at nightfall, after a great deal of suffering. There was a
moment of astonishment. They understood now why the child
could not come out. It was held back by the umbilical cord of
another. And the other was covered with hair, he had a mouth
already full of teeth, he seemed, according to my father, to be
snickering; and he was born with his eyes wide open. *My*
mother fainted. That hideous creature was me.

My mother refused to breastfeed me, and I was entrusted to
a wet nurse as of the second day. Meanwhile, Amédée, who was
jaundiced, was visibly pining away. The doctor's advice, folk
remedies — nothing helped. The Mare was desperate. Then a
servant had the idea of reuniting us. My father, in his diary, uses

the word "miracle." They brought in the Mare. I was turned toward my twin and was stroking him tenderly. Horrified by this scene, she tore me away from him and flung me on the floor. This episode came as a shock when I read it. For I had the impression I remembered it very well.

My father's feelings toward me were no better than those of my mother; what I have read of his leaves no room for doubt in this regard. For him as for her, the child, the only child, was Amédée. I was no more than a thing he required in order to live, a monstrous growth, an anomalous but necessary organ. My father must be given credit for having grasped that immediately. And even though, due to a lack of willpower that Amédée would inherit, he yielded to my mother on almost everything, he remained firm on this point, such that while he lived the couple that we comprised, my twin and I, was in some wise protected. Until at least the age of four, Amédée, as soon as he lost sight of me, would begin to suffocate. He would grope about for me and even fainted at times. We thus shared games, bedroom, outings in the woods, and, when we were of age to receive them, lessons from the tutor, an effeminate young man who extorted from Amédée looks of tender amazement that galled me. My father did not, however, succeed in having me join with Amédée in the voice and piano lessons my mother gave him, and which enchanted him. My shrill voice made her hair stand on end; besides, music for her was something sacred, and had she given me lessons she would have had the impression of scattering consecrated hosts in the mud.

Music was, moreover, not the only thing that enchanted Amédée. He had at a very early age become addicted to the mirror. I often said to him, when we were alone together, "Look at me. Look at me the way you do when you look at yourself."

He would give it a try, sincerely, but soon became vexed: "I swear that is how I look at myself!" "No," I would say with a smile. He would go away whimpering.

I have alluded to his spinelessness. But he was also possessed of a peculiar hardness, one that was selfish, frank, unself-conscious, and which rested on the quiet assurance that he was entitled to everything. He found it natural that I should take the blame for his misdeeds, even though we both knew the punishment meted out to me in such cases was ten times worse than his. At night in our bed he would blow softly on the wounds on my back, just as in the daytime I sometimes saw him blowing on the cat's fur. He would nestle his little body against my chest and fall asleep, while I watched over his slumber. Everything that was ugly in us both I had taken upon myself. I submitted to him, knowing he could be nothing without me, nor I without him. He was the lovable part of ourselves, the only thing in me that I loved.

The Mare, meanwhile, believed I had a noxious influence on him. Whenever my father left on a business trip she would give orders to have me locked in the library. It is there I spent a good part of my childhood. A servant would bring me meals there. When my mother took her nap, Amédée would come with an offering of apples or slices of bread and jam. We would hold each other closely — or, rather, I would hold him close to me. We whispered promises. I dreamed of our freedom when the Mare would no longer be there . . . Amédée listened. But after fifteen minutes or so, terrified at the thought she might catch us together, he fled from my embrace, leaving behind only his scent of fir trees. There were times when this lasted a fortnight. Two long weeks during which I had nothing to do but read, reread, and read again. I was not yet ten years old and already had understood that everything found in books, everything said about God, about the "human heart," about the World, was but a tissue of lies, of futility, and already I sensed that I would one day be brought ineluctably to teach the world a dazzling lesson in truth.

But the Mare did not die — at least, not right away; my father was the first to depart. We were twelve then, Amédée and I. And it was then that I was brutally, irreparably ripped away from half of myself, so that there was nothing left for me to love, and an endless night — a night with no dawn and no way back — commenced for me.

And so, Amédée went off to a seminary to study. The Mare was now free to carry out her plan — which my father had always opposed — to make a priest of Amédée. A priest! At the sight of my brother leaving in a car I flew into a rage. I leaped out the library window. They found me in the chapel overturning the statues. Three men were needed to hold me down. My mother of course jumped at this chance. And it was on that day that my permanent isolation began.

From that day forward I was forced to live in the hunting lodge. A servant was assigned to keep watch over me. He was an ageless, expressionless, almost faceless man, with whom I never exchanged more than fifty words. He was forever at my side, like Pascal's abyss. When I climbed trees in the forest, he climbed with me. When I ate, when I slept, when I defecated, when I was fevered, he was there, imperturbable, showing neither anger, nor disgust, nor compassion: a prison door in the shape of a human being.

But this prison was as vast as the family estate. I was allowed to ramble over the fields, wander through the woods, set traps for wild game. I very soon came to want to prepare my own meals, *for the idea that the Mare wished to gradually poison me seemed to me not at all absurd. I had to let the servant light the fire, since it was stupidly feared I might use the opportunity to set fire to the lodge. As if, were I to burn something down, it would be my own house! There was never any limit to the Mare's stupidity.*

Needless to say, during this time, I never met my mother. There was a statue of the Virgin in the garden next to my lodge. She came there two or three times a week to perform her devotions. I would station myself at the window. Nothing in the world could have kept me from observing this grotesque spectacle. Several times a month she would visit my brother at the seminary. That, at any rate, is my assumption. She left in a car, her face beaming, and came back in the late afternoon wearing a funereal expression. On those nights I could hear her plaintively tinkling at the piano. I learned what it means to be gorged on Mozart, or worse — Chopin.

I communicated with her only in writing, once to request that eyeglasses be made for me. To my great surprise she consented. I wrote her notes addressed to "the Mare of the Twins" and signed "the Librarian." I demanded books, which the Prison Door brought me by the crate-load. Half the library was soon relocated to my lodge. As it was mainly comprised of religious texts, my mother saw no reason why I should not partake of them; what is more, she believed in the power of reading to mollify me: I am sure she died without ever suspecting how deeply mistaken she was. The tomes piled up on the ground and became permeated with kitchen odours; wild geese hung from the ceiling; pigs' heads and sacks of potatoes served as bookends.

The years passed, and I spent them perfecting myself — that is, in my role as a caged beast. I never washed, never changed my clothes, never learned to use a fork or spoon. One day I drafted an Imitation of the Brute, which I dedicated to the memory of Saint Ignatius. Only God is aware of — and still trembles at — the reams I wrote, and burned. I long amused myself with the game of writing to shock the Creator, and when I felt Him shudder I would laugh long and horribly. At the approach of my soul, of the lavish reflections of its monstrosity, God begins to gasp for air, to choke — I can hear Him choking, agonizing; for an instant His moose-like lament fills the entire universe. That is the only music I enjoy.

This was how I lived until the age of eighteen. Amédée had fallen ill, had more or less recovered, but was unable to go on living at the seminary. That is what I learned one morning in a letter from the Mare. I saw the car arriving. I climbed onto the roof of my lodge and scuttled back and forth, waving my arms at him. I shouted his name. Amédée lowered his head as though not daring to look at me. My mother was waiting for him on the porch, and he let her hug him against her bosom.

For days I waited for Amédée to visit my lodge. I was no longer allowed to go out, not even for my walks. Callers in their Sunday best came to greet the one who had returned. I was convinced that once these society chores were done my brother would rush to my embrace. I was feverish. A six-year-old wound suddenly flared up and burned as it had on the first morning. This open wound had to be healed, had to be pressed against his wound, so that one, same blood could flow once again in our two bodies.

I saw him appear one morning in the garden, near the statue of the Virgin. He was holding a spray of flowers. He examined my lodge with apprehensive curiosity. I felt my heart pounding *fit to burst. At times he glanced over his shoulder toward the family residence. Finally, he did something incredible:* he laid the flowers at the foot of the statue and began to pray.

When he arose, I was standing in the doorway. Amédée had never looked so stunning. He was tall now, as tall as I was, and his blond mane was combed back. I could see his pale face, his long, musician's hands, his broad shoulders, his waist as slender as a girl's. Why did he not come to me? He looked at my clothes with a mixture of revulsion and fear. I glanced down at my shoulder: Ligeïa was sitting there, having just come out of my pocket — but Amédée could not be afraid of a mouse, surely! I approached, my arms stretched out. He stepped back. I could not believe it — he was standing there, quaking. I resolutely walked up to him and seized his wrist. Immediately his legs buckled and he began to moan. My throat was in a knot and I was unable to speak. What was going on? Why didn't he understand? I laid my hand on his head; he struggled. I tried with all my might to put my lips to his — wound to wound! He shook his head and cried, "No! No!" I felt a violent blow on the back of my neck and found myself on my knees in a daze. The Prison Door was standing beside me. I raised my eyes. Amédée hurried toward the house, frantic, snivelling, staggering like a drunk.

At that instant I realized I could be no more than a wild animal; this was my fate. And once certain boundaries had been transgressed — the most crucial boundaries — crossing the others was like breaking through a spiderweb.

The first little girls appeared a few weeks later. They arrived in the late afternoon, two or three times over the course of a fortnight, to take music lessons from Amédée. Why only little girls? And why was my brother obliged to teach? Had the family fallen on hard times? These are questions whose answers I do not know.

At any rate, the necessary precautions were taken to ensure that the students remained completely ignorant of my existence. When they were there, I could not even set foot in the garden. I watched them from my window. The lambs arrived in small groups, clasping a violin or a flute; the eldest could not have been more than fourteen. Sometimes they were accompanied by a priest, on choir days. My brother and mother personally greeted them on the porch, bowing like servants. I saw Amédée turning a fretful eye toward my window, and that furtive gaze, treacherous beyond words, left no doubt whatsoever in my mind that he who had been half of me was dead.

But that half remained inside me like a hungry emptiness, a living emptiness. So, to the extent I wished for the return of the child-brother, instinctively sensing that he perforce would ultimately come back to me, in one form or another, to that same extent did I hate this effete and craven Amédée, in every way compliant with his mother's desires, this embalmed Amédée who dared survive the twin whose casket I was, and be no more than the Mare's marionette.

Through the open casement I could hear the song of the lambs, the high-pitched voice of the priest explaining to them the subtleties of the melody, and the music of the two others there, the Mare and her son, playing four-handed! I hated that good priest. I hated my mother. I hated those little girls.

Yet this was not the worst of it. There was, in addition, the first Sunday of every month. At dawn, I was pulled out of bed, stripped naked, had bucketfuls of ice water thrown on my face, was scrubbed, wiped down, and forced to don a ridiculous disguise. For a long time I wondered what drove my mother to want these monthly "family breakfasts." Then I understood that this was part of a complicated ritual in which I was only a tool, and that the display of my brother's beauty beside my monstrous ugliness was for her a source of prurient titillation. I endeavoured not to disappoint her. I ate with my fingers, licked my plate, spilled sauce on my clothes, belched, farted. A servant stood near me for the sole purpose of swabbing my face. Amédée fluttered his eyelids without lifting his nose from his plate, and I, while my mother glared, I laughed and laughed . . .

Then we would proceed to the little family chapel. An aging and deaf priest celebrated the service. I was installed in the rood-loft, with the Prison Door at my side, of course. Amédée and my mother sat close to each other somewhere in the front rows. From the moment of the Elevation, she began to show signs of arousal. She cast moist gazes at my brother, and I saw Amédée stiffen, become more and more livid, until he was overcome by trembling. As soon as mass had been expedited, the whole staff was dismissed until the evening. The Mare gave her orders with short, jittery gestures, her forehead flecked with pink blotches. She and Amédée were to be left alone in the house. Paralyzed by shame and fear, my brother waited off to the side and looked at me imploringly. I responded with a smile of contempt, as if to say, "This is what happens when you spend too much time looking at yourself in mirrors."

The servant brought me back to my lodge. I knew very well what was going on in the music room. And posted at my window, I read quietly and waited. Invariably, after half an hour, no more, I saw the Mare storm out of the house and dash to the foot of the statue of the Virgin. Summer and winter alike, in mud or snow, every first Sunday of the month, on her knees, frantically, she prayed, beating herself on the chest and belly, and from my vantage point, I, the Monster, mocked her, nickering at the top of my lungs.

Yes, I had become a veritable beast, a ferocious beast, who could no longer speak. One day, taking advantage of my servant's nap, I crossed the garden, climbed a tree, and dropped down before a little girl who was coming for her lesson. I was as startled as she was. There was within me a volcano striving to erupt, a torrent of words. Everything was swarming inside my head — the rage, the sense of my own power — and I was left speechless. Then, all at once, these words welled up between my lips:

"On your knees! Admire me! Adore your God!"

I was about to place my hand on her shoulder to force the lamb to her knees, when beside me a stranger sprang up, huge, with fury in his eyes, and beat me off with his whip. Howling, I returned to my lodge.

From this point on certain things elude me — my recollections become murky. It seems to me, in any case, that the Mare's message arrived a few days later. It tersely announced, "Your brother is dead. He hanged himself."

Was there actually a burial? I see things as if in a dream. I was standing on the roof of the lodge, the little procession made its way down the hill toward the family cemetery. My mother was supported by two women. For several days I was stricken, horribly ill. I was incapable of the slightest thought and had only a vague, a very vague sense of being. I sought to lay eyes on the Prison Door. Nothing was present around me any more. But in the end the desire to elucidate this mystery gave me the strength to walk. I crossed the garden, the fields, went by the pinewood, and arrived at the cemetery. There was this small stone cross, brand new. I stepped closer and read. Immediately I turned on my heels, utterly baffled. I headed toward the family residence. I could not believe what my eyes had just seen.

Everything in this countryside had changed, nothing was as it had been before. I found the Prison Door sitting on a hillock, shoeless and in the process of emptying a bottle. I told him to follow me into the lodge. He rose, shrugged his shoulders, and walked off while guzzling some wine. People I had never seen in the house were going in and out. One of them, taking me for a mendicant, shouted at me to go beg somewhere else. I decided to return to my quarters. I was haunted by what I had read on the small stone cross. Was it an error? Had someone wanted to play some sinister joke? The epitaph said, "Jean-Baptiste, aged 19, son of René and Carmen Wilson, brother of Amédée." I no longer understood anything. Who was in the grave? Jean-Baptiste? Could it be that for my entire life I had been mistaken about my own name and had confused it with my brother's? Unless I had been mistaken not about the name but the person, *and in fact was myself Amédée? But then, where did Amédée begin and where did Jean-Baptiste end? It seemed to me I no longer had a face. I latched onto my one certitude, to the only name of which I was certain: I was Wilson.*

One day a stranger entered my lodge and appeared surprised to find me stretched out among the potatoes and the books. The filth and the stench of my abode twisted his face into a frown of disgust. Convinced that he was dealing with a tramp, he commanded me to be off. I asked what had happened to the owner of the estate.

"That is none of your affair — now, get out!"

"I am her son," I said.

He considered me with an air of hesitation. Someone outside yelled, "That's not true, her son is dead! She was even wearing her mourning dress on her deathbed."

"What, has she died?"

"She died of consumption, or grief," the same voice replied.

I was thrown out of the lodge. I crossed the garden, not knowing where to go. As I passed by the statue of the Virgin, I spat in her face. I believe I took the road north, I don't know, everything is muddled in my head. So muddled that at times I wonder whether the opposite was true: that my mother was the one who hanged herself, and my brother the one who died of consumption, unable to bear having survived her. In any event, these are mere details.

What mattered was that my twin no longer existed, nor the Mare, that they had died horrible deaths, and that I was free.

The narrative broke off there; some pages had been ripped out. Séraphon closed the notebook. He had never felt anything like this. His throat was dry, and the blood pulsed warmly, ardently on the inside of his thighs. He considered the notebook with a kind of holy consternation. Shaking as he reverently opened it again, and read with an anguished sob:

I have met this child. His name is Remouald Bilboquain.

The entry was dated that same day. Séraphon skipped over the pages containing only some peculiar drawings, scribbles, long series of numbers, musical staffs.

Yes, as you travelled about, as you chased the horizon, at every stage, wherever you set down your scanty baggage, you would once again encounter the Cross that had followed you there. And the Voice you hear and which issues from the Cross and says at times "I, Jean-Baptiste" and at other times

"You, Jean-Baptiste," which speaks in your stead, speaks of you in the third person, abruptly goes quiet only to begin again sometimes weeks later, the Voice that propels you onward, throws you to the ground, pulls you to your feet, drives you forward once again, batters you, yes, that Voice, you realized, was the wrath of God, God who wants to bend you to His Law, but you resist, you know God never had a purchase on your soul, you know it is you in the end who will win — this is what the Other Voice has confirmed for you, although this other voice, which you believe to be the true voice of your soul, may be — who can tell? — but the voice of He who lies, He who deceives, He who calls to Himself the lost souls, poor fool, in order to lead them farther astray.

Séraphon heard the noise of someone falling, followed by an oath. He hastily put the notebook back where it belonged and, blowing out the lamp, ran to an empty stall. The stable door opened. Wilson.

The lamp wavered at the end of his arm, spreading large, fantastic shadows on the walls. He advanced with faltering steps and rubbed his eyes like a sleepy child.

He came near the secret panel, which Séraphon had not properly shut. He did not seem surprised to find his notebook lying on the ground. Séraphon held his breath. The apprentice sat down cross-legged in the middle of the stable, placed the lamp close to him, and, with the notebook resting on his calves and his left shoulder twitching sporadically as if he were trying to shrug off a burden, he set to writing.

He wrote without let-up, like a man possessed, and while his pencil ran on, his trunk rocked gently, steadily to and fro. There came a distant sound of mewling. Wilson interrupted his writing. He glanced around suspiciously. Séraphon expected Wilson to cry out, "I know you're there!" but Wilson said nothing.

Then, all at once, he half straightened up, his body quivering. The moon had just appeared in the skylight; it was like an eye opening after a deep sleep. Wilson appeared to be racked with fear.

"I thought you would not come. You told me you would not come!"

He fell on his knees and began to mumble, his face lifted toward the skylight. Séraphon could not make out what he said. He addressed the glow, and it seemed as if the glow answered him.

"No, I swear to you!" he suddenly cried. "I swear the thought had not even occurred to me."

He stood up, took a few dazed steps. He stepped back, wringing his fingers. Finally, he let out a scream of horror, a genuine howl, then he keeled over, as though struck down. His skull hit the ground with a thud. His breathing was inaudible.

Séraphon let a long while elapse before daring to leave his stall. He was afraid of corpses and the need to make sure Wilson was not one finally gave him the courage to risk it. But he was immediately forced to do an about-face. The apprentice rose to his feet again, unmindful of what had just taken place. He retrieved his notebook, slipped it inside his coat, and headed calmly toward the entrance.

On second thought, however, he turned around and approached the Nag. He stroked its forehead and by way of jest introduced a finger into its nostril, which made the animal sneeze. Then he rotated his upper body and placed his fist on his hip. "And this," he said, smiling, "is from Amédée." With all his might, he punched the old mare three times full in the head. The creature snorted. Something black spurted onto Séraphon's face; he wiped his cheek — it was blood. Wilson went out, sucking on his knuckles.

Séraphon ran to the window. The night had enveloped Wilson's silhouette. "Tomorrow morning, first thing, I'm giving him the sack!" he told himself. Before leaving the stable, he waited to see a light at the far end of the yard, to make sure the apprentice had indeed returned to his shack and to its walls laden with icons, palm branches, crucifixes, and images of the Virgin Mary.

* * *

WHAT STRUCK HIM first was that in school everything was arranged at right angles — the corridors, the rules, the playing field, the covered playground. One could move about only in single file, along routes as geometrically austere as theorems, from which he might through a half-open door catch a glimpse of the mysterious formulae written on the blackboard in the classroom of the older students. All that he absorbed through his entire being — the smell of the books, the chalk dust, the national anthem sung standing next to one's desk after the morning prayer, the insolent cleverness of the older children and their language rife with innuendo, the implacable schedule, each minute welded to an activity, the brutality of certain schoolmates that kept him from sleeping nights at a time, and the rest, the teachers' frowns, the letters and numbers to be copied, Bible history, grammar, arithmetic, catechism, the nervous excitement of recess — all of this was bathed in the same bracing, exacting, chilly light, like strong salts that his mind was forced to inhale, wrenching him from his home and the sweet sleep of early childhood.

Something unforgettable occurred during the second week in September. They had just been told about the soul, but in terms so strange to him that he at first wondered whether he indeed possessed one. Then he realized that what was called the soul was what he left each morning at the door of the school and recovered only at four o'clock, like a coat in the cloakroom. The two priests had left after blessing the class. To subdue the light that was flooding in through the windows, the teacher had lowered the blinds. And, as the windows reached all the way to the ceiling which was very high, she had used a rod whose presence in the classroom he had until then found puzzling.

The yellow canvas of the blinds was studded with spots of mold. Through it the sunbeams took on a magical, unalterable, unanticipated gentleness. He felt a thrill of happiness run through his body. It was like sitting one summer morning in the middle of an orange. His classmates were no longer lumped together in an anonymous mass; he was one of them, they inhabited the same world, the same garden as he. Each of them was, like him, the only one to be who he was, and they were all together here. How could a beauty such as this, a caress such as this be possible? There was the light that separates, reveals the outlines, marks the differences, the light of numbers and of grammar, of the corridors and the rules, and there was the light — warm, alive, overwhelming in its tenderness — that joins beings together. In that moment he experienced a profound welcoming, like a first dawning of the world, and from that day he drew the revelation that he was on earth to reconcile within himself, Remouald Bilboquain, those two lights.

This thought germinated within him with a vegetal sort of patience. He was for a long time the hard-working student, untroubled and shy, whom one hardly notices and who ruminates on his flowers yet to blossom.

But at the age of eleven he suddenly raised his head and began to speak.

The teachers, male and female, did not always understand the meaning of his questions. "How is it that each thing has a left side and a right side?" That two hands could be at once identical and opposite, when he thought it over, seemed to him altogether disconcerting. The schoolmistress laughed along with the students. Remouald looked at the floor, his face a deep red.

His favourite subject at that time was geometry; the lessons plunged him into unsettling cogitations. He wished to comprehend why Pythagoras's theorem, which was explained on the blackboard with numbers and figures that came out of one's head, applied as well to the wooden frames that held up the roofs of houses, if the textbook were to be believed. The schoolmaster impatiently repeated the demonstration, which Remouald had very well understood. That is not what he wanted to know. We develop laws in our heads, we create an entire abstract, ideal, mathematical world, and in reality things are in every way like those we have imagined: through what wondrous operation did this come about? The teacher settled the matter by saying it was *necessarily* so. Remouald left the classroom alarmed by that adverb.

He spent whole recesses immersed in his thoughts, hugging the walls, away from the team games. The ball would sometimes bounce comically on his skull and leave him stunned and hurt, the laughingstock of his schoolmates. One time, he was urinating and an older student grabbed him by the shoulder to make him turn around. He ran away bent in half, to the merriment of all.

He wanted to love his schoolmates and be loved by them, like everyone else, perhaps more than everyone else, but incomprehensible walls rose up on all sides, ambushes in which the others found it amusing for him to get trapped, and the teachers — he did not know why — constantly chided him for remaining aloof, for not mixing with his comrades. The principal summoned him to his office. Remould answered his questions simply, displayed a gentleness that went beyond good manners and bore witness to a genuine respect for others, and, lastly, impressed the old man by demonstrating in a few sentences, and rather convincingly, that all the virtues could ultimately be traced back to Love. The principal concluded the boy's brain was in no way deranged. "He is a gifted child. He feels somewhat overwhelmed by his gifts, which is natural; time will take care of all that." Months went by and nothing changed, except his questions, which drew him deeper into lonely enigmas. But he was no longer a target for flying balls and his schoolmates stopped calling him Miss Pee-pee. He unwittingly benefited from something new in his otherwise benign gaze, something that kept malevolence at bay.

* * *

IN THE COURSE of repairing a roof, his father, who was a carpenter, fell, and for weeks they feared for his life. Remould spent the nights consoling his mother. He whispered in her ear, "He is going to make it." He thought of the lines of Christmas and of summer and told himself they could not lie.

Remould Bilboquain could not yet even write his name when his father taught him to read the seasons on the floor. There were two lines drawn in chalk. The one in the living room marked the arrival of summer, and the other in the kitchen marked that of the winter holidays. Remould was struck dumb by the precision with which the sun obeyed his father's predictions: on Christmas morning, that was the very exact point where, as they came through the windows, the sunbeams stopped.

While he watched over his father, observing with a blend of love and anxiety whether a breath still swelled his chest, he thought of the lines of Summer and Christmas. They seemed to him to be Signs of trust tying him to the fate of the seasons, which succeeded one another in the proper order, like the laws of the triangle, like the goodness of the heart of Jesus. Life flowed on, each thing arrived at its appointed date and time, like the wish to sleep after the toil of the day, and the sunbeams on the floor. There still remained so many things to do together, Remould was so young, and his father's death would have been a betrayal of the harmony of the seasons. Remould Bilboquain tirelessly repeated this to himself. (Yet he remembered that it had snowed one morning in July. He tried not to think about this.) He brought his hand closer on the blanket and grasped his father's hand.

The carpenter in the end, survived. But walking thereafter was a chore and he had lost the use of an arm. The first thing Remould regretted was that when he came back from school his father would no longer take him on his knees and wash his hands over the basin. Whenever he had felt sad, wounded by an injustice at school, the contact of those rough palms had renewed some undefined promise, which consoled him and once again gave him confidence in life.

But Remould revealed nothing of his bitterness. Every night he reviewed his lessons, did his homework, and went to sit near his father. The man no longer told the story of how he had met Célia when she was only fourteen, and how she had followed him for the sake of love. He no longer recounted the twists and turns of their elopement, the eventual agreement of Célia's guardians, and then the joy it had been for her on her fifteenth birthday to give birth to Remould, who had arrived like a gift. All of Remould's childhood had been illuminated by these tales. But now his father said nothing, and he did not know why. At the age of twelve Remould's memory was already weighed down with regrets.

Remould awaited each Saturday with a fluttering heart, as one awaits Christmas morning. On that day the carpenter taught his son everything he had learned about his trade. Yet Remould did not have the impression of learning but simply of recalling gestures he had always borne deep within himself. When he touched the wood he felt some of the warmth he had been missing ever since his father could no longer wash his hands.

REMOUALD WAS A pious child, and Father Cadorette, detecting a calling, encouraged the boy to visit him at the presbytery. He took out his picture books, spoke of the lives of the saints. He told stories where the Virgin appeared to little girls, where the Devil was disguised as a wolf, where crucifixes had magic-wand-like powers. Remouald interrupted him one day to ask if some things were impossible for God.

"God is all-powerful, my child, and nothing is impossible for Him. Only, He cannot wish evil, which would be repugnant to His holiness."

"I mean, could He make it so that two plus two would not add up to four? Or conceive of an infinite screw or a stick with no extremities?"

"I don't quite see what you are getting at, Remouald, but it seems to me God cannot want absurd things. When we say He can do everything, we do not mean it is within His power to be mistaken. God is Truth just as much as He is Love."

Remouald scratched his nose and swung his leg pensively. The priest wanted to return to the adventures of St. Thérèse of the Child Jesus. Once again Remouald interrupted him.

"If God is all-powerful," he asked, "then that means it is He who determines the course of events?"

"Without a doubt," said the priest, with the tone of voice of a salesman guaranteeing the quality of his carpet.

"But, tell me, Father, when God performs a miracle, it is as though He is, exceptionally, changing the course of events. Right?"

Cadorette was content to just nod his head cautiously.

"In that case," Remouald went on, eyelids half shut, as if he were connecting, disconnecting, and reconnecting the wires in his head, "in that case, if He changes the course of events, then God regards the existing course of events as not . . . the best? It's as though He has changed His mind. But when you change your mind, it's because you think the new idea is better than the previous one, it seems to me. So, if God changes His mind, then, having had that previous idea, He was . . . He was wrong, Father? Or, in any case, He had not from the start found the best way to go about things, among all the possible ways open to Him?"

Cadorette closed his picture book and sank back in his chair. He cleared his throat.

"I find you rather young, my little Remould, to criticize the Lord's good sense."

Remould blushed. He had not at all intended to criticize the Eternal Father.

"You must see, my poor lad, that miracles are not something the Good Lord does on the spur of the moment."

"Yes, Father."

"When God performs a miracle, it's not as if He were tormented by remorse and trying to make up for His blunders with some fancy footwork. His miracles are *signs* addressed to humanity. They are part and parcel of His vast plan, whose purpose we, poor sinners that we are, are quite incapable of understanding. Do you follow me?"

Remould acquiesced but when his eyes met those of the priest, the churchman realized his explanations had not dispelled the boy's perplexity.

Remould had found himself some work: he delivered newspapers and three nights a week ran messages for Séraphon. He thus earned a few pennies for every order he brought back to the wood yard. His father had at first been opposed to this arrangement, for he deemed Séraphon a bad man. But, since his accident, the savings had dwindled, and Célia, in her gentle way, had convinced him to reconsider his decision.

When he had nothing else to do while awaiting Séraphon's instructions, Remould would spend time with the wood yard employees. He was always eager to be of service to them and to share with them his thoughts on God. Ideas for him were not dead leaves; he felt them living, full of warmth, throbbing like a sparrow held between one's hands. Thinking for him was to be stirred by one's thoughts. He spoke to the workers about theology, metaphysical questions (it was the priest who had taught him those words), unable to imagine that anyone might be indifferent to such things. The employees let him think out loud. Some stopped a few moments to listen, then went back to their tasks with a little laugh of wonderment — "You have to admit, he's deep!" — patting him on the head as they passed. The nickname they had given him was the Little Doctor.

Séraphon bent an indulgent ear to Remould's cogitations. He did not lose any sleep over this sort of question, but it amused him to sow confusion in the Little Doctor's mind. The boy was astounded that it was possible to think in such a twisted way, but as adults could not wish to mislead him, nor themselves be misguided, Séraphon's sophisms left him at a loss for words; hence, depressed, disappointed in himself, he would catch himself doubting his own reason.

It got so that he was unable to sleep on some nights. He closed his eyes and pulled his head down under the sheets, in the throes of a dizziness that kept him apart from sleep and the world. He thought: *And what if there had never been anything, if absolutely nothing had existed?* Not even God, not even time, not even space — not even nothing! Like a dog running on a leash, his mind reached its limit at this point and began to strangle him. In those moments, the idea of

Nothing was so present in him, so oppressive, engendered such a *void*, that he had the impression he too had become nothing, that the universe, God Himself, sucked into an abyss, incapable of overcoming this void, could no longer find the strength to exist.

He got up, utterly exhausted, as though he had spent the night wrestling.

Remouald searched about him for someone to talk to. The priest's answers, pale and inconsequent, were predictable and depressed him in advance. His father did not understand his language, and — Remouald did not know why — certain subjects made him ill-tempered. As for Séraphon, his statements were so obscure, his attitude so equivocal, that even his offerings of bread and jam ultimately left an aftertaste of ashes, disease, and death.

REMOUALD WOULD WAKE up during the night realizing that he had been talking in his sleep, and his muttering faded away in a poignant silence. Everywhere, the night held sway over the world. Out of his desire to be heard and in turn to listen, a friendly face took shape in his dreams, and he emerged from sleep with a sense of having been duped by his desire. He felt like an abandoned ship, adrift on the currents of an ever-colder sea and slowly, inexorably, approaching the ice floes.

He hungered for new intelligence. He did not know how to reconcile within himself the high standards of Reason, which isolated him atop a tower where there was a lack of air, a lack of everything, and the need to love, to commune with the beings around him. He clearly saw the two benefits of light: warmth and lucidity. But a strange curse made it impossible for him to be faithful to one without being a traitor to the other and, at times confusing the two virtues as if trying to grasp a flame's heat, he burned himself. His thoughts drew him infinitely far away from his mother, as though carried off by a comet — giddy, uprooted, frozen to the marrow; the very same night Célia would hold him in her arms, bind him to the earth with a thousand fragrant and intimate bonds, of which he was somewhat ashamed and which prevented him from returning to those pure heights where the air was lacking, where everything was lacking, and where his mind awaited him. Why was there in every thing a left side — awkward and warm, below the reach of reason and words — and a right side — inflexible, luminous, icy — that never could meet?

He dreamed of a twin spirit, open to the same horizons and, like him, thirsting for love, like him, refusing all self-imposed barriers. At every recess, fingers entwined in the mesh of the fence, eyes seeking the river beyond the houses at the foot of the hill, he repeated the same prayer, a wordless prayer, a pure call borne along by the hum of the morning, which overlaid the shouts of the teams at play and rolled away with the windswept leaves. The sky was reflected in the puddles, and Remouald thought of the clouds, of those masses of water like ships hovering in the blue. The parched earth would drink the rain, the tree leaves would retain a few drops — this is what had to be done: to join what is below with what is above, the earth and the sky. This is what two spirits who loved each other were capable of, two spirits who drank from the same water, from the same source on high, and who shared the warm nourishment of the light as though it were bread. Remouald felt his heart beating. It seemed to him this bliss was at hand, flitting capriciously about him, and he needed only to turn the right way at the right moment to take hold of it. He was to learn that the most dangerous calls are ineluctably heard, and that a hare running innocently in the snow never notices behind it, following its every move, the gliding shadow of the hawk.

* * *

REMOUALD HAD COME back from school. He had delivered the papers and, while waiting for Séraphon, entered his thoughts of the day in his notebook. He was sitting at the store counter. A rabbit's foot landed in front of him. He raised his eyes.

The young man sat at the top of the stairway. He wore Séraphon's cap, his face hidden by the visor. Remouald looked at him, then looked at the rabbit's foot. He said nothing.

"What are you writing there?"

Remouald was unsure whether this was a genuine question or a rude remark. He shrugged.

"Just some ideas of mine, that's all."

With a curious, slightly anxious gentleness that would soon become familiar to Remouald, the fellow asked, "Would you like to show me?"

He stretched out his hand. Remouald hesitated. He had never shown his notebook to anyone. But no one had ever asked him to see it. He joined the young man at the top of the stairs. The fellow removed his cap and placed it on Remouald's head. He began to read.

"Just some ideas of mine," Remould repeated.

With his narrow forehead, his large mouth arched downward, his enormous eyes (the left temple of his glasses was attached to the frame with a wad of adhesive tape), he resembled at first glance a gigantic red toad. His face was pockmarked. His coat, sheathing him like a pipe, reached down to his ankles. Emanating from this individual was an insistent, endearing odour of earth and mushrooms that reminded Remould of the priest's old tomes. His carrot-coloured hair pointed in every direction in dense, compact spikes as tough as sheaves of hay, and gave him the grotesque, disquieting appearance of a lunatic clown.

When he had finished reading the young man scrutinized Remould's face. His eyes were striking, a hue of green Remould had never encountered in anyone else, as bright as fireflies, and the thickness of his lenses, one of which was cracked, accentuated all that was frightened and distressed in his gaze.

"The rabbit's foot. It's yours. Do you want it?"

Remould accepted bashfully, unaccustomed to receiving gifts.

"I can give you all sorts of things, you know, and much prettier. I know how to stuff animals."

"That must be interesting."

The young man nodded.

"My name is Wilson."

"Wilson what?"

"Wilson."

"I'm Remould. Remould Bilboquain."

"I knew that."

In an affectionate, clumsy gesture of playfulness, he pulled the visor down over Remouald's eyes. Remouald pushed it back with a shy laugh. His eyes again met Wilson's.

Remouald's laughter broke off.

"There are *things* in what you write. But you don't seem to be interested in little girls."

Remouald blushed. He felt this was like mixing apples and oranges, but this very confusion disturbed him.

"I have ideas too," Wilson continued, as though he were talking to himself. "I go about with an abyss in each of my pockets. I've always got thunderbolts ready to hand that I can hurl at anyone I like. But I hold back. I know things that no one knows, that no one wants to know. How about you — would you like to know those things? Are you prepared to hear them?

". . ."

"I'm sure there are lots of things I could teach you. Do you hear? *Lots of things.*"

He uttered these last words dreamily, his voice full of mysterious promise. Remouald consented gravely. He had the impression that for the first time in his life someone was *saying* something to him. Wilson gave him back his notebook. He wiped his nose with the back of his hand. Then he raised his index finger in front of his face in the manner of a censor. Remouald noticed that his fingernails were bitten, some right down to the bottom. Except for the nail of his little finger, which was honed like a knife.

"I think, Remouald my friend, that we were meant to get to know one another."

"Yes."

"There may even be great things for us to do together,

who knows? You shouldn't make light of what I'm telling you. Everybody always makes light of everything."

"That's true," Remouald said.

"And don't you think they all need a lesson in truth?"

". . ."

Remouald hugged his notebook against his chest. Tears welled up in his eyes. "A lesson in truth," he repeated. The apprentice took back his cap.

From his collar, a shiny grey button emerged. Remouald bent closer to see what it was: a mouse. It perched itself on Wilson's shoulder. He picked it up and placed it in Remouald's hands. He gave him a wink.

"The trick, if you want to keep them close to you, is to pluck their whiskers, you see."

Remouald examined the little creature. It ran along his fingers, looking to escape, frantically scratching the palm of his hand.

Wilson stretched out his hand, pinched Remouald's cheek — and stopped dead. His eyelids stopped blinking, his eyes stared like windows opening onto a desert. The seconds elapsed and Remouald was at a loss for how to act. His cheek began to smart.

Then, as though suddenly aware of touching a burning-hot object, Wilson came to and snapped his hand back, leaving white patches on Remouald's cheek. Wilson simply continued from where he had left off.

"There will be no dull moments for us, Remouald my little friend, mark my words."

He pointed at the mouse, which was spinning around and squeaking.

"She always does that, the little bundle of nerves. It's as if

she were desperately trying to warn someone of something."
Then Wilson rolled his eyes jokingly: "Holy moly! my little
friend, don't tell me it's you she's talking to!"

A tear slid down Remouald's cheek. He smiled back at
Wilson.

* * *

TOWARD THE END of the day, Wilson would begin to
show signs of impatience. He became testy, was ill-mannered
with the clients, and even Seraphon would walk on eggshells.

Remouald arrived at the store after his newspaper run.
He had hardly finished relaying the orders when Wilson bore
down on him, hoisted him on his shoulder, and carried him
off like a sack. The other employees no longer had the right
to speak to him. The apprentice took the boy to the knoll
near the freight station. Séraphon watched them from his
window, keyed up and anxious. Wilson paced back and
forth, waved his arms, and the ideas poured out furiously.
Remouald, bedazzled, absent-mindedly tugged on clumps
of grass. They would talk like this until nightfall. Then,
wearing the glum expression of a soldier about to carry out
an unpalatable order, Remouald would follow Wilson back
to the apprentice's shack.

Remouald kept up his visits with Father Cadorette. Wilson
was aware of this. On those nights the apprentice rambled
through the streets of the neighbourhood, and people took
to crossing to the other side rather than crossing paths
with him. Occasionally he would go shout obscenities at
the convent windows. He was suspected of having smashed
some windowpanes at the presbytery and the church. Someone

reported having seen him fighting with dogs. Upon his return to the wood yard he would vent his rage by splitting logs until late into the night.

Séraphon, meanwhile, was like an animal on edge before a storm. He had dreams that had not recurred since his youth, and, more and more often, spent long evenings at the stable. He began to worry, which was not in his nature, and fell prey to bouts of hypochondria that had him wondering whether he was developing one of those ghastly diseases he had been told of as a child, which begin in the loins, are carried through the blood to the head and eventually drive one insane.

AFTER TWO HOURS spent contemplating the ceiling of his room, Séraphon got out of bed, demoralized by insomnia, his head filled with apprehension. It had been a trying day. A female customer had on a whim stroked Remouald's cheek in passing.

"You know, I have never seen such a pretty young boy? Do you know that?"

Then Wilson had slapped her. Séraphon thought back to all the grovelling he had needed to do to convince her to overlook the incident and, above all, to not speak a word of it. Luckily the woman owed him some money. He got out of it by wiping the slate clean.

Séraphon tried to summon his courage. This could not go on — he would have to keep Wilson away from the customers. Yet he knew that, once again, he would speak without daring to look him in the face, the apprentice would snicker, and Séraphon would in the end retreat to his corner.

He stepped up to the sidelight. These were the first days of winter. It had snowed, and the moonlight was splendid. The apprentice crossed the yard and headed in the direction of Rue Moreau. Séraphon waited a few moments before going out, too: he would at last find out the destination of these nighttime excursions.

Wilson moved down the lane and strode over the fence. Séraphon cautiously did the same. The apprentice entered the courtyard. There was no light shining in the house. The blinds had been pulled and the curtains drawn in all the windows, except one, on the second floor. Wilson hesitated. He had removed his coat and dropped it in the snow. He blew into his hands to warm them, with his eyes on the window.

All at once he hurled himself against the side of the building, arms outstretched and head thrown back, as though wanting to embrace the wall. Then, with a nimbleness that astounded Séraphon, he began to climb, his body seeming to cling to the stone.

Séraphon remained in the shadows of the alley. He was shaking, in the throes of an excruciating giggle. *Wilson had stopped at Remould's window and was watching him sleep.*

His face burned in the night like an ember.

* * *

FATHER CADORETTE SADLY observed the child walking ahead of him. Remould Bilboquain had grown thin, and there were dark circles under his eyes. He kicked at the pebbles mechanically, without saying a word, and for such a talkative child to say nothing was an avowal. For the past few weeks he had not responded when spoken to and would mumble to himself, apparently without realizing. The priest witnessed this transformation, helpless and unable to find an explanation.

They went into the churchyard and sat down on the bench near the crosses. It was early evening. The snow had fallen softly, the first snowfall of the season; the sky was clearing now and the cold was not unpleasant. For the last hour the priest had sensed that Remouald was beating about the bush, but for fear of upsetting him he preferred to wait for him to confide of his own accord. Remouald contemplated the crosses. Without turning around, and in that awkward, falsely indifferent tone of voice whereby a child betrays his anguish, he asked, "Are we responsible for the salvation of those who love us, Father?"

For Cadorette, Remouald's questions were nets cast upon the open sea: one never knew what they would bring up. "Yes," he finally answered, "if you mean that we must try to inspire them to follow the path of Good. No, if you mean that we are responsible for the sins they commit in spite of us. Unless I've misunderstood what you mean . . ."

"I don't mean either one, Father. I mean . . . if ever someone did something that got him sent him to Hell . . . his parents, if they were in Heaven, just knowing he was damned amid the eternal fires . . . assuming his father and mother loved him . . . well, could his parents be happy even so? Would they partake of the heavenly peace, knowing he was damned? I mean, the suffering from knowing that their child suffered, wouldn't that be for the parents a suffering worse than being damned themselves, even if they were in Paradise?"

For a long while Cadorette looked at the snow, wearily, then at the stars, where there was more room. He wanted to tell this unhappy child that Hell did not exist. He stood up and walked toward the crosses. How quiet the world was around them. Cadorette read the epitaphs, the dates, the names of the priests who had preceded him in the parish over the past fifty years: it pleased him to think that he would be buried here in his turn.

"There's a sort of emptiness in my head, Father, a kind of pit, and everything I think of to cross over it ends up falling into it, as if I were throwing a stone at something too far away."

The priest suddenly recalled the story of the mummies. The week before, during the bishop's visit, he had spoken to him about Remouald, and the bishop had told him, "Talk to him about the mummies." The mummies? "Yes, the mummies."

"Listen carefully, Remouald. I'm going to talk to you in a way I never have before. Afterwards, if you like, if you feel the need to ask God to be forgiven for something, well, you can confess. All right?"

Remouald was noncommittal.

"Look. You are the most intelligent child I have ever met, and what's even more amazing is that so far it doesn't seem to have gone to your head. That's good, and I congratulate you for it. The fact remains you're still a child. So pay attention. Someone got me to read this in the newspaper, and I thought of you. It appears there are mummified bodies that have been sleeping inside a crypt for thousands of years. People are unaware of this, you see, no one knows they are asleep there, and time has no hold over them. They struck a pose on the morning of their death and haven't budged so much as a hair since then. And why do you think they've lasted and crossed the centuries without stirring? It's because no one knows of them, Remouald. The greatest favour that was ever granted them was precisely to have forgotten them. Because if you open the door to the crypt to see what's hidden there, you'll be disappointed, you'll find nothing: nothing but scraps, ashes, a bit of smoke. The outside air will have disintegrated them, do you understand? All it takes is a gust of air for something that hasn't moved for three thousand years to turn to dust."

He let a few moments go by so that Remouald might take in those three millennia.

"There are things in the human mind, in the mystery of our soul, that are like those crypts, that make us wonder what might be buried there. Yet if we dare to unearth them, out of pride or an unwholesome curiosity, we only succeed in turning to dust what we wished to discover. And we're none the wiser about what's hidden there. We end up deprived of what we've destroyed, without knowing what we've been deprived of. You happen to have that kind of curiosity; you want to open every door. The world is already a little ragged for me, Remouald, but for you it's still brand new. And when you get to be my age you'll understand that a man would give his right arm for the world around him to be still unsullied by the grease of our fingers. But what we lose as we grow older, we gain for eternity. Be careful not to spoil right now that which may be eternal within you."

A bitter grin came to Remouald's face, and the priest feared there was not much of the child remaining in this little boy.

"The eternity of the soul? But when we are asleep and not dreaming, where does our soul go, Father, what happens to it? It's as if it didn't exist. Is that how it is after we die, after life? So what does it mean that our soul is immortal if it isn't even aware of the fact that it goes on existing? If our soul's immortality is as blind, as deaf, and as cold as a stone's?"

He pointed at the cross on which the priest was leaning. Cadorette swung around and came back to the bench. These questions were all so vast, so difficult; only the candour of a little boy could take them on with such fervour. The priest did not feel up to it, and this weighed heavily on him. Remouald continued to look at the crosses, like a mountain-climber who, having reached the summit, scans the world spread out below.

The priest turned toward him abruptly.

"Now, where did you get the idea that the soul sleeps? The soul never sleeps, Remouald; that's only an illusion. Sometimes, when you wake up in the morning, tell me, don't you have the feeling you've just interrupted an important thought, and yet you're unable to recall any of it? You believe you're sleeping, Remouald, you believe you're sleeping with all your soul, whereas your soul is replenishing itself in God and, who knows, hears things, speaks a language we aren't yet ready to hear. And God, in His Benevolence, makes us forget. Forgetting is a fairy, my little Remouald, a mercy that God grants us each morning. We remember only traces, which we take to be dreams. But, no — and this has to be maintained no matter what — your soul never sleeps."

Cadorette slapped his knee with conviction. He himself was not certain of exactly understanding the words he had just proffered, but this bolstered his belief that Someone had inspired them in him. Twenty years after having said them, when Remouald had become what he was going to become and they had taken on an unexpected and poignant meaning, he would still remember them, and whenever he saw the young man of thirty he would recollect every word he had uttered when the boy was only twelve.

Remouald shrugged his shoulders and sniffed. Cadorette moved closer to him. He let his head fall against the priest's shoulder. Cadorette stroked his hair.

"It's true there's no vanity in you, my son. But there is a light inside you, and that light, though you don't know it, is torturing you like a demon. And Satan is never so triumphant as when a person has stopped believing he exists — never forget that in your prayers. You are like a child with a magnificent kite, which he likes to fly higher and higher, so he wants more and more string because he likes to run and feel the sky leading him on: he runs until the kite nosedives, torn to shreds by the lightning, and the wind, and the heights."

A shiver ran through Remouald Bilboquain.

"Forgive me, Father, forgive me."

"God alone forgives, Remouald. Put yourself in His hands."

The wind swept aside the snow; in the moonlight it resembled glass dust, glinting at times like diamonds. The priest savoured this moment of reconciliation. The sky lay on the earth like a cheek on a shoulder, and on his he felt the warm weight of a child's head. Remouald wept silently. There was an aroma of raisins in his hair. The priest raised his hood and, pulling him closer, placed his hand on his forehead.

"There, don't hold it in, my son, crying is never a waste of time."

Someone breathed noisily in the bushes, a greyish mass sailed across the sky toward the chapel: the smash of a stained-glass window. Cadorette sprung to his feet.

"Hey, there! You vandal!"

He chased the shadow to the far corner of the street, then started down the alley, but, out of breath, he was forced to give up. The priest returned to the churchyard. The child appeared hysterical.

"Come now, Remould, what's the matter?"

"No more lies, Father. No more fairy tales!"

The priest tried to hold him but the boy wriggled free. When he reached the entrance of the churchyard he swung about. Cadorette had never experienced a gaze such as this. A soul leaping at your face like a cat.

"You talk of my intelligence, Father, but what do you know about it? What do you know about it? *People don't know how terrible it is to be intelligent.*"

"Remould!" the priest cried. "Remould!"

But the child was now no more than a silhouette running through the snow and the night.

The priest sighed.

He went to the chapel to take stock of the damage. This was the fourth broken window in three weeks. The moonbeams danced amid the shards of glass. Cadorette headed toward the presbytery. His bedroom seemed very far away to him. He knelt before the image of the Virgin. After a few mumblings he realized that his prayer remained rather earthbound, for he was too distracted by the memory of Remould. Why the devil had he rattled off that whole damned story?

"Next time I'll insist that he confess," he promised himself as he slipped under the blankets.

He was far from suspecting that the next time he saw Remould, the boy would hardly be able to recall his own name.

* * *

In the end, Séraphon resorted to drastic measures. The hole left by the old chimney had been covered over by a piece of tarpaper that was concealed under the roof shingles. It did not take Séraphon long to locate the spot and, with a penknife, to pierce the layer of cardboard, so that for a few weeks he was able to see without fear of being seen everything that went on in his apprentice's shack; although, at the coroner's inquest he would swear to high heaven that he had never seen a thing and, what's more, that on the night of the Feast of the Immaculate Conception he was not even at home.

As a matter of fact, he was on the road that night, collecting rent from reluctant tenants. Twenty people had seen him, spoken to him — his alibi was airtight. Afterwards, worn out and shaking like a rabbit, he had taken shelter at the home of his deceased great-uncle's daughter. It was there he learned, the next day, December 9, that the wood yard had been razed by fire. The dramatic event had occurred that very morning. Rumour had it the firebug's imprecations could be heard as far away as the church. He had screamed that he would wipe the damned place off the face of the earth. Some beams had collapsed and he'd died amid the flames. The body had been identified. It was Joachim Bilboquain, Remouald's father.

As for Remouald, it was said he could no longer understand the simplest things, that his intelligence had been shattered. The Costade family had compassionately taken him in, and then he was placed in the school for orphans at Saint-Aldor.

Wilson made a complete confession to the penitentiary chaplain, who was none other than Father Cadorette. He narrated everything without the slightest emotion, with the detachment of a forensic doctor. In spite of the priest's insistence, the apprentice refused all religious succour. Yet he asked to wear a sash of haircloth. After which he pronounced only one more statement.

"But, now, I can't hear the voice any more."

He said this to the guard who brought him the belt of haircloth. It was with this belt that he hanged himself. He had written the word "Hell" on one of the cell walls with the nail of his little finger.

A FEW DAYS after the dramatic events Séraphon was wandering among the still reeking ruins, distraught, his eyes full of tears and his heart wrung by self-pity. His foot bumped against an object. He leaned over to look, and thought he would swoon. The thing seemed to him so precious, so miraculous, that he hesitated before putting his hand on it. When he returned home, he hurriedly concealed it in a cabinet. There followed a fever that kept him bedridden for three days. Unable to distinguish sleep from wakefulness, he would wake with a start, howling. He had the feeling there were wolves prowling in his bedroom, wolves or rats, and that they were going to pounce on him, tear him apart, devour him.

Finally, one morning, he decided it was time to come back to life. He was surprised and delighted at how naturally his thoughts divested themselves of the memory of recent months, and he once again found himself as he had always been, comfortable inside his clothes and quite happy to exist. It was Christmas, he still had one storehouse full of wood; the fire had provided him with an excuse to raise the prices.

"Life, after all," he opined for the benefit of a little girl playing hopscotch below his window, "isn't made up only of bad times!"

For the next twenty years he would not dare to unlock that cabinet even once.

* * *

CÉLIA WAS AT that time a young woman of twenty-six who looked barely sixteen. People who saw her with Remouald often believed she was his older sister. What is more, the likeness of their faces was striking, especially the softness of the gaze. She was convinced Remouald had been touched at birth by the finger of God. Six months earlier he had begun to teach her the alphabet. To be able to read words made her laugh with astonishment.

It was decided that the truth would be withheld from her. "The less she knows, the better it will be for her," Dr. Rocheleau had decreed. Cadorette had protested. But his superiors ordered him to obey the doctor.

For the Feast of the Immaculate Conception, Célia had gone to visit her family at the Reservation. Upon her return, Father Cadorette, two nuns, and Dr. Rocheleau were waiting for her in the kitchen. Célia smiled nervously. Where on earth was her little family?

Cadorette contemplated her with an expression of deep pity. One of the two nuns gently posed her hands on her shoulder and leaned toward her.

"You must be brave, madam."

Célia pushed her away.

"Tell me what's happened? Where is Remouald? Remouald!"

The four visitors kept silent.

She rushed to her son's bedroom. The bureau had been emptied, the chest, the drawers . . . She came out looking terrified.

She began to run from one room to the next. Dr. Rocheleau signalled to the nuns with a nod. Grabbing her by the arms, they sat her in a chair and held her down. The doctor prepared a syringe. Célia struggled. The priest got up, his shoulders sagging, and left the house.

Thereafter, the nuns took up full-time residence in her home, taking turns at her bedside, tying her to her bed when necessary, for she was prone to attacks. She was sedated with injections. The drug left her in a fog. Smiling strangely, she would mumble names. The nuns would go out with tears in their eyes.

The treatment lasted about a year. As the family savings had been depleted, a room was found for Célia at the convent. She did not really communicate with anyone any more. The doctor believed the time had come to stop the medication. The young woman's condition deteriorated. She spent whole days shaking, vociferating: enraged, she would fly at Dr. Rocheleau's face when he came to visit. Then she would calm down and stay for many weeks in a state of near-lethargy. The doctor issued his final diagnosis: "She will never get better." He said he was sorry he had been unable to do more.

And yet, quite unexpectedly, her condition improved. She began to take food again without anyone being obliged to fight with her. She could at last be assigned some small chores. She began dusting and tidying up and finally appeared quiet enough to justify her being allowed to leave the convent. She was found a position as a housekeeper, as well as lodgings in a tiny garret.

Célia would go out every morning armed with her buckets and rags. She was indifferent to the private lives of her clients, who would have seen this as a cardinal virtue in a housekeeper had her zombie-like single-mindedness not ultimately given rise to disagreeable situations. Célia had no consideration whatever for people's privacy and treated them hardly better than pieces of furniture. One day she burst into the churchwardens' dining room with her mop; she obliged the flabbergasted notary to lift his feet as she washed the hardwood floor under the table. Now, the notary, Mr. Robidoux, was right then having lunch with the bishop.

Eventually, people told the nuns that there are limits to charity. But when they tried to dismiss her she would come back two days later, oblivious and ready to come to blows with anyone who tried to stop her from entering the house. The police had to be called in on several occasions. Célia was consequently reduced to doing odd sewing jobs. She began to drink. At first every night, then every morning. She now looked twice her age.

Séraphon appeared at her door one day to collect the rent she had not paid for months. She apparently had no idea who he was. Being penniless, she offered to knit him socks, toques, blankets. Séraphon surveyed the room. There was little in the way of furniture or objects, but everything was neatly put away, even the empty bottles. Pieces of cloth and lace hung on the walls. Pincushions were arrayed on the table amid mounds of fabric and trimming. He was touched by the cozy atmosphere.

He spent the rest of the evening at home swaying pensively in his rocker. He was getting old, his arms grew tired quickly, and his business was rather demanding now that he could no longer afford to hire an employee. He thought dreamily of Remouald . . . Besides, although not stirred by any carnal intentions — he had always been perfectly apathetic in this respect — he nevertheless felt the need (a novel one for him) to be coddled, to have someone serve him his meals, mend his old coats and socks. The next day, he went to see the priest.

Cadorette received regular reports from Saint-Aldor about Remouald. In answer to Séraphon's inquiry he said the boy was doing better. Séraphon flashed a smile of relief.

"That's good news, Father, good news. You see, while I may not be in any way responsible, it would still do me a wealth of good if I could, to the extent my modest resources permit, compensate for some of the harm incurred in my yard, and return a son to his mother's embrace. Business is slow, but, well, we could make do. And anyway, all these years of labour — how sad it would be if none were to profit from it when I go. I have done so little good in my life, Father."

Cadorette pouted doubtfully.

"The thought does you credit, Séraphon," (who responded with a gesture of modesty). "Fine, I'll raise the matter with Dr. Rocheleau and then write to Saint-Aldor to see what they think about it. I'll let you know as soon as I get a reply."

"God bless you, Father. You don't know how happy it would make me to do good."

"No need to lay it on so thick, Séraphon. We'll talk again very soon. There you go."

Célia showed up at Séraphon's house one fine morning: she had finished knitting him a pair of slippers. He invited her to step into the kitchen. He confided in Célia. He talked about himself, of his loneliness, of his old mother whom he so missed, of every person's need to share his woes and joys. Célia stared gloomily at the floor. Séraphon was determined to give it his all. He blurted out that he would bring her son back to her if she agreed to marry him.

Célia straightened up. She asked him to say it again. Her tone of voice was threatening. He repeated. She stepped toward the table like a puppet, her hands trembling, and turned around.

"You said . . . Remould?"

"Yes," said Séraphon, "yes!"

And he struck the table with his fist.

Célia's eyes grew enormously wide, her eyelashes fluttered, she made a vague attempt to help herself, and then she fell over backward. Séraphon triumphantly kissed his slippers.

Two weeks later the priest blessed their marriage.

* * *

SÉRAPHON CHOKED AS he surfaced from sleep; there was a face leaning over him.

"Would yous like a nice cuppa tea?" the Racicot woman asked him.

Séraphon Tremblay looked around him as if it were hard for him to believe he was lying in his bedroom. He began to breathe more easily. For the past week he hadn't been able to fall sleep without his dreams taking him back twenty years. The widow arrived with the bowl of tea. He had to endure the scalding spatters and her placid slaps; he took it all without shedding a tear. He felt lost, as though he were now just a thing among other things. When she stepped toward the door he called her back.

"Stay," he said with a beseeching voice. "Stay with me until Remould returns from the bank. I implore you. Otherwise, She'll come back. When I'm alone, She always comes back."

The widow strained to understand and frowned mulishly. She seemed to surmise that the old man had spoken in jest and she crossed the threshold with a silly laugh.

For the past week, Séraphon had been subject to apparitions. He knew full well his head was playing tricks on him, that these were merely hallucinations; still, he saw what he saw. As soon as he was alone, he would hear Her walking at the far end of the house. He knew it was She. Each time She would put on a different mask — his great-uncle's, a little girl's, or that of his collie when he was eight years old — as though She wanted to impress upon him that his whole life through, behind all these faces, he had always encountered but one: the face of his death. Turning his head away or closing his eyes was of no avail; quite the contrary, he would then feel Her nestle against him, and her embrace was icy and oppressive.

He heard the steps coming from the kitchen. He saw the shadow slowly expanding on the wall. Finally, She came into view. Séraphon groaned. This time She had taken on the appearance of a little boy. His hair was the colour of sawn wood, and he bore in his hand a sheet of paper that he held out in front of him at chest level, like a choirboy bearing a candle. He approached the bed. There was a message written on the paper:

See you soon, on the other side of the lies.

Séraphon burst into sobs. The message was signed "Wilson."

10

CLÉMENTINE CLÉMENT HAD locked herself in the teachers' washroom because she felt an urgent need to speak to someone. She could no longer stand the innuendoes of the other teachers. All day, hints had been dropped here and there about the undue strictness of "certain members of the staff." At little Eugène's funeral, the day before, they had plainly avoided her (and yet at the graveside it was to Clémentine that Mrs. Guillubart had addressed her tortured smile). Clémentine Clément so despised those bespectacled old biddies, those flat-chested, chinless shrews, that she felt compelled to confess.

She splashed cold water on her face and, straightening up, met Clémentine-and-a-half in the mirror.

"I can't bear it any more," Clémentine whispered "I must talk to someone."

Clémentine-and-a-half listened. Brother Gandon loathed her, that much was clear — he found her physically repulsive. "I know, I know, he is a constrained man, but is that any reason to be constantly out to humiliate me?" They looked at each other for a moment without speaking. For the hundredth time in three days Miss Clément tried to catch herself resembling an ostrich. The likeness was perhaps obvious, but it would take someone else to spot it, someone who could watch Clémentine in action, walking, possibly from behind. Was this how she appeared to the captain of the fire brigade? Clémentine shook her head. During the week since they had become acquainted he had paid her three visits. Clémentine did not know what to think. He stayed seated at the table, rigid as a ramrod, his hands resting one on top of the other. She tried to make conversation but he answered in monosyllables. Now and then he would abruptly launch into long, convoluted statements on the subject of wages, savings, investments at moderate but steady interest rates, securities, he said, that will have appreciated at retirement. Clémentine made an effort to stifle her yawns. He attempted a bland compliment on her interior decoration. He added, "You . . . you are different from other people."

"And why am I different from others? Why shouldn't I be like anyone else? Do I have three eyes, two noses, four mouths? Do I have an arm sticking out of my skull?"

Clémentine bowed her head and sighed. She thought back to what had happened on Saturday night. Overwhelmed by Eugène's death, she had wept, which seemed to terrify the captain. He'd cringed as though threatened with a club. Clémentine had yelled, "If you were a man you would take me in your arms!"

"I meant, take me in his arms to comfort me, just to comfort me. Like Papa would when I was a little girl. And I stepped toward him, repeating, 'If you were a man . . .'"

He had stood up, tried to embrace her, brought his hands closer. But his face had collapsed into a painful grimace, and, pushing her aside, he'd bolted toward the door to hide his tears.

"It's the Parade of Constrained Men," said Clémentine-and-a-half.

She had not heard from him since. As it was already Tuesday, she might as well get used to the idea they would never see each other again.

"It's idiotic to talk to yourself in a mirror."

Clémentine paused.

"Yes, all I wanted was for him to comfort me like Papa when I was a little girl. I was so young, I still said, 'Papa's such a pretty lady, such a tall lady, he's the nicest lady.' It made my mother laugh. Then later I said, 'Papa, he's dead.' I had sorted out the genders . . . It's so cold in here all of a sudden . . . Would I have called my son Eugène if he had lived? Eugène, like my father? Or would I have called him my child . . . my Love . . . my Life . . .?

Her cadence had slowed, crumbled, the words fell one by one, like drops of blood. She began to examine her reflection. Someone rapped on the door.

"Miss Clément, are you there?"

Clémentine undid the top of her dress. Her gaze contemplated itself, went deeper, and multiplied in the gaze of Clémentine-and-a-half. She slipped her hand inside her dress. She could feel herself leaning forward, being drawn powerfully, irresistibly closer by her image. She parted her lips and placed them on the cold lips of her reflection. Her saliva had an acidic taste. She let out a weird, swaggering laugh that made her shiver with horror.

"Miss Clément? Answer! Is everything all right?"

She righted herself with a start, suddenly aware of what she was doing. Clémentine-and-a-half cast her an appalled look, the look one gives a madwoman. "I'm going to end up like my mother! That's it!" The idea tore across her mind like a cry! She stormed out of the washroom.

"Is something the matter?" Brother Gandon asked.

The other teachers had left.

"It's nothing," she said, "I just wanted to splash a little cold water on my temples, that's all."

The principal thought she looked odd: she was as white as a sheet and there were purple blotches under her eyes. There was a long, awkward silence that dragged on. Gandon finally spoke.

"I wanted to have a word with you. I think we should talk."

He said this in an extremely sombre tone of voice and was afterwards bothered by this solemnity. Clémentine finished buttoning the collar of her dress. She wished she could dive into a hole in the ground. She limply patted her cheeks. To stand before someone who finds you ugly . . .

"Let's go to my office, if you don't mind," Gandon said.

She did not budge and kept her eyes glued to the floor. Brother Gandon began to be genuinely concerned.

"What is it, Miss Clément?"

Clémentine remained silent. Gandon waited tensely.

"I'm ashamed," she finally said.

"Ashamed? But what of?"

"Ashamed to walk ahead of you."

The principal felt his heart tumbling out of his chest.

"Oh, my friend . . ."

He stretched out his hand. Clémentine shrank back delicately.

"After you," she said, and started away.

It was he who followed her. He did not want her to see his face. This had not happened to him since the time he was eighteen. His father had just died and he was given a four-day leave of absence by the seminary. As he was bidding his mother goodbye, never suspecting he would not see her again either, she said to him, almost absently, "You know, your father never understood why you despised him for being nothing but a poor uneducated worker." God! What a night he spent.

Gandon had not wept since then and was thereafter convinced of being immune, tougher than life. Yet at that very moment he had the feeling that one glance from the teacher, just one, and he would break down. A man in tears — his esteem for Miss Clément was too high to inflict that on her.

Clémentine advanced, head down. They came upon the janitor, who told them jokingly they resembled a pair of prisoners headed for the firing squad. Giving him not so much as a smile, they disappeared down the far end of the corridor.

"Pshaw! Child-tormentors," the janitor muttered.

* * *

A STIFLING ODOUR of pipe smoke and thick blue billows hovered in the room. Clémentine deduced that he had been smoking heavily — therefore thinking deeply — and she was on her guard.

He invited her to sit down and then seated himself behind his desk. She avoided looking at him directly, but kept her eyes set on the half-empty glass of whisky.

"Would you like some?" he said.

"I beg your pardon?"

"Whisky."

She shook her head.

Then shrugging her shoulders, she said yes, why not.

Gandon was not in the habit of inviting anyone to partake of his whisky. He took some solace in this gesture, the pleasure of sharing something with somebody. He poured her a generous measure. Until then, Miss Clément's association with alcohol had been restricted to the finger of port wine with which she would indulge herself whenever she finished reading a novel. It was her way of communing in spirit with the author. This was something writers must do, it seemed to her, after they had put the final touches to a book — enjoy a finger of port wine. Not to have met any writers was one of her regrets in life. And as she grew older regrets such as this had accumulated, so that little by little her whole life took on a flavour of regret and wasted time.

Nor had she ever drunk whisky. No one would be able to say she'd died without having tried that! She took a good slug and found it vile. She felt a fiery snake slithering down inside her; it hit her like a blow to the stomach. But she could at last look the principal in the eye.

Brother Gandon also took a shot, for the long, rough road that lay ahead. He had been drinking since mid-afternoon, something he never did. Clémentine thought he appeared less determined than usual. His cheeks drooped, his expression was blank, his gaze unfocused.

"I'm listening," she said.

She was prepared to hear anything.

Gandon still hesitated. He was hoping for a last-minute interruption — an unexpected visit or a telephone call — that might provide an excuse to defer until the next day this hurtful confrontation.

"You are torturing me," she said.

The principal plunged in.

"I find it most unpleasant to have to tell you what I am going to say, you must believe that. But there are rumours going around about you. And, by implication, about me. You must have some idea as to their nature. They say you persecuted little Guillubart. That is false, of course, but that is what's being said. And that you continue to badger Rocheleau and Bradette with your suspicions."

Clémentine had not expected this. Something cracked inside her. Her certitudes began to break up. After all, what if the rumour were true? True *in part*? Eugène had not seen Clémentine coming that day. He had hardly had time to hide the drawings in his binder. She had smiled triumphantly. At that precise moment, had she enjoyed his fear? *Had she drawn pleasure from the distress in the child's gaze?* She herself did not know; she did not understand herself any more. The image of Mrs. Guillubart smiling at her at the graveside cruelly foisted itself on her mind. She took another swallow of whisky.

Gandon could see all these clouds moving across her face.

"I have known you for many years, Miss Clémant, and I consider you a person of outstanding merit, whose friendship I value enormously. I . . . I know your intentions are commendable, always, whatever you do. But your behaviour of late has perhaps not been the most appropriate. You do yourself harm, as they say. And as a friend, for I am your friend, this saddens me, and I would like to keep you away from needless trouble. I say that sincerely."

A sulking expression of reproach came over her face.

"What does that mean, 'I say that sincerely'? It's as if I were to tell you: 'Take my word, I'm not a liar, because if I were I'd be the first to denounce myself!'"

"Please don't make things harder for me by quibbling over words."

Under the weight of justice, or injustice — she could no longer say which — her spine began to sag. She realized she was going to cave in, that she would ultimately let herself be crushed.

Clémentine hung on to the part of herself that refused to capitulate, the rebellious little girl who said no.

"To accuse me of harassing those children. Me, the one who wants to protect them, to shield them from danger!"

"I know, Miss Clément, I know. But the danger you speak of . . . how shall I put this . . . does it exist other than . . . than . . .?"

He was looking for the right words.

"Other than in my head? Go on, say it!"

". . . other than in your legitimate presumptions. Since the situation, I grant you, warranted those concerns. But all indications are that our suspicions were, fortunately, groundless."

He had subtly accentuated the "our."

"Fortunately groundless," she repeated sarcastically.

Gandon looked at her with curiosity.

"Would you have preferred the suspicions to be justified, Miss Clément?"

She was at a loss for an answer. She took out her handkerchief and wiped her forehead.

"Then what about the anonymous letter the police received? And what I myself saw? The bank clerk? That would be quite a coincidence, I dare say!"

"If people were to be judged on the basis of appearances, you . . . we would be the first to find ourselves in hot water."

The teacher bowed her head. Gandon continued.

"Besides, that clerk has a name: Remould Tremblay. I found that out from Father Cadorette. In fact, I went to meet him today."

"!!!"

"I mean Father Cadorette. The poor fellow, so feisty, so staunch; his attack has left him in a daze. To see him like that, in a wheelchair, suddenly old, I swear . . ."

"You still haven't explained these troubling 'coincidences,'" Clémentine said, shaping the quotation marks with her fingertips.

Brother Gandon poured himself a full glass of whisky. She once again surprised him by sliding her glass toward him.

"Another drop."

"Still, be careful."

"I'm used to it," she said, without batting an eyelash.

The principal began to fill his pipe. "We never really know people," he reflected sadly. On the cover of the matchbook were the words "Davies Hotel, Thamesville, Ontario." How had it found its way into his hands? Nothing travels more, or more erratically, than a book of matches.

A stream of smoke surged through his lips.

"Those coincidences, I believe, are not very hard to explain. Someone got wind of your suspicions and took the opportunity to send a letter of denunciation to the police. Besides, how credible are accusations made by an individual who doesn't even have the courage to sign them? They receive trash like that by the ton. What's more, as far as we know, there was no mention of the name Tremblay."

"But who, I ask you, could have gotten wind of my suspicions? I did not share them with anyone but you."

"Well, there was the captain of the fire brigade. And the other teachers, too."

Clémentine lowered her eyes: true, she had spoken to the other teachers. And had immediately regretted it. Nothing but old gossips!

She drained the last drop and gloomily contemplated the bottom of her glass. The liquor left a rusty taste on her tongue. She was betrayed by everything. And everyone, including Brother Gandon. She seized the bottle shamelessly and poured herself another drink. Pink patches appeared on her cheeks.

"I don't know what to think any more," Clémentine said.

She broke out in a sweat. Lord, how warm it was in that room!

Brother Gandon had not said more than a third of what he needed to say, and the easiest third, at that! He ran his fingers ineffectually through the messy thicket of his hair, like a man getting out of bed. Then he took another gulp of whisky to give himself courage.

"Yesterday, Miss Clément. Fortunately the bank was about to close, and Mr. Judith, the bank manager, was the only one left there with him. Otherwise, just think of the scandal it would have caused in front of the clients, or the other employees. Mr. Judith is an understanding man; I was able to sort things out with him this morning. Still . . ."

"You have no right to remind me of that. No right. I was overwrought. You have no right . . . no right . . ."

She was sobbing, with those snorts Gandon found so insufferable.

"But what got into you, my friend, to go and berate this poor Tremblay like that, without a shred of evidence?"

"I had just returned from Eugène's funeral. I was . . . I hurried over to the Guillubarts', but I didn't feel up to facing his mother. When I arrived at the door I turned around. I said to myself: 'It's my fault he's dead.' Then — I don't know why, I told you, I was distraught — I thought: 'I'm not the only one who killed him!' I ran to the bank, I wanted to denounce that man, that . . . that poor Tremblay, as you put it! That poor Tremblay whom I surprised again last week with a little girl whose face was covered in bruises — am I making that up as well?"

"That was Mr. Judith's niece. He told me so himself. She had fallen down and hurt herself."

Clémentine pounded her fist on the desk. "I don't believe it! This Judith must be in cahoots with him! Or . . . !"

"Let's try to keep our heads. That is precisely your problem: you are too quick to lose your composure. You are going to make yourself ill. Can you imagine what you looked like, yesterday, screaming, and banging on the window of the bank? And half barefoot, no less, in the snow. Do you remember that? *You had forgotten to put on one of your boots!*"

This detail, of which she had been unaware, left her speechless. Gandon continued, reluctantly.

"There is also what you did on Sunday, which cannot be ignored. Rocheleau's father sent me a letter, and Bradette's uncle telephoned to give me an earful, pardon the expression. These are actions that I shall have to take into account, and I shall be obliged to mention them at the next meeting of the school commissioners."

"Fifteen years of teaching and love . . . fifteen years . . . fifteen years!"

She repeated these worlds in disbelief. Gandon felt as though he were operating on living flesh without anaesthetic.

"Forgive me, Miss Clément, but I have no choice but to ask you for your version of these events."

The principal waited.

"What is so comical?" he finally asked, with a hint of amusement.

Clémentine was convulsed by a grotesque fit of laughter. She jerked in her chair as if she were being bounced over a washboard road. The seconds ticked by. Brother Gandon got up from his chair. He was going to call a doctor.

"He kicked me in the behind," she said at last.

Gandon was not sure he had heard right.

"Someone . . . you . . . ?"

Yes, she nodded.

"Who did?"

Racked with laughter, she was unable to answer. He took the glass of whisky from her hands.

"Get a hold of yourself, please. Who would dare do such a thing?"

She managed to calm down and with a cynical sort of joviality took up her glass.

"Bradette's uncle. He put his boot to my rear end. Can you picture it? A lame woman with a mashed rump! Chugging along like a locomotive. *Choo-choo, pshhh. Choo-choo, pshhh.*"

The principal could not believe his ears. Striking a woman! And in that way — and Miss Clément, of all people!

"But that's . . . that's unacceptable!"

The schoolteacher shrugged her shoulders in a detached, good-humoured way. Took another nip. Gently patted her stomach.

"I had first gone to Dr. Rocheleau's house to express my fears to him. He listened with an angelic smile. Then he simply replied it was impossible, that I did not know his son very well, that his son could not have done such a thing. He told me about a seraph who always watches over his child, explained something about a pin, said that the lad's mother is more alive than you or me . . . He gave me the impression of someone with bats in the belfry."

"Judging from his letter he does indeed seem somewhat bizarre."

Then she had gone to see Bradette's uncle, believing she had a better chance of being listened to there. She had not yet finished her first sentence when the man started to insult her. He got up from his chair and chased her to the door, bumping into the furniture along the way.

"And then, by way of a sendoff, he booted me in the bum. There you have it."

There were tears in Gandon's eyes. As he lifted the glass to his lips, his hand fairly trembling with indignation, Clémentine exclaimed in a shrill voice, "He said I was sleeping with you!"

"What's that you say?"

"Bradette's uncle. He said I was sleeping with you! And when I went to buy bread yesterday at noon I heard the baker's wife repeating the same thing behind my back!"

Brother Gandon wondered whether he was dreaming. He stepped back around his desk and sank into his chair.

"You don't say things like that. It's not possible. How can anyone say such things?"

"Well, as a matter of fact, everybody has been saying it! For months now! They're always together, they say. Isn't that strange? Well, it's because they fornicate seven times a week!"

"Be quiet! Can't you just be quiet!"

Clémentine snickered into her glass: it felt good to lie.

"They say my skin smells of you! They say we're like animals! They say that . . . that I give you hickeys!"

She did not quite know what the word meant, but she liked the sound of it; it sounded right. He was on his feet, arms raised, ready to strike. She burst into hideous laughter, intoxicated with defiance. The laughter crushed him.

"You are drunk. And you are losing your head."

She sprang to her feet so abruptly that her chair overturned. Her toque had fallen, strands of hair zigzagged down her cheek, her lips were tumid with blood. The principal was terrified. She was spluttering in his face, and her spittle fell on his half-open mouth like drops of vinegar. He was terrified because she was terribly beautiful.

"Hit me, go ahead! Why don't you hit the ostrich if you think it's going to stop people from talking! But they'll keep on saying we're lovers! They'll keep on saying I've been in love with you for five years, since the first day I saw that face that I detest so much I wake up at night to detest it! Just as I detest the smell of your pipe, of that awful whisky, of your unwashed body that I find when you're out of your office and I bury my face in the coat there, in that closet! And do you know what else they say, what people say? *They say you come to my house, that we have a code, that you can come up through the back if I light the lamp in the kitchen!* . . . They say . . . ! They say you're my superb, generous lion! And they say other things, too, they chatter, people do, if you only knew! They say we get drunk together, and that I dance for you, for you alone, to excite you — just like this!"

She moved into the centre of the room, nearly tripping over the upset chair. She pushed it aside. Her arms began to undulate over her head, she did a few steps, swaying her pelvis in the way she imagined Moorish women did, based on her readings. Then she lost her balance and her weak leg gave way. She crawled to him on all fours and clutched his cassock at the hips.

"They say I love you, my love. And that soon I'll be old. And that I was beautiful and am turning ugly now . . . Do you hear what they say? That I'm perishing for the love of you? And that I couldn't care less about the captain of the fire brigade, since everyone says you're the one I love, do you hear? Answer me, my love, answer me!"

She sobbed as she drummed her forehead on the principal's abdomen.

Up to that point Gandon had seen only flashes of lightning, heard only screeching. Suddenly he realized what was happening. She was climbing on top of him. She toppled him over backwards on his desk.

He tried to extricate himself but she was strong. Her lips darted over his neck, his cheeks, she nibbled his ears, mumbling, "Gaston, Gaston . . ." A profound feeling of repulsion swept over him. He shoved her away with all the strength in his arms. She flew to the far end of the room and hit her head on the wall.

Gandon was on his feet, provoked, his muscles ready for battle. *Come on, get up!* he thought. He felt a savage desire to fight with her — yes, for them to pounce at each other, to lash out! to roll on the floor, to pummel each other's face, to pin each other down, to fight to the finish! and then to lie stretched out on the ground, torn, panting in separate corners like dogs licking their wounds . . .

But his blood cooled, his breathing slowed, and he saw

the situation in all its hideousness. He clasped his head with both hands.

Steps rang out in the empty school. He listened to them approaching in time with his heartbeat. He heard the knocking: once, twice. He did not react. The door opened.

It was Remouald Tremblay and, behind him, the janitor.

"I'm sorry, sir, but this gentleman here wishes to see you. I just came to collect the wastepaper basket, but . . .

The janitor stopped short upon noticing the schoolteacher. Remouald looked at her incredulously. The top of her dress was wide open, she was slumped against the wall with one of her breasts exposed. She seemed completely unmindful of her surroundings. She was using her sleeve to wipe away the blood dribbling from her mouth.

The principal should have had the simple reflex of going to help her to her feet. And that is exactly what he wanted to do. But he was unable to move.

"Sorry for having disturbed you," the janitor said with an unpleasant smile.

Gandon heard the footsteps of the two men fading away.

* * *

THERE WAS A prolonged silence. Gandon was unable to shake off the silly thought that he would have to empty the wastepaper basket himself.

He said, "Five years of friendship and this is what it has come to."

"I thought you were a man. But you're not a man. You've got no heart. You don't even have a body."

She said this very softly. Gandon seized the bottle with

an urge to drink from it directly, but he felt a sudden repugnance toward it and placed it back on the pedestal table. He stepped toward Clémentine, who refused his help. She hobbled over to her glass. The alcohol set her bruised tongue aflame and she winced.

"I implore you not to drink any more. And also . . . there . . . your dress . . ."

Clémentine buttoned her collar. They were standing by the desk. At times their shoulders touched and their exhaustion was such that they tended to lean against each other. What sort of leave-taking could there be after an evening like this? Gandon found it impossible to think; there was nothing inside his head now but haze.

Clémentine maintained the unwholesome poise, full of suppressed violence, of someone who no longer cares about anything and is prepared to prove it. Gandon looked at her. Her unkempt hair, her clothes in disarray, everything that a moment ago had lent her an aura of wild, brazen beauty gave her the sorry mien of a madwoman now that her fury was spent. The principal turned away.

She straightened a lock of hair with a slow, mechanical gesture. Her tone of voice was jaded, with a kind of dreamy indifference about it.

"Are you angry with me?" she said.

Gaston Gandon hesitated.

"Yes, I am."

She quietly conceded.

"I guess that's natural. In any case, I'm not afraid of you. Why should I be afraid of a little boy who hides behind a dress?"

"Stop insulting me. I am asking you nicely."

She ignored him, as though addressing Clémentine-and-a-half.

"Why did you become a school principal? To stay inside this little world, the only one you knew, with its retreats, its refectories, its hockey teams and early mornings in the chapel, and also its books. You ran away from life because the only problems you could face were little-boy problems. You *are* a little boy. Your habits, pastimes, enthusiasms are those of a little boy. Real life — its pain, its pleasures, its realities — is something you reject. You prefer to ponder questions of theology or go off on excursions with your knapsack and your little friends singing 'Valderi, Valdera'. In fact, I wonder if you might not be attracted to them. For the same reason you hide behind a dress. For fear of women, fear of life . . ."

It was a matter of honour for Gandon not to lose his temper.

"I am warning you once again, politely. If you persist . . . I shall hate you."

"You? Hate? Do you think you're strong enough for that? To love the springtime, your grandmother, the little birds, that's fine! But to hate, do you even know what it means? The strength of character it requires? The clear-sightedness, the courage? It's easy to love everyone when you go around with your eyes set on boy-scout ideals, doing your daily Good Deed without paying attention to what you're stepping on, without seeing the hurt, the suffering, the hell that life is for the people around you."

"One night, I happened to be at the hospital with the doctor of some friends of mine. There's no reason for me to tell you his name, but I will, just the same: Daniel Langevin.

Langevin, just like this school. We were having a drink in his office. I asked him if I could see the children sleeping. We were already tipsy, otherwise he would have refused, and, besides, I would never have dared. But we went. In one room, there was a child sleeping apart from the others. He looked like an angel. That isn't just a cliché, Miss Clément; I've known enough children in my life not to confuse them with angels. This child, though, was truly an angel. Blond, curly-headed, the kind you see playing John-the-Baptist in parades. My friend pulled back the blanket. Over the entire surface of his back there were purple lumps the size of golf balls. Daniel whispered in my ear, 'He's four years old.' He had only a few excruciating weeks left to live."

Clémentine acted unimpressed.

"Why are you telling me this?"

"To show you that I, too, have eyes to see. *A man's eyes.*"

She smiled wearily, not so much at him, it seemed, as at the pictures hanging on the walls. Her arms were folded over her chest in the kind of embrace intended to keep oneself warm.

"Your paintings are dreadful as well. Clumsy, puerile, like the women they portray."

"I have no illusions about them."

She shrugged.

"Men and women are not meant to get along."

"Leave," he said with subdued firmness.

Clémentine grabbed her cloak, purse, hat with the same stiff movement that she might have used to pick up vegetables at the market, carelessly put her toque back on, and walked casually to the door. She turned back one last time toward Gandon — a smirk, a suggestive glance, all calculated to torment him through the night. Then, oozing dignity, she limped in the darkness toward what remained of her life.

Gandon stayed standing in the middle of the room, stabbed through the heart by a woman's scorn.

At this point, his rage, his qualms, his distress, everything rose to his temples all at once. He ran to the janitor's room: the light was out, the door was bolted, the man was gone. Gandon knew he was in the habit of ending his workdays at the tavern. His drinking mates would certainly have a juicy tale to share with their wives when they got home! The principal returned to his office, perspiring, panting, at his wits' end.

He opened the closet to take his coat. He saw the gouache he had painted for her and had wanted to give her as a present. It was a portrait of Clémentine that he had toiled over all day Sunday. He held himself back from putting his foot through it.

"I'll never forgive her. Never!"

There was something glutinous at the bottom of his pocket. He pulled out a long blood sausage bought that same day and immediately forgotten. He bit into it. He disliked raw blood sausage, but he was in the mood for irrational behaviour, as if he were telling God, "You wanted me to abhor raw blood sausage, eh? Well, I'm going to eat some nevertheless!" When he bent over to slip on his boots he noticed that, earlier, he had ejaculated.

He was in a murderous frame of mind and grumbled as he headed toward the school exit. Remouald loomed up from the shadows. At the tip of his nose a drop was turning to ice.

"What do you want from me?"

"To talk," said Remould, and he looked so piteous that Gandon's anger fell a notch.

"What do you have to say to me?"

"I don't know."

The principal looked at him ironically. Remould wiped his nose on his sleeve. He wore that overfed ass's smile of his. Was he drunk or something? He waited without saying a word.

"Were you born like that or have you been practising? Come on, what is it you want from me?"

"To tell you," Remould said.

"Yes, to tell me what?"

"That I've been cured."

"I'm so delighted. Cured of what?"

"It's been years now. Tell your friend the schoolteacher. So she stops thinking what she wanted to say to me yesterday when she banged on the bank window."

"And what exactly did she want to say to you?"

"I don't know."

"That's splendid. Congratulations."

"She didn't have the time to say it. And you, too. Don't think it, even though you came to speak to Mr. Judith this morning."

"What you're saying is not very clear, do you realize that?"

Gandon was beginning to have doubts as to the other man's mental health. Remould rubbed his hands and stamped on the snow to warm himself.

"Also, I wanted to tell you a secret, for your schoolteacher friend."

"Oh, I see. Well?"

"I don't know any more."

Nothing surprised Gandon at this point, so this left him unruffled.

"I mean, I don't know if I want to tell you any more," the other man added.

"You're a nice fellow, you know. You ought to run in the next elections."

The brother started away. Remouald followed suit. He walked slightly behind, thrashing his upper arms to beat off the cold.

"I'll come this week to tell you the secret, because tonight I'm not in a position to. I'm not in a position to tell you because I don't want to. But now I'd like to tell you something else."

The brother stopped; he was quite irritated. Remouald in turn came to a stop in order to keep his distance.

"My woollen scarf," he said.

"What about your woollen scarf?"

"You've got it around your neck."

"What?"

Remouald reiterated. Gandon untied the scarf and examined it in the moonlight. Indeed, it was not his.

"This morning, at the bank. Without realizing it, Brother, you walked away with my scarf.

He pulled the principal's scarf out of his pocket.

"Good Heavens, you're quite right. I do apologize. But you could have worn mine in the meantime! Look how cold you are."

"It wasn't mine," Remouald said, with that smile of his.

He bowed slightly and went away. Gandon put his scarf back on. An object had stayed caught in the folds of the fabric. He looked: a rabbit's foot. It slipped out of his hands.

He searched, to keep his conscience clear, but was unable to find it in all that snow. "Too bad," he told himself. He was once again besieged by his worries. The janitor. The whispering. Miss Clément.

"How will I ever find the strength to see her again tomorrow?"

The principal walked more quickly. He desperately called up in his mind the image of Christ on the Cross. To be incapable of forgiving someone spawned within him an infinite distress.

But the next day Clémentine did not show up at school. Nor the following day, for that matter. Nor even the day after that.

11

He had looked everywhere for it.

Under the bed, under the furniture, in every imaginable pocket of his clothes, in his boots, in the breadbox, even in the places where it was impossible for it to be . . . He tried to recall the last time he had touched it. The previous day, no doubt. But where? Did he still have it on entering the principal's office? He remembered having squeezed it in the palm of his hand the moment he caught sight of the schoolteacher. But when he was waiting for the principal outside, did he still have it? He glanced at the clock. Not yet seven in the morning. He left without taking any tea, without even telling Séraphon, who was still asleep.

It had snowed for part of the night, and trying to spot a rabbit's foot put a severe strain on his eyes. His head was spinning due to the alcohol he had imbibed the night before. He advanced, hunched over, scrutinizing the ground. In this manner, he arrived at the École Langevin. He straightened up and the mere effort of it made his heart race; for a moment there were stars dancing before his eyes.

The schoolyard seemed to him like a white desert, vast

and disheartening. "Little rabbit's foot, little rabbit's foot," he hummed. He scattered some snow with the toe of his boot.

He noticed a silhouette at the far end of the yard and followed it with his eyes. A short woman, all chest and buttocks. She unexpectedly stopped and bent down. Then, seeing Remould bearing down on her, she started away, tucking her bread under her arm together with her all but penniless purse. But the young man overtook her and blocked the way out of the yard.

"Have you found something?"

Remould, gazing intently at her, waited. The woman stepped back.

"Tell me what you picked up, and in exchange . . ."

He rummaged through his pockets.

"And in exchange, I'll give you some matches."

A nutcase! thought the by now desperate woman.

"Would you like to know in how many leap years the Feast of the Immaculate Conception will fall on a Friday? Tell me what you've just picked up and I'll calculate whatever you like."

The woman's voice was stretched very thin.

"There is absolutely nothing I want you to calculate for me!"

She was afraid he would start chopping her up into little numbers with a knife.

"Or postage stamps. I've got some at home and I can give you some. Pictures of the world . . . Please, ma'am."

The woman said nothing. Remould had run out of bargaining chips. His face grew sombre and he pulled his hands out of his pockets.

"Give me back my rabbit's foot."

The woman took another step back.

"Your rabbit's foot?"

He walked up to her and struck her shoulder with his fist.

"My rabbit's foot," he repeated, and held out his hand.

The woman drew the rabbit's foot out of her coat and flung it on the ground. She scurried away, her hands on her chignon and her bread forgotten. Remould knelt down. He blew on the snow-covered rabbit's foot, placed his lips on it. "My poor little thing. Do you realize? This was the first night we have not slept together."

When she came through the door of her house, the woman ran to the kitchen.

"Armand! Armand!"

Armand was badly hungover and fought with his eyelids to keep them open. There was a cigarette smoking in the ashtray in the bedroom, another in the kitchen, and a third between his fingers, which looked as though they had been soaked in iodine.

His wife gave him a detailed account of what had happened to her on the way back from the bakery. She acted out the episode with sweeping gestures, her chest heaving and she herself in the role of heroine. She mimicked Remould by rolling a pair of large, sinister eyes, and raised her arms above her head, as if she had just come face to face with the Abominable Snowman.

Her husband listened in the manner of a husband listening; he told himself that, just like the ones before, this dreary tale would in the end come to an end. Then all at once his eyes lit up, and he showed some interest in the anecdote. Buoyed up by this unexpected success, the woman laid it on even thicker. And when she had had enough of repeating the same things, she fell silent and waited for his response, arms folded across her bosom.

Armand was in no hurry at all. An elusive smile floated on his lips. As he headed toward the sink, he coolly let the words fall from his lips.

"Your nutcase — I think I know who he is."

This left his wife gaping. He savoured this initial triumph. But he had far more succulent tidbits still in store for his old lady this morning! He splashed some water on his face, towelled himself, and came back, stretching and groaning with contentment.

Armand was the janitor at the École Langevin.

* * *

SARAH HAD THAT little girl's quirk of pulling her woollen stockings up as far as possible above her knees, so at any given moment the stroll would have to be interrupted for her to perform this ritual. At times a detail would capture her attention: the shape of a cloud, a sparrow pecking at an old shoe. Remouald began to comprehend the language of her eyes, and this was very often clearer for him than if she had used words to speak. Sarah's eyes, like those of an owl, made visible what they saw.

Otherwise, she showed almost no interest in anything. Not the animals they came across — the squirrels, the horses, the dogs, not even the small ones — nor the toys in the shop windows. The games that the children gathered in the alleys to play in the late afternoon meant nothing to her. They never had a destination but followed, rather, the meandering pathways of the avenues. Sarah no longer held

Remouald's hand. She walked, beating her mittens together in a slow, absent-minded tempo, for the pleasure of joining and unjoining her hands, of uniting and separating, to lend cadence to the passage of time.

So why this sudden interest in the Cornes Bleues? She had raced across Rue Saint-Catherine and glued herself to the butcher shop window. She shaded her eyes against the sunlight to have a better view inside. Remouald joined her. She wanted to go in, pulled on his sleeve with both hands. Remouald finally yielded.

Bruised cuts of meat, laid flat on the display counters, in quarters or slices, protected by the glass, like a museum of wounds and injuries — and Sarah stopped in front of each one, ceremoniously, as though at an exhibition. The beheaded fowls, with their air of opera singers, plucked and rosy, chests puffed out, were held by hooks down the length of the wall. The butcher was in the process of carving chops. The clucking of chickens could be heard on the other side of the partition, along with the scraping of claws on the wire cages. Hams and sausages hung from the ceiling. Remouald pulled up his nose-warmer. A rank odour of meal, sawdust, and blood had made him gag the moment he walked in.

The butcher stepped up, wiping his hands on his apron. Rather short in the legs, massive shoulders, a large chin. Remouald wondered whom he resembled. He was unaware that this was Siméon Cadorette, the priest's youngest brother.

"What can I do for you?"

"Sarah wanted to come in."

Siméon looked at the little girl. He had a peculiar asthmatic laugh, a bronchial whistle that sounded like a board being sawn.

"You're hungry, is that it?"

"She's just eaten, sir."

Sarah was content to smile.

"What's the matter? Cat got your tongue?"

While Remouald was explaining to the butcher that she was mute, Sarah slid along the counter and moved toward the back of the store. She hopped and clapped her hands. Remouald tried to hold her back.

"No, no, let her go. She's probably interested in the caged animals."

They followed behind her.

The chickens squawked and ran toward the yard — a rooster hugged the wall, its spur raised up. There were feathers flying everywhere, as if a pillow had been disembowelled. Sarah went up to the cages; the rabbits lying prone with their snouts between their forepaws, red-eyed from lack of sleep, seemed resigned to ending up on a plate, slathered in mustard, with a potato in their teeth. Sarah scratched on the bars while making faces at them. She began to knock the cages with her fist.

"Hey, what are you doing there, little girl?"

Sarah yanked on one of the hutches with all her might, and it crashed to the ground. She charged at the others, ramming them with her shoulder. The framework collapsed. She launched into chasing after the chickens, kicking them in the behind; she caught one by the legs and swung it like a bell.

The butcher tried to right the cages, swearing all the while. Some rabbits managed to escape. Remouald, wanting to help, succeeded only in trampling on a snout: a star of blood appeared beneath his heel. He very nearly passed out.

Sarah stole back to the shop and scooped up a slice of

veal. She climbed onto the counter and set about whipping the hams with the veal slice.

"You're not nice, Sarah! Come on, get down from there, will you?"

The butcher came back, fuming, into the shop.

"What in the world is this calamity!"

He approached with the intention of bringing her down from her perch himself; Sarah suspended herself from a ham and wrapped her thighs around it. She swung above their heads, sticking her tongue out at them.

"Do something or I'm calling the police!"

Remouald turned toward the girl.

"If you come down I'll buy you some candy!"

She answered with her mischievous eyes, "*I don't like candy*."

Remouald had a flash of inspiration. It was as though someone else were speaking in his stead when he heard himself say, "I'll take you to the movies, then! If you come down, I'll take you to the movies!"

Siméon had picked up his telephone; he was just about to dial the number of the police. Sarah, rocked by the peaceful swaying of the ham, pouted haughtily, capriciously.

"*Okay, the movies it will be,*" she finally signalled.

She let herself drop softly into Remouald's arms.

Remouald removed his hat and wiped his forehead with his sleeve.

The butcher looked at Sarah in disbelief. She walked up to him and politely deposited the slice of veal in the palm of his hand. Her gaze said thank you. She went back to Remouald and pressed her cheek against his thigh. She smiled at Siméon.

"Well, then, thank you, sir," Remouald said in a tiny voice.

"Hey!" said Simeon. "Don't play the fool. What about this slice of veal — who's going to pay for it?"

"The one who's going to buy it, I suppose," Remouald replied, taken aback by how obvious the answer was.

"Oh, and you think I'm going to be able to sell it, do you?"

Remouald, as a matter of fact, could not see how this could be a problem.

"Look at it! Your daughter has completely shredded it!"

"She's not my daughter."

"I don't give a damn! You've got to pay for this slice of veal!"

Remouald handed him a few coins, convinced he was being taken advantage of, as usual, but haggling with a merchant was more than he could manage. Siméon hastily wrapped the piece of meat in waxed paper and thrust it against Remouald's chest. Sarah grabbed it.

The butcher tapped his temple with his forefinger.

"It's because she doesn't like meat very much, I think," Remouald said.

Siméon cursed and returned to the back of the shop. Sarah and Remouald went out of the butcher store.

As soon as she had it in her hand Sarah put the ticket in her mouth and swallowed it. The usher would hear none of Remouald's explanations, even though he had seen what the girl had done. "I need a ticket, that's all there is to it." They entered the nearly empty hall after making another trip to the ticket booth.

Remouald had never had any great fondness for the cinema. It gave him the impression of an existence chopped into pieces, with accelerations, troubling shortcuts, gigantic faces that were forever grimacing, and horrifying characters who suddenly appeared holding a knife. He found it strange that people would waste their money in exchange for the anxiety this afforded them. As for him, he preferred to close his eyes and listen only to the piano. Eventually, he fell asleep.

* * *

A CALL RANG out and Remouald opened his eyes. The Madonna of the icon was leaning over him and smiling.

"Who are you?" he murmured like a dreaming child.

"You have to leave, sir, the show is over."

Sarah had also dozed off, huddled against Remouald. The pianist spoke in a low voice so as not to wake her too abruptly. She repeated that they had to leave.

"Yes," Remouald said, without moving.

Sarah woke up with the sulking gestures of a little cat, and the same smell. Remouald took her in his arms. The pianist went out of the hall. Remouald hurried after her.

"Miss Vilbroquais," said the usher, "something has just arrived for you."

The usher disappeared behind a door and came back with a bundle of dirty, dog-eared letters that seemed to have passed through many hands.

"It came from New York. The sender knew only that you worked as a movie hall pianist. So the letters went around all the theatres. But look, there's no mistaking your name."

Justine Vilbroquais appeared utterly surprised. She opened one of the envelopes. Remouald was standing behind her. When she lowered her forehead she resembled even more the image on his icon. She immediately skipped ahead to the last page of the letter.

. . . for I know, my love, that we shall meet again after these twenty sleepless years, the twenty years it will have taken for you to be able to forgive me, and on that day, no matter where we may be, it will be as though we had at last come back, after a thousand futile labyrinths, to the house of my childhood (surely you have not forgotten: I was nine years old and would send you greeting cards signed "House of Oaths, 1909 rue Moreau" — fifty years ago!), the house of our childhood, when I was yours alone, when you were mine alone, when Heaven was in its place! I ask you to meet me in front of that door, soon — I am partial to December 22, your birthday! — and you will come, won't you? I will be ugly because I am old, and you too, perhaps, will be ugly, but there I shall be, there the two of us shall be; should you not come, I do not know what I will do — hang myself, who knows? (is that what you want?) — slit my throat — after burning down that cursed house . . . For my life would be meaningless without this final reconciliation with you. It would be meaningless if our love turned out to be but a lie. Do you hear what I am saying? I have had enough of remembering. But I know that you will come. Do not forget: the 22nd of December.

Eternally yours,
Rogatien

With her gloved hand Justine dreamily crumpled the sheet into a ball. Remould, who had gone pale, continued to peek over her shoulder. She noticed this and buried the bundle of letters in her coat pocket.

She walked past the ticket booth looking preoccupied. Remouald followed her with his eyes until she had crossed the street and vanished behind the garden wall. He remained standing near the door.

"Pardon me," said the usher, "but I must insist, since we are closing."

Sarah had transformed herself into a rag doll. Remouald tried to get her to put on her coat, but she would not make the least effort to help him. She kept her eyes languidly closed and teetered on her legs. He took hold of one of her mittens and immediately flung it down in disgust.

"Don't throw your garbage on the floor," said the usher.

Remouald retrieved the mitten and, stepping into the street, shook out the slice of veal that Sarah had hidden in it.

He was still trembling when he came back. Sarah had collapsed on the floor, and he lifted her in his arms. The clock showed four o'clock. It was time to bring back Mr. Judith's niece.

The pianist had gone up Rue d'Orléans, heading north, and that was the route they took as well. Remouald, hearing horse hooves behind him, quickened his pace. Sarah felt heavier and heavier.

"Do you think you can walk?"

She nodded yes, and he stood her on her feet. The horseman had overtaken them and was blocking the way. This was the fourth time in less than a week that he was making his presence felt in this way before riding off without a word. Remouald turned back, but the horseman called out to him in a husky voice.

"Hey, you pervert! You know I could squash you like a turd if I chose to? Eh?"

Remouald had taken Sarah's hand in his own. Sarah advanced while looking back at the horse.

"If ever the police find out it's all true, those stories about the little boys, then I advise you not to let me get my paws on you, you bastard . . . Hey! You could at least look at me when I talk to you!"

Remouald turned around. Atop his mount the captain of the fire brigade grinned down at him. And with his thumb cocked, he aimed his index finger at him like a revolver.

* * *

Remouald sat waiting for Mr. Judith to have finished with his last client. Squatting like a duck, Sarah amused herself by spreading Remouald's fingers, twisting them, and tickling the palm of his hand with a lock of her hair.

Mr. Judith came out of his office, preceded by Charles Hudon, one of the owners of the spinning mill. Short, stony, and rather thin-skinned, he was reputed to converse with dogs and horses, bestowing extravagant titles upon them, but he was nonetheless his brothers' brother and his father's son. He was plagued by an imaginary fly buzzing around his nose, which would give rise to unexpected halts when he walked, and Mr. Judith, who was bowing and scraping at his heels, had to take care not to collide with his back.

"So until tomorrow, of course, with your brothers . . . And best regards to Mrs. Hudon!"

The businessman bade him a quick farewell — perhaps to be rid of the fly — and Mr. Judith came back with his pinky planted in his ear. He then noticed Remouald, stopped, and spread his arms, looking deeply dismayed.

"If you would be so kind as to come into my office, my dear friend, I have something quite unpleasant to tell you."

Remouald followed him.

The manager did not take up his station behind his desk. His meeting with the factory owner had left him with a touch of humility; he positioned himself directly in front of his employee, eyeball to eyeball, as one does when speaking man to man.

"This afternoon I was apprised of some very sad news. Oh, my little Remouald! When things start going wrong . . ."

Remouald raised his guard.

"I didn't do anything. I simply told him to give me my scarf and I gave him his."

Mr. Judith, who was preparing to pour his heart out, stopped short and tried to make head or tail of what he had just heard.

"What's all this about a scarf?" he finally asked.

"The school principal. And Miss Clément, the teacher."

Judith looked vexed.

"That whole affair is behind us; this has nothing to do with that, my friend. But with Sarah."

"I see."

"Her mother"

"?"

"She is on her last legs."

He let the appropriate period of silence elapse. Remouald stayed true to form.

"Do you mean she is going to die?"

(*No, I mean she is going to play the banjo*, thought the manager.)

"The doctors fear she has no more than a week to live."

Remould tried to feel sorry for Sarah. But he was prevented from doing so by a nasty suspicion, which was beyond his control. He realized now that, although Sarah's mother had been mentioned to him over the past week, he could not bring himself to believe in her existence. He was no longer listening to the manager's interminable monologue.

Suddenly Judith joined his fingers together in a posture of entreaty:

"Dear Lord, don't let her die without having seen her child again!"

Then, having addressed his Creator, Mr. Judith sedately came down to earth, as one descends a stairway.

"Is Sarah going to leave?" Remould asked.

"She will have to, in any case. And that is where my problem lies. You must believe me, Remould, I would go myself as a matter of duty if I did not have a meeting of the utmost importance tomorrow with people like Messrs. Hudon, Justice Lacroix, Mr. Costade . . ." He placed his hand on Remould's knee. "So it's you who will be going."

"Going where?"

(*Dot every i one at a time*, thought Judith with a sigh.)

"Going with Sarah to visit her dying mother."

"Where?"

"At the sanatorium."

"Where's that?"

"In Saint-Aldor."

"Where?"

"The Saint-Aldor sanatorium . . . Don't you see, meeting her mother will be such a trial for Sarah: she will need to have someone she is fond of by her side. What's the matter, Remould, you're trembling? Is what I'm asking you so terrible?"

"What you . . . what you ask is impossible."

"Listen, we are not going to go through that again the way we did last week! I can't see who else it could be aside from you, Remouald. A mother is on her deathbed — are you going to deprive her of the presence of her child? Will you tell me what on earth could be tormenting you like this? For heaven's sake, you look like you are about to faint."

The manager got up, stepped out of his office, and returned with a glass of water.

Remouald took a drink without giving it any thought, obeying out of habit. He choked and pushed away the glass.

"I can't, I won't, I've never left the parish, I don't know a thing about the outside, I'll get lost!"

He pressed his arms against his stomach as though suffering from cramps. The manager's patience ran out.

"Stop whining, damn it! I've already worked everything out. The route will be explained to you when you get off the train — there's nothing to it. Look here! Enough is enough, eh?"

Judith took a deep breath, just as his doctor had instructed him, and counted to ten in his head, slowly, conscientiously. When he opened his eyes he felt more accommodating. The virtue of numbers.

"You lack self-confidence, Remouald. You say you have never left the Nativité parish? Well, then, what could be better! This will be an edifying experience for you."

Remouald was holding himself tightly, legs entwined, and biting his thumbnail.

"So, it's yes?"

". . ."

"It's either that or you're out the door! You can go work at MacDonald Tobacco like everyone else. Or at the spinning mill, if there are any jobs open, which I doubt. Mr. Hudon has just informed me his brother will be laying off some thirty workers after the holidays. He would rather not tell them right away, as he's not a bad man and wouldn't want to spoil their Christmas. At any rate. The choice is yours!"

Remould's body went slack all at once and unknotted itself, like a dying boa. His face had turned livid.

"When do you want me to leave?"

He might have used the same tone of voice to ask, "At what time are they going to hang me?"

"This very night," Mr. Judith said as he gathered his coat. "You can go by your house if you like, then we'll dash to the train station. Barring any unforeseen delays, you ought to be in Saint-Aldor before dawn tomorrow."

Remould tried one last objection.

"I can't leave my dad alone at home tonight. He's always frightened these days. And then there's his soup . . ."

"Then ask a neighbour to bring your dad his meals. You'll be back late tomorrow night. It won't kill him, after all."

Mr. Judith slipped on his coat. He stopped short, his arm in the air, halfway up his sleeve.

"Well! Hurry up. There's not a moment to lose."

Remould stood up slowly, reluctantly it seemed. He clasped his hat humbly against his stomach. Sarah was hastily dressed, the manager picked her up under his arm, the little girl's coat was buttoned askew. In the manager's car (Remould had never been in an automobile), they settled on a plan. They would stop at Séraphon's, the situation would be explained to him, then they would go immediately to the freight station.

"The problem," said Judith as he tried to pass a truck, "is that the next passenger train for Saint-Aldor will not be leaving before tomorrow morning. The freight train leaves in a half-hour. The stationmaster is a friend of mine; everything has been arranged. All right, it may not be the most luxurious ride, but you are young, after all. Look on the back seat," the manager continued. "My beaver coat — take it along, in case the little one feels cold. And another thing: Sarah's mother's name is Tétreault. Can you remember that? Julie Tétreault."

They arrived at Séraphon's house.

As Remouald did not know how to open the car door, the manager had to open it for him. Remouald clambered upstairs to his house.

Sarah sat stiffly beside Mr. Judith. He observed her out of the corner of his eye. He sensed that he was nothing to her. She never displayed the slightest hint of gratitude or affection. She cared only for this Remouald! . . . Although he was indifferent toward children, even annoyed by them, managing at best to give them an official smile in front of clients, he was galled by the mere fact that his clerk might be preferred over him. What's more, she was impudent, and insincere: she peed in bed, pulled faces when his wife's back was turned, and the day before yesterday he had caught her playing with matches — one would have thought she was trying to set fire to the living-room curtains! . . . For thirty years of happy wedlock, despite the occasional indiscretion — once right in the kitchen while twenty guests waited for them in the parlour — Mr. and Mrs. Judith had cautiously avoided having a child. And a week with Sarah had not made them regret their decision!

But what would he do with her now? He had discussed it over the telephone with his wife after reading the telegram to her: "Julie Tétreault dying. Wishes to see Sarah for final adieux. Please notify concerning arrangements. Signed: Saint-Aldor Sanatorium." He still had scruples. "Life is so good in the orphanages," his wife had said to him.

The minutes passed and Remould had not yet come back down. Mr. Judith honked.

Remould burst from the stairway, red-faced, and thrust his head through the partly open window.

"He doesn't want to! He doesn't want me to leave him! He's screaming!"

Mr. Judith got out of his automobile and saw Séraphon. Face flattened against his bedroom window, the old man was sobbing.

"Tell him I'll take him to my house!"

"He won't go! He won't go!"

Sarah had begun to cry. She wailed so that the veins in her neck bulged, but no sound escaped from her mouth.

"If your father refuses to stay with us, well, take him to Saint-Aldor with you!"

Remould looked aghast. Mr. Judith wagged a menacing forefinger.

"You have no choice, Remould! The train leaves in thirteen minutes. Take the old man with you!"

Remould hopped up and down, wringing his hands. At last, he bounded upstairs.

The manager returned to his seat.

He said to Sarah, "Stop squirming or I'll let you have it!"

By way of response Sarah stuck her tongue out at him. The manager twisted her ear with a vengeful cackle and then went back to drumming impatiently on the steering wheel.

Sarah had removed her beret in exasperation, and when he inhaled the fragrance of her hair Judith suddenly experienced a peculiar sensation of warmth. He looked at the little girl. A tempting, silly idea blazed across his mind. He sat taller in his seat. He looked around him, out the door, in the rear-view mirror, making sure there was no one about. Then slowly, meticulously, with scientific zeal, he pinched Sarah's breast. The little girl's agonized grimace, her silence, filled him with a strange, somewhat disquieting emotion that throbbed to the very tips of his fingers. He released her abruptly and began to scratch his beard pensively. And nice little legs, besides. *What if I were to adopt her, after all?* . . . The idea, which at first amused him but which he could not take seriously, suddenly alarmed him, and he stuck his head out the door.

"Are you coming or what?" he bellowed.

Remould appeared with the wheelchair in his arms and Séraphon in it. The chair was placed on the back seat and, sitting down beside it, Remould took Séraphon on his lap. There was a new smell in the car. Sarah had folded her legs up, wrapped her arms around them, and leaned her head on her knees. She could be heard sniffling quietly. The automobile sped away.

They crossed the former grounds of the wood yard. Mr. Judith could see Séraphon's haggard face in the rear-view mirror.

"Why don't you come stay with us, Mr. Tremblay?"

The old man seemed not to realize that he was being spoken to.

Remouald repeated the question. Séraphon moaned.

"As you wish," Judith said.

They were expected. Séraphon, Remouald, and Sarah were loaded onto the train, which was carrying bundles of felt from the mill — they could always stretch out on them should they have the urge to sleep. Sarah, who had not eaten since noon, was given some milk to drink. The manager thanked the stationmaster, who was thinking of his mortgage arrears. "Why, think nothing of it, not at all," he said.

Kneeling inside the wagon, Remouald looked at Sarah, Sarah looked at Remouald, and they smiled at each other. A railroad worker slid the door shut.

"It's dark," Séraphon whimpered.

"Life is like that," Remouald said.

They felt the train lurch into motion.

* * *

As soon as he crossed the threshold of his house Mr. Judith forgot the tribulations of the day. True, the next day's board meeting was of some concern, but the prospect of spending the evening without the little girl, alone with his wife, filled him with a sense of well-being. He bent down in the hallway to remove his boots. A shadow approached him on tiptoes and grabbed him by the crotch.

"Peekaboo!"

"Grrr . . . you little scoundrel! You don't realize how risky it can be to do such things."

Judith put his lips on the nape of his wife's neck, pretending to be a big, gluttonous bear. She seductively disengaged herself from his embrace and went off to the kitchen. Her body was moulded in a short, blue satin dress. Judith barked lustfully.

"You have the same ass you did thirty-five years ago!" he trumpeted. "Come back here right away so I can take a closer look!"

He heard her crystalline laughter fade away in the corridor.

He went into the parlour in a humming frame of mind. He took a cigar, spat out the end, and lit it. Then he flicked the match into the crackling fireplace. He sat down on the leather sofa, stretched out his legs, and felt young. He puffed on his cigar and twisted his earlobe as if working a pump: the smoke poured out of his mouth in rings — a gag he had seen performed at the music hall. Then he began to dream of pleasant things, letting his fantasy run free: the archbishop, at a reception, chortling at one of his jokes; the Minister of Finance recognizing him at a restaurant and inviting him to his table; the Mayor decorating him with the city's Order of Merit for having saved some orphans from a fire . . . when he heard the doorbell ringing. Judith scowled with displeasure.

His wife went to open the front door. He heard a cry of surprise, then laughter, an excited and confused babble of voices. Who could it be? His wife came into the parlour. Pale as a corpse, nostrils flared, quivering all over — as a rule it was only in bed, just before her bliss, that she looked like this.

"What is going on, Simone?"

She was speechless. She raised her arm limply and pointed toward the vestibule. The visitors appeared, smiling.

"Forgive us for this surprise visit, after so many years, but since we were in the neighbourhood . . . Now, Uncle, I don't believe you've ever met my husband, Alphonse Tétreault. And here, this little pest is my daughter, Sarah. Come Sarah, be nice. Cat got your tongue? Say hello to my uncle and aunt!"

The little girl, whom Judith and his wife had never seen, was hiding behind her mother's skirt. She uttered a shy hello.

Mrs. Judith remained dumbstruck in the middle of the room. She finally whispered:

"But the letters, Julie . . . that telegram . . ."

"Letters, Aunt? What letters?"

"But, Julie, how is it . . . ?"

Simone heard a dull thud behind her.

Uncle Judith had just blacked out.

12

IN THE COLD and the dark, the clamminess and the rolling of the train, the wind spilled through the gaps in the sides of the car, snoring like a jailer bloated with wine. There were abrupt jolts, and the felt bundles tumbled down from their shelves and bounced on their heads in a shower of dust. Piercing and furious and monotonous and unrelenting, the wheels ranted on. Rocked by the slow swaying of the car, they heaved over the track joints as though buffeted at five-second intervals by a small wave of nausea.

The stops were few, and each time the question: is this the one? Sarah's hand sought his. She squeezed it, let it fall, lost it. Then sought it once again, like a patient losing her memory. And Séraphon, wrapped in the manager's fur coat, whimpering sporadically like a dog dreaming.

It lasted an incalculable length of time. Overcome by the rocking, Sarah eventually brought up the milk that the stationmaster had fed her. The sour, pasty odour of an infant's vomit. Remould wiped his bespattered hand on his trousers. Séraphon slept. He gave off a smell of kidneys. Remould hugged Sarah against himself. None of them knew where they would end up, what awaited them, what they would do there. They had been sent far away; they accepted this unquestioningly. The three of them were fated sooner or later to find themselves together like this, Remouald thought.

Screech of steel. The train once again coming to a halt. As before, they waited. Hoping they had reached their destination, yet, at the same time, that it might be even farther, even more remote, on the far side of the earth. The door of the car opened. A fine spray of snow gusted inside, hard as star salt. Remouald rubbed his eyes. With infinite respect he unknotted Sarah's arms from around his neck — she had fallen asleep enfolding him with her whole body — then, exhausted and stiff, he climbed down from the train.

He was greeted by a clear, sumptuous night, embroidered in princely fabrics and hang the expense. Remouald took a few moments to register the shock. Swollen and glittering, shot with green and blue: the belly of a fly about to lay its eggs. He turned his thoughts to the sky in his favourite stained glass window in church, so beautiful as to be excruciating: the Wise Men on the road to Bethlehem. There were woods on either side of the field, dark and dense to the left, and to the right, farther away, more sparse and receding into the mountainside. In between, the snow stretched as far as the eye could see. No dwelling place was anywhere visible.

The railwayman instructed Remouald on the route he must take. It was straight ahead, through the field, about an hour's walk. All they had to do was follow the edge of the woods on the left. They would come to the top of a hill; there they would see a huge house with vaulted windows, like a convent: the sanatorium. You could not miss it. Remouald pretended to listen but did not hear. The landscape entered him through the eyes and mouth and filled his ears with a sort of droning.

He got Sarah to come out, her eyelids still heavy. The railwayman helped him carry Séraphon out. Wrapped in the beaver fur, the old man looked around uncomprehendingly. Remouald also unloaded the wheelchair.

"It won't work," said the railwayman.

"What's that?"

"Your mother. You can't trundle her about like that in a wheelchair." The man spat out his wad of tobacco. "At times you'll be walking knee-deep in snow. You won't be able to budge that chair. Do you understand what I'm saying?"

Remouald did not reply. He was looking at the moon. Quivering, full of luminous wrinkles, it seemed to have been forgotten there amid the mountains, abandoned like a glass slipper.

All that could be heard was the panting of the train.

"Hold on a minute," said the railwayman. "I've got an idea."

He went off in the direction of the locomotive.

"Do you think you can walk?" Remouald asked Sarah.

"Where are we?" said Séraphon.

These anxious words were the first he had pronounced since they had left.

Sarah reassured Remouald.

"Sure you're not cold?"

No.

"Where are we?" Séraphon repeated.

"In Hell," Remouald answered.

His father wriggled in his seat like a maggot.

The railwayman came back with a sharp-edged object on his shoulders. A sled.

"You'll be far better off with this."

He paused.

"By the way, is it your mother or the little girl you're taking to the sanatorium?"

"Children's pyjamas," Remould replied, "with musical scores printed on them."

He was looking at the sky.

The railwayman pouted delicately, in a way that meant, "Let's pretend I never said a word."

"Anyhow, here, this is the rope. You just pull the sled with it."

Remould pondered for a long time before asking, "What about the wheelchair? What are we going to do with it?"

"I could leave it in the village, and you could pick it up some other time."

"There won't be another time."

"I could take it back to Montreal, if you like. I'll entrust it to your friend the stationmaster."

"Tell him to give it to Father Cadorette."

The man promised he would.

They laid Séraphon on the sleigh. Strapped him down. The old man looked like a hunted beast: Where are they taking me? Who are these people? Where could Remould be? Sarah waited, playing unhappily in the snow.

They were ready now.

"I advise you not to dally along the way. Take advantage of this opening. It's a clear night, the weather is still fairly mild. But hurry, before it gets overcast. Otherwise you won't be able to see a thing."

Remould looked at the clouds, as yet stationary, coiling in on themselves, seeming to champ at the bit and to rear with impatience.

"Goodbye," Remould said.

"Wait, just one more minute."

The man went to the head of the train. He returned with a package, which he opened.

"Here. An oil lamp. And here are some matches. This may come in handy."

Remould handed over a few of the matches to Sarah. Not knowing what to do with the lamp, he finally wedged it between his father's thighs.

"Goodbye, sir."

"I wish you good luck. And don't forget: straight ahead! As though you were following a rifle bullet. Let the woods be your guide!"

They were no longer listening to him. The man went back to his locomotive carrying the wheelchair. Before climbing back up he cast a final glance their way. Remould was leaning into the effort of hauling the sled. Behind him Sarah moved unevenly, in zigzags, hopping like a cold-footed sparrow in the snow.

The railwayman warmed his hands by the purring stove. He uneasily eyed the clouds on the horizon. *So long as the wind doesn't rise*, he thought.

There were three whistle blasts, the baying of an animal, the squeal of the tracks, and in a billow of steam gushing from every corner of the locomotive, the train started away again.

The wind rippled through the forest in a vast mare-like shiver.

* * *

REMOUALD HUFFED AS he pulled the sled, pausing occasionally to raise his eyes toward the clouds. It had been fifteen years since he had last seen the countryside, and everything was bursting with bigness, with deepness, as though the night were making itself at home, having fled from the cramped corridors of the city. He looked around him, dazzled, awestruck by so much space. The country seemed to be hooked onto the firmament by the treetops. There was sky from one end of the earth to the other. There was no room left for suffering, no room for anyone — the giant beings, primal in their simplicity, their indifference, occupied the whole space, had regained possession of the universe. Remouald was a speck of life adrift in the infinite.

He strove to keep to the forest's edge. It was getting colder by the minute, and darker as well. The snow came up to their calves, sometimes to their knees. Streaks of snow crossed the sky, sparkling, diamantine; they were great anonymous dreams, dreams that on this night no one would have, dreams escaped from prison, which passed majestically, mysteriously above their heads.

Sarah advanced erratically, higgledy-piggledy, stopping to wave expansively, as if giving orders to the clouds. Remouald asked her to stay close to him; the clouds were the colour of ashes, they looked as stern as judges, and he was afraid for Sarah. But the little girl insisted on keeping to her own path, which went in every direction. He saw her jumping with both feet, as though defying the sky and trying to leap to where he was. She plunged into the darkness, excited and giggling, playing hide-and-seek with companions that existed for her alone.

Soon Remouald felt neither cold nor tired. His perseverance had turned to euphoria. His body had been transformed into something infinitely free, and he himself was now nothing but an intoxicated will. He moved forward blindly, borne along by some grandiose and mad adventure of which he had only a vague notion and in which each of his steps, breaking through the crust of the snow, plunged him knee-deep in stars.

"Where are you taking me?" Séraphon asked.

"Nowhere. Up there, ahead."

Séraphon recognized the voice.

"Is that you, Remouald? Oh, my little boy. What's happening to us? Where are we? I'm afraid."

Séraphon waited in vain for a response.

"There are so many things I would like to say to you, Remouald. So many things . . . To have a good talk one of these days, my little Remouald, my son . . . You know what I thought about the other day? I thought about the kitchen cabinet . . . the one with the padlock . . . You never knew . . . Nor your mother. Yet I must tell you . . ."

His voice had grown so faint that Remouald could barely hear him.

"There is nothing to say, Dad. There hasn't been anything to say for twenty years. I have an appointment — that is all I know. An appointment in the house of oaths, the house of my childhood."

The wind lifted the snow and flung it in his face. Séraphon sobbed and asked to be forgiven.

"The stars have lost the race, Dad. We will reach the sky before them," Remouald said.

He felt like laughing as children laugh.

"So, are we there?" said Séraphon. "Is it here, then?"

The ensuing half-hour of silence lasted forever.

* * *

THE CLOUDS, WHICH had invaded the sky, appeared to lie on the earth like the body of a man on that of a child. It was impossible to see anything two paces ahead. Sarah struck her matches and planted them in the snow. They flared for a moment, then went out. Remould stopped. He had lost sight of the little girl. The sled, propelled by its own momentum, knocked gently against his calves.

"Sarah! I can't see where you are any more! Light a match! Sarah!"

His call ricocheted from every tier of the mountain, sifted through the snow, returned empty-handed . . . Remould picked up the rope and set off again. He could not distinguish any footprints in the snow. The sled now seemed weightless to him.

SUDDENLY HIS HEAD bumped against a tree and he lost his balance. He realized he had gone astray and he looked around him. It was completely dark. The only sound he heard was that of his own breathing.

The snow had begun to fall. He felt it without seeing it, covering his face, his shoulders, dropping down his collar. He called again. He saw a brief glimmer among the trees.

"I am here!" he cried.

He fell into a fit of coughing.

He remembered the oil lamp and groped about for it. It was difficult to light. In the blossoming glow, Séraphon's face appeared. His fur hat had slid down over his cheek; his left eye was closed, the other gazed into the void, he had rime on his lips and in his nostrils. His skin was the colour of stone, with touches of blue. Remouald stood up and raised the lamp over his head.

"Look, Sarah! I'm here! Come back!"

There was another flicker issuing from the depths of the forest. It went out almost immediately.

"Hold on tight, Dad. The going will be a little harder now."

Remouald took up the rope of the sled and entered the wood.

The flickers reappeared, scattered and unpredictable. One flared up behind him, obliging him to retrace his steps. They set alight the treetops like St. Elmo's fires. He careened down ditches, stumbled, scraped his face and fingers on fir needles, and went on. The sled nearly capsized several times. They came upon a clearing.

In the centre of the copse was a broken-down cabin, a loggers' cabin. It had a dirt floor, a roof riddled with holes, and it contained only branches stacked in faggots. He pulled the sled up to the cabin. He had walked for such a long time that he had no idea where he might be. "Sarah will come back," he told himself. "She will see our light." The snow had stopped falling. He felt confident. This is where he had been bound. For twenty years, this had been the appointed meeting place.

Séraphon's head had dragged through the snow and the muck of dead leaves: he was lying half out of the sled. Remouald righted him again, swathed him in the fur coat that had opened to the waist, and gave him back the lamp.

"Are you cold?"

He had sat down a little farther, with his back against a log.

"Are you cold?" he asked again.

Séraphon's body blended with the lines of the sled. His neck was broken and his chin rested on his chest. Remouald imagined a severed head placed on a table beside a lamp.

"You wanted us to talk, eh? Well, there are a few things I could tell you, too, Séraphon my old friend."

". . ."

"Sarah may have lost her way, and we are also lost, but that does not matter any more. Do you hear me, Séraphon?"

Many minutes passed without a word being said. Through the crooked planks of the roof the stars swirled their lights. Remouald was less and less able to feel his limbs, which were slowly succumbing to the cold. It was good to be in this copse, in this cabin, sheltered from the vast spaces, and from time, perhaps. Nothing now had any weight, thoughts floated within him, a little of him was in each of them. He no longer felt anything but an irresistible urge to sleep.

He turned toward Séraphon. The lamp was askew and there was oil spilling from it. A circular flame was spawned in the old man's coat of fur.

"I knew you were aware of what was going on in the hut when I ate with Wilson. Because from where I sat the mirror let me see your face in the framework. And that night — I mean on the night of the Immaculate Conception — Lord, how you bolted! . . . There, that's all I wanted to say to you. Lord, how you bolted! . . . But I bear you no grudge, Séraphon. I no longer bear you any grudge."

Remouald closed his eyes. Yes, Sarah would come back. *Whatever happened, from now on, he knew, Sarah would always come back.* He had the impression he could hear her steps, out there, among the branches. There was a noise of shattering glass. Remouald turned his head toward his father. In a single swoosh Séraphon's whole body was set ablaze.

Remouald closed his eyes again.

He did not quite know where he was any more. Images came back to him — the Grill aux Alouettes, the fire — images as sharp as photographs. The barman had placed the icon of the Virgin behind the counter. A customer who had acquired it that afternoon had brought it. Everyone came to kneel clownishly before it. It was a harmless joke. But the drunks repeated it relentlessly, more and more grotesquely, trying to outdo one another's buffoonery, and feelings that had until then remained unfamiliar to him took shape inside Remouald: vexation, exasperation, a muted desire to put an end to the foolishness once and for all. He offered to buy the icon. The little money he had in his pockets he laid on the table. He was shaking. They laughed in his face: you could get three times that amount at the second-hand store! Remouald went out covered in scorn — desperate, revolted, irrevocably at odds with life, smothered by the sensation that up to that point the universe had done nothing but mock him. In the stairway he came across a very short, thickset man, his face all jaws and snout. He asked Remouald if he had any matches. And yet, Remouald had seen the jerry cans of gasoline.

"In any case, I was not put on earth to save anyone," he mumbled, and he closed his eyelids more tightly.

The cabin started to burn; the flames crackled among the dry branches. It was like birdsong in the morning, tender and peaceful. He experienced that nascent dizziness that would come over him as a child when the ride in the amusement park was set into motion, his mother's hand trying until the very last moment to hold him back — that instant when he would at last abandon himself to the movement — and the entire world began to spin; after a while he would no longer know where his body ended; he had the impression he was leaving the earth, falling into the middle of the sky, carried away in a whirlwind of clouds and blue — and that laughter, singing in his ears, Célia's laughter.

The flames crept closer. This was, he knew, the beginning of the agony. But this beginning was the end of another agony that had lasted twenty years. Twenty years of a greedy, petty agony, during which each second called out for the great, ultimate agony as for a liberation. Twenty years of a sentence to live in the hope of atonement. Yet now, just when all hope was exhausted, that mercy which he had despaired of ever earning was granted him. He welcomed the punishment gratefully. The heat reached his feet, his knees, ascended his thighs: his body would suffer. But from this suffering he had nothing to fear. He was prepared for the reconciliation, prepared like a traveller on the pier who has waited, valise in hand, for twenty years. The flames raised their towers as high as Forgiveness. He would never have believed the sky could rise to such a height.

All the moments of his life gathered around him, everything he had lived through in confusion, every event and every crisis, all of it suddenly took up its proper position, like notes on a staff. Remouald opened his eyes. The firmament itself was nothing now but a musical score. But this was nothing yet: he all at once recognized the place where he was. He was no longer in the loggers' cabin. He was in the votive chapel that he had built near the factory wall. And that little chapel had grown to be as vast as the world! He would not have thought it possible — it was unhoped for. He had taken boards, a hammer, some nails, and, alone, in the far corner of the yard, with his own hands and the wish to silently bear witness to everything he had endured, he had built a palace that reached to the stars.

"Thanks," he murmured.

And in the centre of that world, of that cathedral raised up by the flames, there shone the face of the Virgin of the Musical Scores. He saw her. She was laughing like a young girl who has been presented with the child to whom she has just given birth, full of wonder at the joy of loving. And Remouald abandoned himself to that laughter. *He found himself at last in that instant before time, that instant that had preceded the beginning of time for him, when Remouald was nothing, when no one was anyone yet.* That time before time when he lay in his crib and his mother leaned over him laughing. An entire life could not succeed in erasing that laughter, in erasing the memory that he had been the object of that joy, and at last he understood. He understood that that laughter was Memory itself and that the crime he was expiating was, above all, that of having wanted to forget. Now all was clear, as on the first morning. He had tried to forget that laughter. Now he recalled everything, even the worst things, even the ghastly things, with a kind of gladness. The horror that had encased him in ice for twenty years had melted, and for the first time he breathed without feeling an evil hand, his own hand, crushing his heart. The Virgin watched over the fire, she perked up the flames with small, indulgent touches, as one touches up a bouquet. Joachim, his father, was in the habit every night when Remould came back from school of washing Remould's hands, and after the meal they would dance a jig and his mother, sitting in her rocking chair near the stove, would laugh and keep time by clapping her hands.

The flames glided over Remould's skin, caressing him. He half opened his eyes, closed them again, opened them anew, like a happy child falling asleep in the arms of someone he loves. He felt as though he were between two worlds: a world that already no longer existed and another world that did not yet exist, that perhaps might never exist. But which present? which future? These words no longer signified anything. The fire began to engulf his trousers, then his coat sleeve. He found the strength to search through his pockets. He wished to throw away whatever was in them, to be rid of it, no matter what it might be. He wanted to die like some legendary beggar, dispossessed of everything, his coat studded with stars. Forgiven. He pulled out a lottery ticket that he did not recognize. It seemed to him like an enigma of awesome proportions, a Number that perhaps might bear on the very secret of the universe . . . He gave it up to the fire, to the scorched grass, resigned to letting the mystery elude him — was there anyone who, at the moment of their extinction, could claim to have understood everything?

Remould clutched the rabbit's foot in his fist as he went to sleep. And his smile radiated intelligence.

13

(The first part of this document has no bearing on the story.)

So, just imagine, on that very afternoon I went down to City Hall. I never go there without donning a pair of gloves (the doorknobs are always greasy), and I try to look as ingenuous as can be — Aladdin entering a palace in A Thousand and One Nights.

One of these days, if He Who Does Not Exist grants me the opportunity, I will speak in praise of the corridors — their human dimensions, the impression they give of always leading Somewhere, that there are places worth going to — and the stairways, which are their giraffe-like extensions. As for the doors, only when opened at random can they be fully savoured. Behind them, greenish beings with tadpole skulls, preserved in the formaldehyde of formalities, show me the way — always the right one, never the same one — with a curling of the lips. Some of them, when I approach, crawl back even farther into the depths of the damp shadows where the gestating cocoons and the archives slumber: I disturb them in the middle of laying their eggs. More corridors (the same perhaps), a staircase. A door opening onto a hallway that opens onto another hallway, which in the end opens onto a lavatory — I am not making this up. Retreat toward the central corridor. Perspiration and nervous tension. I retrace my steps. And just when I collapse on a bench no doubt intended for that purpose, my brow in a sweat, sagging under the weight of dereliction — suddenly the star of Bethlehem! a sign, arrows — THE *door, at last.*

I enter. I proceed along some desks where a galley-folk, scribes of a sacred language, hands flecked with pink due to ritual anemia, dream of improbable, obsessive, minuscule exceptions and investigate the hidden meaning of things (paper clips are unbent, bent anew, mysteriously), chained to the chairs at the calves, mucus-eyed, pecking at ink spots and ingurgitating preserves of paper that ruin the appetite and damage the liver. I notice one sucking pensively on his pencil, which he holds with both hands like a flute (I expect at any moment to see surfacing from among the stacks of file folders, the mesmerized, obtuse head of a python). Finally, I arrive, bedazzled and trembling, about to slip into a trance, at the holy of holies, the throne of desks in whose direction all the others are pointed like prayer rugs. There the Toad Queen sits.

A venerable figure in shirt sleeves, plump, bedecked with bow-tie and fob watch, both out of fashion even thirty years ago (but here time has stopped, frozen to the bone); plump, indeed, ample, covering an area of twelve square feet, four high by three wide; sympathetic and cynical (sympathetic in deploring the unjust consequences of a regulation, cynical in applying it nevertheless); a skull as smooth as a buttock, marvellous lamp that one must rub to release the genie of the Civil Service — the Queen can read a person's mind. She interrupts my explanation with an august wave of the hand, indulgent, as one might be toward a child, of my clumsy attempts at speaking her delicate language full of arcane refinements, whereby a comma can shake kingdoms to their very foundations. She has already been apprised, she knows all, I defer; she rises and disappears behind a bookcase. I wait. I let my gaze wander. I admire these drones gathering their ration of nectar from their assigned paperwork, their brains simmering, concocting the honey they will later disgorge into drawers. I start. A head rises: a civil servant has just been visited by the idea of a Reform — a napping cow abruptly standing on its hind legs, eyes fixed.

Albert Cousinet — that is the name of the Queen — has returned. Across the surface of his ink-starred blotter — in a gesture of nonchalant familiarity — his short, pudgy fingers slide toward me the forms on which, in order to obtain what is coming to me, I set down, in two burin-like strokes, my signature. I am handed a carbon copy. The Queen files the documents in a folder, sacerdotal in its griminess. She has the beneficence to bid me goodbye. I get up. And through the magic emanating from the Superior Manes, keepers of fabulous secrets, the door behind her leads directly to the exit on Rue Notre-Dame.

Thus, the two bodies were to be delivered to me that very Saturday.

There is no true captain but the one who can perform every task on his ship — the ordinary seaman's as well as the helmsman's — who knows the yard and the ropes as well as the sextant; that is why I enjoy loading a corpse on my shoulder, as in the days when I was my father's ship's boy. Soucy assisted me and we went down into the cellar. We took them out of their burlap bags with professional caution. The bodies gave off a stifling odour. Soucy took down the bottle of ammonia from the shelf and proffered a mask to me. I brushed it aside and asked to be left alone.

How can I describe the warped flesh, mummified by the flames, covered, as it were, with a layer of tar? I don't see this sort of thing every day. Unusual protrusions, startling contours, and novel, elegant, inexplicable cavities — one wonders how a fire manages to discover all of this. The different body tissues — lungs, liver, guts, and callus — do not all burn alike. Shreds of skin, not very attractive, curl up like garlands and wrap themselves around bone; or desiccated flesh, fragile as dead leaves, dangles and needs to be cut with scissors. I scratch the tip of my nose thoughtfully.

One of them, the younger, the taller one, has stiffened into a curious posture. He is sitting, legs apart, knees slightly bent, arms opened as though he were receiving a spray of flowers — his left hand is closed in a fist; head tilted back, neck swollen, like a force-fed goose, he is looking skyward. One cannot tell whether his mouth is open or shut. His features, though substantially altered, have nevertheless retained a kind of expression of . . . I was about to say enthrallment; of tranquility, at any rate, and (do not laugh) of piety. When one considers what his final moments must have been like, an expression of this sort is enough to make a man wonder. On the other hand, this may be nothing more than the effects of the disfigurement.

As for his father, he puts me in mind of those recent paintings you described to me and which are supposed to be all the rage in New York, that scandalized billionaire of a town: one must scrutinize him at length in order to distinguish where the skull is, where the hands are, where the feet are. After a while, one gets caught up and begins to search for the ears, the nose, the two eyeholes (I cheated: I used my fingers). This corpse, if truth be told, no longer resembles anything. A log perhaps, a scorched tree trunk. I will most likely be unable to do very much with it, no matter how skilled I may be. The piece has been cooked like a ham, wrapped in its fur. I have no idea, moreover, why he is tied up this way, like a sausage. He himself must not have been any the wiser when he died. In short, may God rest his soul. There must, after all, be a little bit of it left.

I step closer and bend down toward the more interesting son. I assess the sort of work that will have to be performed on him, not to make him presentable — it is understood that we will not show him to anyone — but he must at least be straightened out in order to fit into the coffin. This will be no mean feat. With that affectionate, playful familiarity I am known for, I pinch the tip of his nose and tell him in a reassuring voice, "All's nil that ends nil." The nose comes off between my thumb and index finger . . . (let that be a lesson to me). I look at his closed fist. Taking a screwdriver, I pry it open as though it were an oyster: the brittle bones give way, and inside, almost intact, I discover a rabbit's foot. "Gain not base gains; base gains are the same as losses." And I am, as you know, an Honest Man. But good-luck charms, like women, bring bad luck if they are spurned. I slip the rabbit's foot into my pocket.

At this point, I have no idea that these two corpses will from one day to the next become local celebrities. As they lie side by side on my table, withdrawn into themselves, bonded by some enigmatic understanding, like two chunks of scoria thrown up by the same volcano, every newspaper in the city is already talking about them. They were found near the village of Saint-Aldor. They are presumed to have gone astray in the woods, and then, no one knows why — exhaustion, no doubt — they burned in a cabin, to all appearances unaware that it stood only a few paces from the open field (I thought you might enjoy the irony of the situation). A fresh snowfall prevented the *fire from spreading to the rest of the forest, a testimony to God's goodness. Apparently, it is the priest, said to be at death's door, who insisted they be returned to the parish.*

Now, the real nugget in this whole business is that they were accompanied by a little girl of whom not a trace has been found. Intensive search efforts involving the entire local community have so far proved fruitless. In a word: Gone! Vanished into thin air!

She had hitherto been believed to be the niece of Mr. Judith, that cuckolded poltroon originally from Lyon — I have told you about him — who passes for our bank manager. Well, it turns out that is not the case. Mr. Judith's real niece, whose name is indeed Sarah, showed up at his home in the meantime, in the company of her father, who Judith thought was dead, and of her mother, who Judith thought was dying in a sanatorium. I realize that, presented this way, all of this must seem rather muddled, and yet, in point of fact, that is how it is. Mr. Judith has since withdrawn to the country, on compulsory sick leave, and his psychiatrist forbids the press from speaking with him. I have been told his wife never leaves his side, not so much in order to comfort him, I believe, as to latch on to something herself, because she fears for her husband's condition, and when she is afraid — I know her quite well, and I mean that in all senses of the term — her husband is her only refuge. I had some flowers delivered, along with my wishes for a speedy recovery.

Nothing more was needed to stir the popular imagination. You know the folks of Hochelaga. Spirit-rappers are a local specialty. Knots of people began to prowl around the victims' house. Anyone and everyone had a story to tell. Neighbours claimed to hear repeated thumps through the walls, or to notice luminous balls around their windows, which upon bursting released pestilent odours. The latest rumours have it that the old man had been dead for ages and that his ventriloquist son lived for years with the gaffer's remains. Get the picture? One continues to hear all manner of nonsense. Children pester their parents to be taken to see the Haunted House.

The cobbler's son, more daring than most, managed to get inside the house, expecting to find who knows what there — perhaps a sorcerer's instruction book, the Holy Species of Magic. The police had to assign an officer to watch the front door. The boy, however, asserts that he noticed a padlocked cabinet inside the house — what could it possibly contain? Some reporters seized on the affair, which was dubbed the Case of the Padlocked Cabinet. The police have refused to comment; the cabinet will be unlocked in due time.

All of this to demonstrate how small the world is, for, you see, the two individuals lived in the house of your childhood, 1909 Rue Moreau.

I HAVE SPENT the entire night writing this to you, dear Rogatien; the sun is coming up, and the two corpses are ready, on either side of the pages you are now reading; in a few hours they will go off to the church. As for me, I am going to sleep a while, to refresh myself, for I expect the day to be an exciting one. The air has been electric since yesterday, a pre-storm atmosphere that has the neighbourhood buzzing like a sheet of tin. You see, tonight, December 8, the feast day of the Immaculate Conception, in the courtyard between the police station and the fire hall, they are going to execute the man who burned down the Grill aux Alouettes. Things may turn ugly. There was a scuffle last Thursday at the Hudon spinning mill. A group of workers opposed to capital punishment came face to face with another group who were demanding retribution and had rallied round the brother of that Blanchot fellow (you know, the one to whom I sold your icon and who perished in the blaze). Punches were thrown, and some property was damaged. The police had to step in.

In any case, the person who stands to gain the most, as always, is yours truly, since the firebug will end up here tonight, on this table where I am setting down these last few lines. As a matter of fact, I have completely remodelled this room — all in the most modern style — you ought to see it. It will be an inauguration of sorts. A housewarming with a still-warm hanged man! And here is where I leave off.

[WRITTEN A FEW hours later, just before going to the execution grounds.] I am enclosing the neighbourhood newspaper, as you requested (I suppose it is for your novel); it is hot off the press. You will note the banner on the front page: "WINNER OF THE LITTLE MAURICE LOTTERY STILL SOUGHT." By way of explanation: a lottery had been organized for the orphan of a fireman; the winning number was drawn last Friday, but the ticket-holder has still not come forward; he is being given one last chance, until tomorrow. There, now you know everything.

Now, I was about to forget the most important thing. Justine Vilbroquais — your "sister" as you say — came to see me earlier at my office! We had not spoken for the longest time. Without taking the time to say hello, she snapped, "Would you mind telling me what's gotten into that old codger, writing to me after twenty-five years?" (So, my dear Rogatien, when I informed you that she had come back to the neighbourhood, I was not speaking to a brick wall.) She is no longer young, of course, but her gaze has not changed since you rendered it on the icon; it is just as blue, just as striking. She appeared nervous, somewhat embarrassed by her attire, and that is understandable: her skirt is as criss-crossed as a railway map for having been mended so often; around her neck she wears a leprous fox as stiff as a three-day-old sock. I thought back to her younger days, when she dreamed of a career, do you recall? Tours, ovations, bouquets carried on stage by little girls, wrenching breakups with Russian princes in every European capital . . . I asked her what had brought her back to the parish, after all these years. She whipped her fox around, as if to screw her head on tighter. She lost her husband recently, and then her son. Nothing compelled her to come back, other than the lack of anything better. We spin and spin, Rogatien, we drift giddily toward the peripheries, then, drawn, sucked by the depths, we finally fall back into the same hole, we are nothing but a marble in a funnel. This will not come as news to a morphine addict like yourself.

But it was not for my pretty face that she came to visit me. She had a message for you. It seems you had asked her to meet you? Well, you may as well forget it, old man. As for the letters you wrote her, she told me to tell you she has thrown them down the drain.

Do not be too upset by this, Rogatien. All of us have in some corner of our lives someone who, without saying a word, would publicly slap us in the face, yet in whose presence we would nevertheless lower our eyes in shame. That is how it is for everyone.

R. Costade
Businessman

P.S. By the way, have you just about finished your novel? I gather, based on your last letter, that our dear Vilbroquais will be one of the characters. With your "vow" as the epigraph, I think this would make a nice title, wouldn't it: The Tidings Brought To Justine*!*

Do finish it for December 22, her birthday; it would please her so much, I am sure.

* * *

CLÉMENTINE CLÉMENT, WHO had been feeling queasy since that morning and had not been able to swallow anything but a little broth at noon, was once again overcome by dizziness. She had to hold on to the prie-dieu.

The students of École Langevin filled the pews to the left of the nave. Those on the right were reserved for the little girls of École Marie-Reine-des-Coeurs. Her colleagues, Miss Robillard and Mrs. Désilets, lighted votive candles, while Misses Baril and Pichette, kneeling behind them, recited the rosary. All this for the repose of Guillubart's soul, Clémentine well knew, but, no, she would not light any votive candles for the repose of Guillubart's soul. Her mind was now quite made up concerning this sort of sham; her fellow teachers could think whatever they liked, she had sworn to herself she would have no more to do with it.

The new vicar, in the ambulatory, ambled about, showing signs of agitation. He had been assigned to the parish in the wake of Father Cadorette's heart attack. He was a small priest, recently ordained, easily embarrassed on the subject of women, motivated to the point of trembling by the wish to do well and as yet unpossessed of that authoritarian poise that constitutes 90 percent of a priest. Clémentine did not think kindly of him. He had retained the bloodshot eyes of the conscientious seminarian, tormented by his dreams, viewing everything as a trial, and still unclear at times as to what exactly His Saviour expected of him. For fear of not looking his part, he wore a pod of a beard, pasted below his lip like a cedilla. He paced up and down, head bowed, fiddling with his crucifix. This fidgeting annoyed the teacher. She would gladly have grabbed him by the chasuble and forced him to sit down with a cuff to the back of the head. She averted her eyes from the priest and inconspicuously stroked her belly.

The little saints were tardy in showing the tips of their wings. The delay was due, as every year, to the abundance and the meticulousness of the preparations that the Feast of the Immaculate Conception demanded: paper bouquets, cardboard halos, candles, and confetti, in accordance with how the good sisters and the teachers envisioned the joys of Paradise. A plaster Virgin awaited their offerings, her head crowned in candles. The boys were growing impatient. They elbowed each other, smothered fits of laughter. Too weary to react, Clémentine did nothing to stop them.

Bradette, for one, could not keep still. He had been impudent and had clowned around incessantly; since that morning Clémentine had more than once held herself back from slapping him. She was also concerned about Rocheleau. He had looked so fraught earlier, subdued, more fragile than usual, on the verge of tears. He had run away from school during recess and had not come back.

Bradette suddenly rose and swaggered toward the statue of the Virgin. Miss Clément opened her eyes wide. He had taken a cigarette from his pocket and was about to light it off a candle. The schoolteachers, aghast, turned toward Miss Clément. Clémentine leaped up, to the extent she was able, and snatched the cigarette out of the child's hands.

"Do mind your pupils, won't you?" whispered one of her colleagues in a prim tone of voice.

Flushed with humiliation, Miss Clément crossed the nave tugging the student by the arm. She reached the pews to the rear behind the transept and roughly pushed Bradette into one of them. She sat down beside him, determined to mete out a penalty at the slightest bit of foolishness. The youngster put on an air of quiet superiority.

A lectern had been set up near the font. On it was placed the reproduction of a renowned maternity scene. Clémentine did not know who the painter was. But the face of the Virgin made a profound impression on her. What the pupils were taught, and what she herself had been taught just like them, about the simplicity of the Christ Child, his filial obedience, his admirable docility before the humble demands of each day, carrying Joseph's tool basket, helping his mother knead the bread, all of it appeared to be gainsaid by this picture, by Mary's sidelong, almost depressed way of looking at her son, arresting in its authenticity, which seemed to say, "Now, what new woes has this boy got in store for me?" The Virgin's lips were pressed tight, as though God's fingers had sewn them together, while Jesus, full of himself, an infant already set to lecture the whole world about life, turned a deaf ear to her.

Clémentine Clément closed her eyes. Poor Mary. For centuries now she had been endlessly celebrated, honoured with the most eminent names, yet she remained the great forgotten figure of the Gospels. The Annunciation, the weeping at the foot of the Cross: a fistful of sand, nothing at all. Despite the supernatural quality of her fertilization, the hand of the Father, as far as one could tell, had not spared her the all too corporeal pain of birthing. Had she been given foreknowledge of the horrible end awaiting her son? The nails transpiercing the bones, the final humiliation? How delightful to give birth being aware of all that, and in a manger to boot. Who knows what she may have told him as she nursed, when she was so near to him that God Himself could not hear what she said? Perhaps she beseeched him. To pay no attention to the affairs of the world, to not cast his nets beyond the humble bounds life had allotted him in having him born a carpenter's son. But he had only to look at her, with those eyes emanating their awful intelligence, to silence her. She smiled faintly, with infinite sadness. He, his eyelids lowered, continued to suck peacefully on the gourd of flesh.

Yet perhaps she in fact did not know. For it would have been a miscalculation on God's part. Mary believed simply in what she had heard in her dream, that her son was called by an uncommon destiny, and she reassured herself with sweet thoughts, hugging him closer to her bosom, repeating to herself that one day he would be a great prince, arrayed in precious cloths and stones, who would lead his people like Moses.

And he grew older, and taller, and became an adolescent of admirable beauty. His grace alone would have sufficed to make him famous throughout Galilee. Clémentine took pleasure in imagining the handsome man he must have been. Mary would have liked to know what was going through his head. About Yahweh, the prophets, and the rest — she had so many questions which stirred her with wonderment. She did not dare address the learned men. She had always known her place. But now that her son was himself to become a rabbi? While she prepared her cakes, she tried unobtrusively to engage him in conversation. Lying on his stomach, his nose buried in some scribbled notes, he answered with impatient mutterings. Mary did not insist. She told herself these great matters were no doubt not for her. She was careful not to make any noise that might disturb his sleep, after his nights of visions, dreams, and wakefulness. It meant falling behind in her chores, but no matter. She approached with measured steps, soundlessly, and knelt down close to him as he slept, to inhale, eyes closed, the heavy perfume of his blond hair.

When he left on his travels, she would let a few hours elapse and then go out in turn, following behind. He was so splendid that the women turned around as he passed. At the market she occasionally succumbed to the temptation of whispering to the female vendors, "That is my son, you know . . ." Then she would blush from so much vanity. Off he went, and she continued to follow, always in the rear, devoutly picking up a tassel which he had left behind. He was no doubt glad she followed him in this way; a good part of his performance was intended for her alone, perhaps. He never let on. When he came across her amid the crowds to whom he preached, he looked at her only with indifference and never said a word to her. He paid more attention to a prostitute whom he had met one day and who, also, now followed him. Sometimes they would exchange a vague smile. At night, when all were asleep, he and his disciples alike, Mary kept watch. She well understood that she had been deceived. True, she had not given birth to an ordinary individual, she had not been lied to on that account. He had a gift for magic. But she saw the turn events were taking. She fretted over the evil things that were said of him along the way, over the reproofs directed at him by the priests, who must after all have known what they were talking about, and who gathered together in grim conclaves. All Jesus's words were at odds with the religion in which she had been raised, in which she had believed her entire life.

Workless, always traipsing about with his friends, head-strong, proffering in an irritated tone of voice unbelievably pretentious proclamations, he repented only at the eleventh hour. Finally acknowledging the grief he had inflicted on Mary, as she wept at the foot of his cross, he pronounced the most touching, most humble of prayers, one that appeared to be an admission of defeat; he asked his disciple to regard her as his own mother. And in the end, after all the sacrifice, all the indulgence and silent consent, which had never been repaid, what did she obtain? A martyred corpse was laid in her arms, limp as an eviscerated frog, a base criminal, who died knowing it had all been a lie, that at the ultimate moment the one he believed to be his Father had forsaken him. It was raining. Her dress covered in mud, Mary sobbed on the breast of her only son who had sacrificed himself for a cloudland.

The apostles had used it all as grist for the mill, had fabricated a fantastic story; in short, fishermen boasting at the tavern. For a moment, Clémentine considered writing for herself a Life of Jesus, the Gospel revisited by a woman. She let herself be charmed by this idea, as sweet as revenge. Just a few days ago, such thoughts would have throttled her with terror. But now . . . (Clémentine stroked her belly. Smiled inwardly.) . . . Now she was *free*.

Clémentine realized she was attributing her own features to Mary — she opened her eyes again. She felt a cold mass on her thigh. Bradette had placed his hand on her knee. His eyes stared and he was panting. Clémentine thought he was about to vomit. She moved her hand close to his cheek . . . She was horror-struck. As he held her thigh, Bradette was engaged in the activity that little boys as a rule undertake only in bed, beneath the blankets, in total darkness. Clémentine flattened her hand against his face. Bradette pounced on her and tried to bite her breast. She toppled him and the two of them rolled into the aisle. Bradette stood up. He laughed hideously. He began to shout:

"I got you, you poor cow! I got you! I got you!"

The schoolteachers came running. Clémentine remained prostrate, appalled, stricken with disgust. Bradette looked about him. The aisle was blocked on one side by Miss Baril and on the other by Mrs. Désilets. Miss Pichette stepped toward him gingerly, moving sideways like a crayfish. Already, pupils were coming to lend a hand. Bradette strode over Clémentine and started to vault over the pews using the backs for leverage, nimble as a monkey whose yelps he actually imitated, in the throes of a demented exultation. He stopped suddenly.

"The Father, that's me! I am the Father!" he howled while thumping his chest with both fists.

His foot slipped on the back of the pew and he tumbled to the ground. Dazed, he had difficulty standing up again. Miss Robillard thought she could hold him down. He landed a punch to her lower abdomen. The teacher doubled over. Bradette made for the exit. The new vicar was waiting for him there, his cassock hitched up to his knees, in a wrestler's stance. Bradette slipped between his legs and the priest dropped on his backside. The church doors were flung wide, and there were the little girls of École Marie-Reine, their shoulder blades adorned with small paper wings. Bradette charged headlong. Halos went soaring, along with shreds of skirts; he sent the wings of half a dozen of them flying and some hair as well. The nuns frantically waded in. They sought him among the dishevelled white dresses, the beleaguered young girls, the cries of terror and surprise. Bradette was no longer there. Bradette had fled.

THE VICAR BEGAN to wonder into what madhouse of a parish he had landed. The seminary had not prepared him for such situations. The little girls stamped their feet and wailed at the top of their lungs. He announced to the nuns that he was cancelling the pageant. He straight away removed his chasuble. Then, bristling, he headed toward Clémentine.

The teacher had regained her pew. She sat with her hands crossed, elbows resting on her knees. She stared at the floor.

"Are you hurt?" he asked.

She made no reply. The young man rocked back and forth in his soutane. *A priest's hands cannot part for a moment without joining once again across his stomach*, she thought despondently. He had beautiful hands, slender and bony, like those of Brother Gandon. Clémentine had the impression she recognized them, and in spite of her efforts, with a spontaneity that revolted her, the tears welled up in her eyes.

The vicar exploded:

"What in the world did you do to that child?"

Clémentine shrugged. Her attention was focused entirely on her four colleagues assembled near the baptismal fonts.

"Please excuse me, Father."

She rose, casually pushing him aside, and walked directly toward them. The priest felt the sweat trickling down his neck. He tried to fall into step behind Clémentine but stumbled pathetically.

Clémentine grabbed Miss Robillard and swivelled her around. The others recoiled.

"When I have something to tell someone," she said, "I say it to her face."

She waited, arms folded.

"So then, you have nothing else to say? Cat got your tongue? Well, don't let me interrupt! I know very well what you say behind my back. That I'm the one who drove little Bradette mad! That I drove him mad just like I persecuted Guillubart until he fell ill! That's what you were telling each other, isn't it, go on, admit it. And that Rocheleau ran away this morning when I came near because he was afraid I would bite him! And that I was the one who sent Guillubart to his grave!"

Miss Pichette traded furtive glances with the other teachers, then delicately placed her hand on Clémentine's forearm, the gesture of a woman who understands another woman.

"Come, now, my dear Clémentine," she said softly. "Why would you imagine such things?"

Clémentine curtly disengaged herself.

"Oh, you of all people, don't you touch me! *I don't share the customs of your little girlfriends on Rue Darling.* As for the rest of you, you've always resented me, you've always envied me, because I was young, and pretty, and men turned their eyes in my direction, even priests, even my pupils, even Gaston Gandon!"

Clémentine abruptly fell silent; she was devastated. For weeks this was precisely what her colleagues had been waiting for. For her to get carried away, to break down, to confess. Miss Robillard wore a sly, triumphant smile. Clémentine decided not to give a damn about any of this.

"You can say what you like about me, have me thrown out of the school while you're at it, I don't care. Old maids like you don't have the slightest hold on me! Do you hear? *Not the slightest.* Poor you! If you only knew what has happened to me! If you only knew!"

She broke out laughing in a voluptuous, somewhat forced way, then left without a goodbye. The closing of the church door reverberated on the stone slabs.

"Oh, my dear Lord," said Miss Robillard, "it walks; it even talks!"

They found that one quite good, the schoolteachers did, and wiped away their tears of hilarity with old kleenexes. This was a special occasion. They decided to go all together for some pastries. Only Miss Pichette preferred to go home.

"At once!" chuckled Miss Robillard. "Let us go at once!" She mimicked a lame woman.

This was a breach of good taste, and it dampened their mood. They went to find the little vicar.

They found him in his chair in the sacristy, shattered, his cedilla trembling. The pupil named Carmel was standing near him.

The priest finally composed himself a little.

"Don't you understand? What the little Bradette screamed in the church, what he was trying to tell us. It's horrible. He bragged about it this morning to his friends. Go on, Carmel, repeat what you just told me."

Carmel, intimidated, pointed his nose downward, as though guilty of something. The vicar spoke instead of him, sobbing from time to time.

"That Miss Clément . . . Bradette says she is expecting! Do you hear? *He says she is carrying his child!*"

* * *

IN THE WAKE of her quarrel with Brother Gandon the previous week, Clémentine had stayed in bed for three days. For years she had been a trooper, withstanding hell and high water, buoyed by the idea that all *this* was merely a long and painful ordeal so that she might be worthy of Happiness, but now her reason for living, for struggling, had been run through the heart, and the rider thrown from her saddle. It was no use doing anything any more. She was resolved to stay just where life had abandoned her, her bitterness and rage directed at nothing, to not budge again, to pine away.

She left her bed only when driven by a malaise, a stiffness, a restlessness in her limbs, a train of thought. She nibbled whatever was at hand, moping about in her kitchen, her bathrobe undone, as though seeking to punish herself, to take revenge on herself, on Brother Gandon, ultimately on all the ugly things that lined her existence. And she neglected her hygiene in the same vengeful, disgusted spirit. She felt like that squashed wedge of lemon that had been stranded on her kitchen counter for a week.

The first night, the doorbell rang. It was Miss Robillard, come to ask after her. Clémentine had forgotten to advise the school of her absence. She opened the door no more than a crack, so that only the tip of her nose appeared. Miss Robillard tried to see over her shoulder. Clémentine said she was indisposed and would not be in class for the rest of the week. Miss Robillard went away with a mysterious air about her. Clémentine pulled a face when her back was turned.

Her sole longing was to sleep, but she managed to do so for only a few minutes at a time. Twenty-four hours a day she went through these aborted slumbers, dragging herself from the bed to the sofa, falling into fitful naps in the kitchen rocking chair. Seized at times by a brutal craving, a malicious fury, she pleasured herself. She panted, she panted, stifled a final groan in her pillow. Then her muscles relaxed and she burst into sobs.

Or she mused, rooted in front of the living-room window. Her gaze drifted among the debris of the Grill aux Alouettes. She mentally wrote and rewrote an interminable letter to Brother Gandon, by turns contrite, forceful, full of demands, imploring, vindictive, useless in the end, for it always died before reaching the page. Occasionally propelled to her desk by a wave of revolt, an inflamed vestige of pride, Clémentine took up a pencil and pulled a sheaf of blank paper from the drawer: she would pour her heart out, tell all, give a full account, name names! But after three pages everything became muddled, she had lost control, the pen fell from her hands, she went back to the sofa to lie down, racked by morbid tremors as though she had just committed a murder.

One night she surfaced from sleep, haunted by the noise of a kettle on the boil. She jumped out of bed, found nothing on the stove, then realized that that snoring kettle was her own head. She held it between both hands to muffle the vibrations. The most distant, most humiliating memories, the indistinct plots she sensed around her, lurking in the shadows like the eyes of wolves, the atrocious prospect of her future, all of it coursed through her again and again in a movement she was incapable of interrupting, of reining in with a *thought*. She felt in her stomach, in the pit of her bosom, a malevolent presence, thoroughly viscous and contorted. She succeeded in calming down through an act of will so painful she felt it in her bones; then she looked around in terror: she was sitting on the porch of the house next door, in her bathrobe, barefoot, with her bum in the snow.

FINALLY IT WAS Friday, and things changed altogether, a kind of peace swept over her.

She had suffered so much that it was like not suffering at all any more, as though suffering no longer had any meaning. Everything was on the same plane, levelled out. She hovered over her life with a tranquil gaze, like a disaster that has run its course, bounded in space and time. She felt no pity for herself, her own hurts no longer affected her, no longer weighed on her. She was as light as a hole.

Around her, her bedclothes emitted a noxious odour of fever and medication. An odour arose from her, too, of saliva on skin, one that had disgusted her as a child. Without moving from bed she looked through the window. It must have been around two o'clock in the afternoon. One could see the steady gleam of the clouds, an uncertain whiteness, and everything white in the room — the paper on the table, her shirt draped over the back of the chair, her sheets — reflected that luminescent, grey pallor.

In that instant she realized she would never suffer again.

And she saw herself sitting before her, as if she were facing someone else. She saw herself at the same time standing by the window. She heard herself moping about in the idiocy of her kitchen. She saw herself weeping as she wrote at her desk. From the middle of her bed, Clémentine saw all these figures of herself emerging one last time before vanishing one after the other into a nothingness from which nothing returned. Without any sort of emotion she proceeded to abolish these Clémentines, like a monarch who, having recaptured the throne, revokes each and every decree of the vanquished usurper. Clémentine-and-a-half was dead. She remembered a line of poetry she had read in the journal *The Rubicon of Lonely Souls*: "You called for the Night, it is descending, here it is." That was it exactly. Her Night was this Friday afternoon. The Great Deliverance at last. Henceforth, nothing could sap her strength. She felt hard, strong as wickedness, indifferent toward herself, free. She again looked through the window. She recognized in the colour of that sealed sky the definitive colour of her soul.

At this point she decided to go out. She felt the need to test her new shell — her brand-new, seemingly indestructible armour, the as yet undefined power she felt welling up within her — like the Japanese warriors of old who, it was said, impatient to try out a new blade, cut off the head of the first peasant to come along. That jubilant ferocity, that sovereign discounting of scruples, titillated Clémentine with a perverse shiver, and around eight o'clock, in a conquering frame of mind, she finally went out, with a cynical smile on her lips that placed her in a special breed and raised her in her own eyes to a superior rank.

But where to go? The destination she chose, or, rather, that forced itself on her, confirmed for her that she had indeed become an utterly different species of Clémentine. She would go downtown. Where there was a *nightlife*, where there were Americans from Chicago, where there were the big department stores, where the women wore satanic hats, smoked cigarettes as long as carrots, spoke English, and recounted the mad nights of New York and Paris. Clémentine boarded the trolley at the corner of Sainte-Catherine and Préfontaine. At the next station it was the captain of the fire brigade who climbed aboard. Their gazes met. She proudly averted her eyes. The captain took a seat at the back of the car. Clémentine adjusted her chignon.

She alighted at Rue Papineau and headed west. She sensed a presence behind her, looking at her; a strange warmth radiated over her, from the small of her back to the nape of her neck. She dared not turn around. How could the captain of the fire brigade, who had behaved so lamentably the night of Guillubart's death, stammering and whimpering, how could this man trouble her, trouble the woman she had become? No, she was not afraid of him. She hurried along and arrived with relief at the broad, brightly lit streets.

The illuminated signs, the throng, the holiday commotion: Clémentine was dazzled. She had never come this far at night. A hurried bit of shopping on a Saturday afternoon once every two years to refresh her wardrobe and a just as hurried departure, that was all.

But today, there she was. A delicious tension took hold of her. Everything drew her out of herself, called her to forget herself, to let herself swim on a great anonymous and wild surge of Happiness. It was enough to be there, to soak it all in. How simple it was. To become like these people, to be one of them. Her sole regret was to be so shabbily dressed: she realized she had unthinkingly put on her most thread-bare, mud-stained coat, which had buttons missing: she looked positively down-at-the-heels. She was sorry, also, that her body was perhaps not impeccably clean; and there and then, with startling violence and intensity, she was overcome by her perpetual fear of smelling bad. Clémentine floun-dered. She began to hug the walls. She tried to catch her own odour by surprise. She inspected her fingernails: they were black. She buried her hands in her pockets. She started to feel faint. How long since she had eaten last? She looked for a bench. The flowing crowd bore her along. She hesitated in front of a club: everything appeared so marvellous inside — the marble and glittering glass tables . . . In the end, she backed down, because a man seemed to have scoffed at her attire, a handsome fellow at that.

Clémentine went into a department store. She walked the aisles blindly, managing to kill a few quarters of an hour, and finally ended up in the lingerie department, where she blushed like a fool. She rushed outside. In the entranceway of another store she halted and watched the crowd stream by before her; breathless and dazed, she had the sensation that her whole person was falling to pieces and being set adrift. She needed to go in somewhere, anywhere, to go inside, sit down, try to be like everyone else. Were she to return home — to run away yet again, to run away as she had always done — she knew she would be unable to bear the sight of her face in a mirror. Clémentine fought back the urge to cry. She thought, *I must look demented, rooted like this in front of this door*; and that thought drove her onward.

She set off again. She tried to imitate someone who knew the area well, with no idea of the effect. There was a green glow filtering out through the windows of a café. Clémentine took a deep breath and stepped inside.

She felt like a chimney sweep entering the residence of His Lordship. A thick fog hung before her eyes. She sat down at the first empty table, located next to a column. She ordered a crème de menthe, and the waitress, whose makeup was beyond anything Clémentine could have imagined, looked at her as though she had just asked for the moon. Glancing around, Clémentine noticed the other customers were drinking nothing but beer. Nevertheless, a bottle of crème de menthe was fished out for her. The waitress set down a minuscule glass, for which she requested a sum that nearly knocked Clémentine out of her chair. She paid, telling herself this was how it was in fashionable spots and wanting above all not to appear unaware of this. The waitress gave her her change and remained standing near her, scratching the inside of her thigh. Clémentine wanted to know why she stayed there; she flashed a suppliant smile.

"Service is not included," was the waitress's comment.

"Why, of course, what was I thinking!" said Clémentine with a false laugh.

The waitress returned a disagreeable smile. Clémentine placed a few coins in her hand by way of a tip, ludicrous in the waitress's view. As she walked away, Clémentine heard her say to someone, ". . . and has the nerve to order crème de menthe, no less."

The schoolteacher began to sip from her glass. She did not have the courage to look around, with everyone surely pointing fingers and mocking her. What had become of that

Clémentine made of steel, armour-plated with her haughty indifference? "You called for the Night, look, Clémentine, here it is." An interior voice, so familiar in cadence, too close to her mother's, churned out its obsessive refrain: "Why can't you see yourself as you are, a lame, conceited, old maid? Get out of here! Run and hide! Hold on to at least a shred of dignity!" But her whole being rebelled with a terrible cri de coeur, and she found the strength to lift her head.

The captain was sitting directly in front of her, a glass of beer in his hand. His smile said, "I have been following you all along."

THEY SPENT THE evening talking, drinking a little, basking in each other's company, and laughing (laughing!). She had never seen him like this. He was another man, so poised, reassuring, attentive, appreciative of humour. The captain in fact spoke very little, occasionally making a few somewhat uncouth remarks, but he knew how to listen, he shored up her sense of her own importance. A good half of what she told him about herself was, moreover, fabricated, but she did not feel she was thereby deceiving him in any way; she made things up because the situation was made for it. She was not signing an affidavit before a judge; she was executing a *pas de deux*. Grace had gone dancing ahead of truth.

Pausing at times, she cast him a sideways glance like the flap of a wing, and she was off again. His fine, masculine nose, his dense moustache, his gaze inhabited by a somewhat bulky strength, but whose bulk was like a handful of good earth, everything about him inspired Clémentine, who by contrast felt a lightness that made her head spin. She discovered she had a talent for caricature. She mimicked the other teachers, their old maids' foibles, their small, pinched mouths, and in so doing enjoyed the pleasure of a woman displaying a bit of malice in the presence of man who is fond of her.

The captain paid for the drinks as they were served, each time leaving a tip amounting to three times what Clémentine had left earlier. After the fourth glass Clémentine's mood darkened, something she had not seen coming — a drop in the wind. She came close to slipping into confidences concerning her stillborn child. But at the last instant she was restrained by a sense of modesty and recovered her merriment almost intact. The time came to leave the café — that moment when coats are reluctantly put on again, when the little statements that make all the difference are uttered, those that echo the longest in memories, because they sum up, without seeming to touch on, what one would have wanted to be able to say, to have the courage to say in the preceding hours.

She said, "I know who you look like. It has just now struck me. The moustache, and the forehead — you look like Guy de Maupassant. Really, really, I assure you."

He did not know who that was, and Miss Clément was moved by the simplicity of this admission.

They walked home, taking quiet streets where their footsteps resonated as in a corridor. Clémentine, directing her eyes downward, or far ahead, or high up, harboured only one wish — to look at the captain's face. She sporadically caught a glimpse of only his profile; if he turned toward her she would immediately turn away. He kept, she noted, to the curb side, as is proper when walking with a lady, a custom of which Brother Gandon was apparently oblivious. The streets were unfamiliar to her or she no longer recognized them, so different in the captain's company was the language things seemed to speak, full of murmurs and secrets.

"You called for the Night, it has come, here it is," she sighed.

After a long silence she added, "The sleeping houses resemble faces dreaming."

The captain cleared his throat.

"You . . . you are a poet."

He said this in that timid, slightly sulking tone of voice that means, "You are making fun of me, taking advantage of your superiority." He did not see her blushing.

"A poet?" she said, "Yes, perhaps."

The rest of the way was spent in silence. They found themselves by her door, facing each other. Clémentine's gaze darted over the massive face with a sort of frenzy, as though covering it with kisses. The captain's eyes shone with a soft, peaceful glimmer. The eyes of a loyal dog.

"I wanted to tell you, Captain . . . This evening . . . for me . . ."

His mouth, too, was beautiful beneath the moustache, fleshy and red. His curly hair. Tears came to Clémentine's eyes. She bit the corner of her lip and shook her head, not knowing what to say. She pushed her fingers through the captain's shock of hair. He leaned down and kissed her hand. She made a small, ineffectual gesture to keep him from going and found herself once again alone, suddenly chilled, lost in her tender turmoil.

She raised her eyes toward the window of her bedroom. The prospect of returning there filled Clémentine with distress and disgust. For a moment she considered rambling until dawn, even catching up with him, why not? "Don't abandon me." But the captain was probably already far away. Clémentine bowed her head. She slowly climbed the stairs. The boot on her right foot was a different colour from the one on the left.

* * *

THE NEXT DAY, Saturday, she awoke from several hours of profound and dreamless sleep such as she had not experienced for weeks. She felt hungry enough for a slice of bread with butter and half a bowl of porridge. She brewed some tea. Then she was shocked to see it was past noon. Oh, well, too bad. There would be no visit to Mother today! She decided to clean her house from top to bottom.

Once her work was done the floors were clean enough to eat on, the pots sparkled, the windows were draped with fresh curtains. Clémentine, impeccable from her hair down to her toenails, put on her loveliest dress and, sitting near the piano with a Sully Prudhomme anthology in her hand, waited for the captain. No rendezvous had been agreed to. But she waited. She had the impression that since yesterday the wind had started to shift: henceforth only good things could happen to her. The captain did not show up. When she went to bed Clémentine felt guilty, of what she did not know.

She slept not quite as well as the night before and woke up bemused. She drank a cup of tea while looking out the window. It was a dreary morning. Fog patches blurred the rooftops; it was as though a drawing had been left unfinished out of boredom. Images of Brother Gandon came to mind intermittently; she chased them away. She noticed on her night table, leaning against the portrait of the exile of

Guernsey, the latest issue of the *Rubicon of Lonely Souls*, which she had not yet opened. She absent-mindedly read a few isolated paragraphs here and there. It all seemed so silly to her now. Yet she was arrested by these words: "free verse." Clémentine began to read more attentively. It was as though she'd been slapped.

> *Past days, you raise up before the desperate surge*
> *the wall of wool, the wall of mist, more undoings;*
> *memories, you rehearse the cold night, the evenings*
> > *of triumph,*
> > *the evenings of useless and futile triumph;*
> *memories, with jaded fingers you undo necklaces*
> > *of celebrations.*

Clémentine felt as though she had been ripped from the ground. She feverishly reread the lines. Next to this, Victor Hugo seemed all at once a noisy gorilla! She went to lie down, quaking from head to foot, on the living-room sofa. This was how one ought to write, how one ought to say things. She got up, cheeks aflame. She wrote in a single stroke:

> *When I return from these roads, like a child at last Happy,*
> *we shall sow in my garden*
> *the traces of our eyes, my love, and the mysterious defeats*
> *of our hands.*

She reread what she had written, hardly daring to believe it. She continued. The words poured from her pen — dictated, sovereign, without let-up — for two pages. At the end, she set down her signature. Crossed it out. Wrote instead: Clémanthine de Kléman. Then relished a moment of ecstasy.

She fell asleep during the afternoon and dreamed of fauns, of English gardens: young boys in ancient dress dancing around a fountain. Then an idea jolted her as she slept. She opened her eyes: what if she were to go off to Paris? There, in exile, she would write, become known. There, she would be understood. She imagined herself being welcomed by enthusiastic young poets with long hair and blond beards. In a smoky Montmartre café, looking haughty and worldly-wise, indifferent to the surrounding conversations, the Prince of Poets suddenly sees her, learns who she is from a young painter, and in a single gesture rises, places his beret over his heart, and declares before the mesmerized bohemians, "I salute you, Canadian sister!" Clémentine gaily, wrathfully threw her head back: "Ah, if only Gaston Gandon could see that!"

Later, coming back from church at nightfall, Clémentine collapsed, crushed by the weight of her solitude.

It was too late to leave; that was the sort of thing one did at twenty. The page where she had written her poem lay on the piano. It was all misshapen from being held so long in Clémentine's hand. Should she burn it, in a grand gesture? She reread the lines, stopped at the second verse, disgusted with herself. A wave of heat swept over her at the idea of this being read in Paris. How they would have sneered. "In Canada, they plant hands in the garden!" Miss Clément poured herself a generous glass of porto.

At a quarter to nine, the captain of the fire brigade rapped on a pane of her kitchen window. He could not stay. But he promised to come back the next day; he would have his whole evening free. "Here?" she said with a shiver. He answered only with his eyes. Toward midnight Clémentine read her poem again, which she had not done for almost five hours. She regarded it with greater indulgence. It appeared to glow with new, mysterious meaning, full of promise. She delicately stored it in the drawer of the writing desk.

The Feast of the Immaculate Conception fell on a Tuesday, but it was the Monday that had been set aside as a holiday. "It's going to happen, it's going to happen," Clémentine repeated to herself with a mixture of panic and hope. Her visits to the washroom were unusually frequent. She was constantly washing her hands. To allay her fretfulness she thought it best to go out for a stroll.

She had put on an elegant dress, her fancy boots, her most stylish coat. She walked for a long time, one street leading to another. Eventually she stopped in a café. It was cold and she wanted something hot to drink. Sitting on a stool, she observed the décor with disdain: she was a patron of downtown nightclubs. Around her people were whispering. She distinctly heard someone say, "That's her, the schoolteacher . . ." Clémentine held her head high. She went out. She felt above all that.

She walked, and the kerchief around her neck floated on the wind; she found it suited her perfectly. She would have liked for the captain to see her. Indeed, she behaved as though he were spying on her. She put on airs, struck poses on the street corners as she waited for her traffic light. Yet she was anxious; she felt a rough knot in her stomach, and there was nothing for it. She went up Rue Moreau, astonished to see it so crowded. She inquired from a policeman, actually quite a handsome man. He informed her of the death of the bank clerk and his father. Shaken, Clémentine turned around and went back home.

The captain arrived at seven o'clock. He had to rap on the window three times. Clémentine could not manage to stand up. She contemplated an oil stain on the floor with taut fascination. She breathed deeply, then ran to the door, frantic at the thought he might have retreated. He was there. He had brought a bunch of carnations as well as a bottle of wine. And he had waxed his moustache.

She had gotten the living room ready especially for him, but he instinctively headed toward the kitchen. The atmosphere at first was funereal. *How tiresome he must find me*, thought Clémentine as she held herself back from crying. The long seconds dripped by one by one. She sadly noted that he had lost his Friday verve; he once again had the appearance of a little boy intimidated by his teacher. There was, however, something indefinably hard in his gaze. Clémentine sank her forehead and twisted her fingers.

She remembered the whistling of the elves and was tortured by it. When she was a child, this was the expression her mother would use whenever they boarded the train: "Have you remembered to make the elves whistle?" Clémentine felt an irrepressible urge. The toilet was located in the kitchen, directly behind the chair he was sitting in. She was certainly not about to let him hear that! She nervously suggested they move to the living room. The captain rose with a slightly listless docility. As soon as he was installed in the settee, she dashed to the kitchen and made her way to the toilet.

When she came back, vastly relieved, he had filled her glass, which she drained in one go. She found the wine bitter.

"This deposit at the bottom of my glass," she joked. "You aren't trying to drug me, are you?"

"Those are the lees," he said.

She poured another glass for herself, and for him as well, and as she gave it to him their fingers brushed together. She snatched her hand away so sharply that he jumped.

"Would you like me to read you one of my poems?" she asked with a fervour that was quite uncalled for — she might as well have been shouting, "Fire! Fire!"

The captain looked at her with some dismay. Clémentine reddened and went to fetch her poem.

She read it to him in an unsure voice and from the very start she felt as though she were churning out heaps of obscenities. Nevertheless, she carried on bravely until the last line, then looked at the captain pleadingly. The captain was at an obvious loss for words.

"You don't like it, do you?"

He made a vague gesture of protest.

"It's . . . I would have to reread it . . . with a clear head. Another day, of course. It's . . . it's more complicated than *The Dairywoman and the Pail of Milk.*"

The reference amused Clémentine no end, which caught the captain off guard. But the schoolteacher's laughter improved the atmosphere a great deal, and he joined in.

At this point she became expansive. About her plans to travel to Paris, where, she said, she was already in touch with poets and painters, through correspondence, of course; about her plans also to find a publisher there. The captain listened politely. The names she cited — and she stopped short of none — meant nothing to him and echoed like drums. Clémentine was touched by this. Evidently, the wine was tasty. It fired Clémentine's imagination, her senses, too: how handsome the captain was! Her exaltation soared to such heights that she eventually began to reel in her chair. She halted. The captain asked her if she was all right. She said yes but her eyelids grew heavy.

"I don't know. It may be the alcohol . . . alcohol . . ." She let out a drunken titter. "I feel a little sleepy all at once — how silly."

"It's nothing. We'll take a few steps together and it will pass."

She let herself be pressed against his muscular chest, dropped her head on his shoulder; it was good to be all limp and leaning on something so firm, the gladness of an octopus embracing the coral. Entwined, they walked down the hallway.

"I'm happy," she said breathily. "I was waiting for you."

The captain bent his perfumed moustache down toward her and planted a long kiss on her lips. She shivered and nearly lost her footing.

"Come," he murmured, and he led her to the bedroom.

Clémentine disengaged herself: all of a sudden she felt very sick. She locked herself in the toilet. She had the impression of being twelve feet tall — she saw her feet, her hands as if through the wrong end of a pair of binoculars. *How long have I been here?* she thought. Then she realized it could have been forty minutes — or seven seconds. She felt hot, her teeth were chattering. She undid her skirt; it slid down her thighs, down her calves, in a dizzy fall that lasted an eternity. She had nothing on now but her shirt; below the waist she was naked. Had she undressed? But when? She was sitting on the porcelain of the toilet bowl: she had not lowered the seat. She felt she was slipping away, that she was on the verge of fainting. The toilet door was wide open, the captain was standing before her — how long had he been there? He seemed so far away. Clémentine was naked, sitting on the bowl. He took her in his arms, like a bridegroom carrying off the bride. She was in her bed. She moaned feebly, her voice childlike: "I don't want to sleep." A spasm traversed her whole being as he lay down on her. She tried to extricate herself, to roll out of bed, she thrashed about like someone drowning. Then her limbs no longer responded. She yielded her body up in a final swoon, hardly sensing the abrupt burning between her legs. The burning softened, grew warm, and deep. She continued to fight against the drowsiness. But the very desire to sleep only added to her bliss. An "'I love you'" escaped from her lips just as she relinquished her last ounce of strength. She fell into a sleep more soundless than death.

SHE HAD A host of bad dreams, along with a fever. She was tied down at the bottom of sleep amid noises, restless lights, motion that strove bewilderedly to become form but to no avail. In the end it was the cold that woke her. Her bedroom window was gaping. The wind lifted the curtains. It was early dawn.

She got out of bed, shivering. She tottered toward the window, closed it, then sought the captain in every room, shouting his name. He was gone. Clémentine crumpled at the foot of the bed and let out a cry of surprise: a remnant of semen was oozing down her thighs.

She paced up and down, saying to herself that she was born to go round and round in her kitchen. She was certain of having spoiled everything, of having ruined her last chance. The captain would never come back again.

There was a message waiting for her on the kitchen table, wedged between the mustard jar and the sugar bowl. She suddenly noticed it after passing by it three times, and she was petrified. She instinctively knew, given the state she was in, that even the most remotely hurtful phrase would leave her worse than dead. All her fears, all her hopes had shrunk to the dimensions of this piece of paper. Her hand quivered as she reached for it.

Thanks for the plesure we shared. I did not wish to wake you on leeving. I watcht you sleepin for a long time. See you soon mi amor!

Yours,
Big Roger

The joy exploded inside her like fireworks. She hugged the note against her heart and began to waltz around the kitchen floor. *"Mi amor!"* He had written, *"Mi amor!"* And he had written, "See you soon!"

Humming merrily, she slathered a slice of bread with mustard — she felt grateful to the mustard jar — she was happy, and her appetite was the kind born of happiness. "See you soon *mi amor!*" she said to the sandwich as she was about to bite into it. Yet, without warning, her gorge rose and she dashed to the toilet.

She nevertheless managed not to bring up and she splashed some water on her face. She leaned over the sink and took deep breaths. This reminded her of the time she was pregnant. At breakfast, under the wily and watchful eye of her mother, Clémentine had heroically controlled herself until Mrs. Clément had finished her meal; then, on the pretext of having something to attend to in the cellar, Clémentine had scurried away to regurgitate the eggs which the florist forced upon her, fully aware of Clémentine's particular loathing for eggs.

Here, a suspicion arose. A few quick calculations led her to the conclusion that these were her fertile days. When she was eighteen, then too, one time, just one, had sufficed . . . It all at once became an inexplicable, intuitive, absolute certainty within her. She posed her hand on her belly and smiled. The future unfurled before her in a mystical vision. The captain would marry her, for she was pregnant. She would give up teaching. He would be the breadwinner, and she, she would raise their child, their two children, perhaps — it was still possible at her age; she would write poems, and the captain would come to comprehend and love them; Roger had kept his childlike simplicity, that was the main thing — he was a little boy in the big, beautiful body of a man. She imagined him, evenings, in his bathrobe, smoking a pipe by the fireplace. Tears of delight slid down Clémentine's cheeks.

She looked at the clock: it was time to leave for school. The day promised to be a trying one. It was the Feast of the Immaculate Conception, and, as every year, she would have to take the students to church for the ceremony prepared by the little girls of École Marie-Reine-des-Coeurs. Clémentine despised the whole thing. But after the three-day holiday she had granted herself the week before, she could not reasonably prolong her leave of absence. Besides, the prospect of seeing Gaston Gandon again (*What a ridiculous name!* she thought) no longer affected her. What could he do to her

EPILOGUE

ALONG WITH THE night, the snow fell in large flakes on the vast Côte-des-Neiges cemetery. Remould and Séraphon's caskets were buried side by side in the same pit, a single headstone for both their names. Not far away, a very small, white cross, with only the given name "Joceline."

* * *

BROTHER GANDON HAD spent part of the afternoon drafting a letter in which he accused himself of attempting to violate Miss Clément. He took the blame upon himself, exonerating her completely. The schoolteacher was reputed, rightly or wrongly, to have some savings. If ever — as there was every reason to fear — the janitor got the notion of blackmailing her, threatening to tell everything he had seen the previous week in the principal's office, he would forward this letter to the competent authorities. What could happen to him? He would be sent where he could be forgotten, to some distant mission in Africa, or Japan, or among the Eskimos: "Bah! I wouldn't be the first." Brother Gandon had tears in his eyes. And to think that all of this was due to the schoolteacher's madness, to her stupidity!

The principal left his office and made for the presbytery. He had promised Father Cadorette he would pay him a visit. He hoped to bring his friend some comfort and in so doing banish some of his own torments. He left the presbytery deeply disturbed. Now that Remouald Tremblay was dead and that he himself was not long for this world, the priest, no longer feeling bound by secrecy, had acquainted the principal with the truth about the bank clerk. Brother Gandon was still in a state of shock. God, what a life he must have endured, what agony for all those twenty years!

The principal donned his beret, tied his scarf around his neck, the scarf that Remouald Tremblay had held, perhaps worn. He fancied he could detect a scent. Gandon started off, eager to be home again. He crossed the church square. Then he stopped in his tracks, she slowed her pace, and they observed each other for a long while without exchanging greetings. Miss Clément was coming out of church; she had just had her outburst before her fellow schoolteachers. It was their first encounter since they had quarrelled.

"You were ill last week?"

"It was nothing at all," she answered with icy civility. "Merely a cold. I'm feeling much better now. Unfortunately for you."

"Well, better luck next time," he said, showing his teeth as he smiled.

She held down the sides of her cloak with deliberate nonchalance. She had covered her head with the hood, which was very large and lent her a madonna-like air. Gandon was struck by her beauty. She reminded him of the ladies whom as an adolescent he would see coming out of the theatre on Saturday nights, sombre and graceful, and who so stirred him that he would hurry away. Where could she be going, to which soirée, in such elegant attire? He suddenly noticed she was wearing eye makeup. And she had appeared like this before her students! It did not occur to the principal to be scandalized by this. He had the impression she led a parallel life, one full of lights, balls, and music; he felt wretched in his mended cassock. He thought of the captain of the fire brigade. And he resented the teacher even more.

"Oh, well, you'll have to excuse me," she said, "but I must go home."

Gandon stood there without saying a word. She set off with a shrug. The brother followed her.

She walked along, poker-faced, completely detached, as though she were telling him, "Go ahead and follow me, I don't care the least bit." He marched behind her at a short distance. His mouth was twisted into a sneer.

The streets were more congested than was customary at that time of day. They paid no attention. People were streaming out of their houses, hailing each other across the street, walking in the same direction. Clémentine and Gandon followed the current.

He asked, "Have you heard the news? I mean, concerning Mr. Tremblay, the bank clerk?"

"Of course," she said coolly. "I don't live on the moon."

"You must surely remember the anonymous letter? The one received by the police and on which you set such great store . . . Miss Clément? Are you listening?"

She straightened a lock of her hair.

"I hear you."

Gandon laughed bitterly. Clémentine, who guessed what was coming, kept walking at the same unfaltering pace.

"It was written by Remould Tremblay," he said at last.

"So what?" said Clémentine, unable to suppress a shiver.

"It proves we are often wrong about people, don't you find, Miss Clément? You thought you had caught him red-handed with those children, when he was just a witness to that hateful crime. A witness, Miss Clément, not a criminal."

"It also proves that I was right: someone had indeed committed that crime. I find it strange, however, that you should credit that testimony now that you know it was the bank clerk who wrote the letter."

"Granted. But Father Cadorette is categorical: Mr. Tremblay was incapable of lying. At all events, we know what's what now. We can set to work on Bradette and Rocheleau."

They had to stop for a moment, as the throng was creating a bottleneck at the corner of the street. An altogether absurd idea crossed Clémentine's mind.

"What about the offender? Who is it?" she asked apprehensively.

"No one knows yet, unfortunately."

The schoolteacher looked at the principal without speaking.

"Why on earth are you looking at me like that?" Gandon said furiously. "You don't actually believe I'm the one!"

Clémentine made a gesture of exasperation, one that meant, "What a fool you are!" Yet her face was red. They set off again in lockstep. Gandon was irate. They skirted the droves of pedestrians, avoided the children who scrambled past them in both directions armed with their hockey sticks. Clémentine noticed that no little girls were anywhere to be seen.

"And where did you come by all this information?" she asked him again.

"Father Cadorette, I already told you. As he was the only one to know Remould well, the police relied on his statements. But that was not all he told me concerning the bank clerk. He related another story."

They reached the corner of Darling and Sainte-Catherine. A man was crossing the street and, without looking at them, heading in their direction. He was a little frightening — a tall man with a pockmarked face and coal-black eyes — yet handsome. His kinky hair provided a sort of cushion for his top hat. Clémentine recognized him: Raymond Costade, the funeral director. *To think he is to be my brother-in-law*, and this thought moved Clémentine. They greeted each other but kept their distance. Gandon glanced at the object Costade was holding under his arm.

"An icon of the Virgin, you see," Costade said, feeling obliged to offer some explanation. "It was lying in the alley. Some children were using it to slide on the snow. I don't know how it ended up there. Strange. It's actually a relic of my youth. A childhood friend of mine painted it; he lives in New York now. As it happens, on the day of the fire I had entrusted it to that poor Mr. Blanchot, may God keep his soul. I was sure it had burned as well. It's odd how certain objects find their way back to you."

They listened to him with some embarrassment, for Raymond Costade was afflicted with a conspicuous stutter. He went away after a short while, ill at ease himself. For a few moments Gandon contemplated the gangling silhouette. *The man who embalmed his own mother*, he thought, shuddering.

The crowd resumed its flow, carrying them along to the

courtyard shared by the police station and the fire hall. The windows had been arrayed with torches.

Gandon did not know if he had the right to disclose the bank clerk's secret to Clémentine. He said to himself, *She judged him so severely, I must rehabilitate him in her eyes so that she may gauge the gravity of her error.* But he also knew that what he would say would aggrieve the schoolteacher and that this was no doubt his true motivation. Gandon began to recount everything he had learned about Remould's childhood, the intelligence that had been his, his awful passion for ideas and, finally, his relationship with Wilson. The cult of blasphemy. The parodic masses they celebrated to mock the Virgin. And the carnal practices that this inevitably involved.

Clémentine listened with growing distress. If the priest was aware of all this, why had he not intervened?

"The fact is, he knew nothing," Gandon replied. "He learned all this when he went to Wilson's cell to hear his confession, before he hanged himself."

"Oh, so now there's a hanged man," Clémentine said with disgust.

"The most terrible part," Gandon continued, "is that Wilson was insanely jealous. He stalked that poor Remould, going so far as to watch him through the window of his bedroom at night as he slept. But Remould did not sleep alone."

Gandon paused. Ever since his conversation with the priest, he could not put the image out of his mind. It was a primal image, prior to all memory, like that of the crucifixion, of which someone — Pascal perhaps or St. Anselme — had said that it continued to be present at every moment of the universe. This, too, in its own way, marked an absolute beginning. And Gandon sensed that now it would remain with him for the rest of his life. That image of Wilson in a sort of night preceding the world, his features crazed with jealousy, gazing through the window at two children asleep.

Suddenly he became aware of the place where they stood. He clutched Clémentine's arm.

"Let me go!" she whined.

"Where are we? What are we doing here?"

They had ended up in the middle of the courtyard. The throng behind them made all retreat impossible. The gallows shimmered in the glow of the torches. The mob generated a din of shouting, fierce gaiety, and howls of hatred; effigies jiggled in the air: "Death to the arsonist!" Brother Gandon attempted to turn his back to the scaffold. He was obliged to yell. Miss Clément tried to move away, but he held on to her: she needed to hear the story out to the conclusion.

"Finally, one night — are you listening, Miss Clément? — finally, one night, exactly twenty years ago today, Remouald was twelve years old, it was the Feast of the Immaculate Conception . . . Wilson had prepared a special ceremony for the occasion. He said he had stolen a lamb from the slaughterhouse."

"What?"

He shouted to be heard above the roar. "It was part of the ritual, he would present Remouald with all kinds of talismans — a rabbit's foot, the ear of a hare — but he would first prepare the game he had hunted, or the meat of stolen animals, and then feed it to Remouald. Remouald received his amulet only at the end of the meal. That night, Wilson told him, 'Look in the bag to see what you've just eaten.' Then he withdrew . . . And Remouald opened the bag."

Gandon paused. The commotion now resembled the clamour of all the noises of the world at once. Clémentine no longer heard the words, she saw them, saw them fall from the principal's mouth one by one.

"Her name was Joceline . . . Joceline Bilboquain. She was seven or eight years old. She was Remouald's sister, and . . ."

Brother Gandon grabbed the schoolteacher by the shoulders.

"Well, what? Say it!" she screamed.

"Inside the burlap bag . . . was the little girl's head."

* * *

THE ARSONIST HAD just been led onto the scaffold. His hands were tied behind his back. Shrieks of horror rose from his throat, a hoarse, ridiculous wail, barely audible above the tumult. A shudder ran through the crowd, packing it even more tightly together.

"But it was His hand that guided me!" screeched the condemned man. "It was He in person who handed me the matches! I swear! I swear!"

No one heard him. Gandon and Clémentine were driven back against the wall. A torch came loose and fell at their feet, nearly setting the principal's robe on fire. Buffeted on every side, he managed to stamp it out with his heel. Faces bore down on them, grimacing and sneering. Half stooped, Clémentine sought to protect her belly. She was jostled about by the swarm. Gandon strove with all his might to extricate himself. Clémentine's face was pressed against his, locks of her hair tickled his lips, against his chest he could feel the hard tips of her breasts. The pressure of the crowd welded them together.

"You had no right to tell me that story!"

It was almost a scream. Gandon thought he was about to lose consciousness.

Suddenly there were shouts: "There's Roger Costade!"

Gandon saw Clémentine's cheeks go aflame. The crowd shifted once again and they were freed from each other. Clémentine nervously searched all around with her eyes. Then her face lit up.

Captain Costade's wagon, drawn by four animals, appeared next to the gallows. Beside him sat little Maurice. On his shoulder lay Big Roger's solemn, shielding hand. The arsonist was dragged to the noose.

Brother Gandon at last understood. Clémentine regarded the captain with an expression of such bliss and hopefulness that she was irradiated, transfigured, still more beautiful. The principal closed his eyes and leaned against the wall, enervated by the violence of his hate.

By way of a signal, Roger Costade softly raised his hand in an august, Roman gesture. "Oh, how handsome you are, my captain!" Clémentine murmured, certain that these words sent floating from her lips would reach him: she thought she noticed his moustaches rise, as if he were smiling discreetly. The trap door was slow to open. The arsonist seemed to dance a jig; the disappointed public jeered.

Maurice looked at the captain of the fire brigade with sadness and disquiet and supplication. Big Roger answered with a fatherly wink. The little boy cast him a timid, albeit pale smile, but a confident smile nonetheless. And was there anything in this world more beautiful than the smile of a child? Clémentine Clément caressed her belly, where the future was beginning.

Brother Gandon had not yet opened his eyes. He was nailed to the wall, arms spread wide, haunted by a luminous image, searing in its intensity. He no longer heard the ferocious uproar. He was thinking of a night when the first snow was falling. Two children, a little brother and his young sister, have put on their pyjamas embroidered with musical notes; they are having a pillow fight on the bed they share, their cheeks afire, and they are reeling under the avalanche of their own laughter. (Through the window, Wilson saw this.)

The locked cabinet contained only the shoe of a little girl.

New York, December 22

Anansi offers complimentary reading guides that can be used with this novel and others.

Ideal for people who love talking about books as much as they love reading them, each reading guide contains in-depth questions about the book that you can use to stimulate interesting discussion at your reading group gathering.

Visit www.anansi.ca to download guides for the following titles:

The Immaculate Conception
Gaétan Soucy
978-0-88784-783-7
0-88784-783-8

Atonement
Gaétan Soucy
978-0-88784-780-6
0-88784-780-3

The Little Girl Who Was Too Fond of Matches
Gaétan Soucy
978-0-88784-781-3
0-88784-781-1

Vaudeville!
Gaétan Soucy
978-0-88784-782-0
0-88784-782-x

Gargoyles
Bill Gaston
978-0-88784-776-9
0-88784-776-5

The Law of Dreams
Peter Behrens
978-0-88784-774-5
0-88784-774-9

The Tracey Fragments
Maureen Medved
978-0-88784-768-4
0-88784-768-4

Returning to Earth
Jim Harrison
978-0-88784-786-8
0-88784-786-2

True North
Jim Harrison
978-0-88784-729-5
0-88784-729-3

Paradise
A. L. Kennedy
978-0-88784-738-7
0-88784-738-2

The Big Why
Michael Winter
978-0-88784-734-9
0-88784-734-x